GINGER
HILL

GINGER
HILL

By Sarah S. Allen

JOHN F. BLAIR, *Publisher*
Winston-Salem, North Carolina

For
Bill, Will, Foy,
and Reynold
and
In memory of
My brother James
and
With thanks to
Guy Owen
and
Ida Mae

GINGER HILL

PART ONE

13

CHAPTER ONE

*A*bout four o'clock every afternoon I went to the Big House called Ginger Hill to help Mama fix supper and set the table for Miss Lou and all the family. In the summer the road was usually muddy and I went barefooted, carefully holding my old black patent leather sandals in my hand. The sand and mud felt good between my toes and I'd wade through the big puddles, being mighty careful not to splash my dress or Mama would skin me alive. I'd have to watch where the teams had been through, too, leaving the fresh-smelling mule piles. It was only a quarter of a mile from our house to the Big House, and I could see the wide Chilliwan River nearly all the way with lines of blue-green forests on the other side.

> River, river, flowing by,
> Cutting land to reach the sea,
> Running, singing, joking river,
> Run and sing with me.

Mama never knew that I made up poems about the river and the whole world. She would have thought I was spooky, and anyway, I wanted it for a secret.

To keep the cooking fumes out, the kitchen was separated from the rest of the house by a long, high back porch. I helped rush the food to the dining room so the wind wouldn't cool it off before the family could enjoy their hot supper. We had plenty of covered dishes, most of them silver. Everything they used at Ginger Hill was beautiful and mysterious, almost like in a church. Mama used to tell me it was a great honor for a colored child to get acquainted with all those things. On Saturday mornings I even helped Mama polish the old silver, but once I dropped a candlestick and dented it a little and Mama slapped me and sent me home crying.

By the time I was thirteen I could pass the biscuits around to the family without trembling or making a single mistake, always from the left so they could reach over with their right hand. With Leighton I would go to the right, for I knew he was left-handed, and he'd smile and say thanks. We all knew each other so well and felt so at home with each other it wouldn't have mattered if I had made a mistake.

"Is your cold better, Ophelia?" Miss Lou would ask me. Those were the days when we didn't stop doing things because of colds.

"Yessum."

"Did you get the snap beans picked this morning?"

"Yessum, but they're getting scarce."

"Ophelia, will you pour me some more tea?" Mr. Lockwood would ask on summer nights, and I would carry the ice bucket around again and refill the glasses with tea.

There was Mr. Lockwood and his wife, Miss Lou, and Leighton, sixteen, all earthly saints, and Janet, fourteen, a living devil. One summer night when I was passing the macaroni, Janet tripped me and I fell sprawling with the hot cheese spilling all over the richly colored carpet. In the candlelight no one saw what she had done. Some of the macaroni scalded my leg, and I could hear Janet laughing as I ran with tears in my eyes to get Mama and some scouring cloths.

"Never mind, Ophelia," Miss Lou said. "We can do without the macaroni, but do try to be more careful. Hush, Janet. Accidents are never funny."

4

Mama belted me across the head when we got back to the kitchen, and she carried in the blancmange herself. I went howling out into the rainy night and fled down the road with my shoes on. I waded through mud, stepped in some mule droppings, and was drenched through before I reached our little tenant house. I went in, groped on the table for the lamp, found a match, and lighted it. It was in the thirties and we were still using kerosene lamps because the electric wires hadn't yet been run through the farm.

The lamp bathed the room in a rosy glow and created long shadows behind everything. The house had just two rooms, the living room and bedroom combined, and the kitchen. Our furniture consisted of hand-me-downs: one old easy chair, a rocker, and four straw-bottomed wooden chairs, a green wardrobe with the paint peeling off, and an iron bed. Mama had made us some cream-colored net curtains for our three windows and hung two pictures of chubby pink babies cut from calendars on the pine-board walls. Miss Lou had given us a folding screen, a real luxury, for privacy when dressing or bathing. The house wasn't much, but it was ours and it was home.

I went back of the screen, kicked off the smelly shoes, and pulled off all my wet clothes right down to the skin. I would have taken a bath but there wasn't any water heated. So I rubbed off on my towel and looked at myself in Mama's cracked hand mirror. My face was tear-stained and my hair tousled, and the water on my dark eyelashes made me look sad. I began to feel better as I gazed in the mirror. My skin was the color of fresh pine straw; my nose wasn't flat or my mouth too big. I was growing tall and my breasts were growing out. Every month I could tell a little difference in the way my dresses pulled. I had seen the boys at school looking at me, especially Bucky, my best friend's brother.

> Grow, little breasts,
> Over my heart.
> Make me a woman,
> With a secret part.

I hugged myself and grinned with satisfaction. I looked in the mirror again. My face wasn't like Mama's. I knew why—my daddy had been a real light West Indian. My hair wasn't kinky, but wavy, and my skin was pretty. Oh, Mama, I know you hated him, but you did something for me when you got me my daddy. Then I felt ashamed to have such a thought. I frowned and my face did have a resemblance to Mama's after all. And I loved her so; I loved my Mama so much. She was the best person in all the world.

I put on my faded purple nightgown and was combing my hair when Reverend Halleck called from the door, "Cassie, you home?"

He came every Saturday night without fail.

"One minute, Rev'rend," I called back and put on my wrapper. "Come on in. Mama ain't back yet."

He came in with his big black umbrella that hooked over his arm and gave him tone. What a lovely umbrella, and it could be a useful weapon if needed in the dark night.

"Let me put your umbrella in the kitchen to dry," I told him and took it in there, being careful not to hold it over my head in the house because that was the worst luck on earth.

Reverend Halleck had a big, shiny-black, honest face and a beautiful gold tooth that sparkled like the promise of heaven. His hair was grizzled, looking like a soft wig, and he had a deep resounding voice that the folks all loved to hear. He had found his calling all right, and thank the Good Lord for people like him. He could bring Moses right down out of the sky and make us hear the trump of Joshua. He could singe us with the fire from Elijah's chariot or send the breath of Daniel's lions to blow down our necks. Oh, it was a delicious shiver he sent us!

He handed me a package wrapped in newspaper.

"Three nice chub." He grinned, with his gold tooth emphasizing his delight. "Had a *very* successful afternoon. Fish just love to bite in the rain."

I unwrapped the package. "Beauties!" I cried. "I'll go put them on."

He sat down in Mama's big chair with the stuffing bulging out and picked up an old *Liberty* magazine that Miss Lou had given us, holding it sideways in the yellow lamp glow.

I made up the fire in the cookstove. We burned wood, and it was quicker than you think. I put some lard in the pan and put it on the stove, and in no time I had the fish frying and the coffee perking. People could say all they wanted to about hard times, but we never were hungry, not a single time, and we always had a fire, too. We were lucky, I guess.

"Got a leak in here," the Reverend called.

I took the washpan and put it under the drip. It went plop, plop, plop in the pan, very cozy, while the Reverend looked at some pictures of ocean fishing in the magazine. The good smell of frying fish and boiling coffee filled the air. "Smells mighty good," he confessed.

I fried some sweet potatoes and made a little corn bread. Pretty soon Mama came panting in with a newspaper over her head, all soaked, her shoes in her hand, and two servings of blancmange. She had had to wash all Miss Lou's dishes without my help and was still peeved with me, but when she saw

7

Reverend Halleck and smelled the fish, she smiled and her little gold tooth on the side flashed at his big front one. She went behind the screen and put on her grape-colored second-best dress and her shoes, and we were ready to eat.

The rain beat down harder on the tin roof of the kitchen when we drew the chairs up to the table, giving us that cozy feeling of being fenced in where we wanted to be. With the delicious fish on the old cracked platter before us and the coffee steaming on the table, along with plenty of sugar to go in it, we were as content as folks could be.

"Oh, Lord, thank thee for thy glorious bounty. Never let us forget the needs of the poverty-stricken. Save us for Paradise. Amen," the Reverend intoned in his melodious voice while Mama shooed off the flies. Then we ate.

After supper, I washed the dishes while Mama entertained Reverend Halleck. Mama had a prized possession and a special talent to go with it, and she got both from her mama. One was a foot-pump organ, and the other was the ability to play it. When old Miss Emmy Lockwood found out that Mammy Bunny, my grandmother, had a natural talent for the piano, she gave Mammy the old organ. It's been hauled about to every church around in wagons, carts, and trucks, but Mammy always made them give it back. Mama could play it almost as well as Mammy, and how she loved it. She would pump away with her thick legs working like pistons and her big brown arms busy as beavers while she threw out her bosom like a bellows and sang with great fervor. I used to feel my chest getting tighter and tighter, and I would nearly burst with pride when Mama played and sang, knowing that only one in a thousand knew how. It made me feel very special, like having my hair wavy instead of kinky.

The Reverend set the lamp on the organ while Mama removed the red-and-yellow streaked scarf that she kept over it. Then she opened it up and struck a few chords up and down, laughing happily. They sang "The Church in the Wildwood," "River Jordan to Cross," "I Come to the Garden Alone," and "My Hope Is Built."

I listened to them sing as I finished the dishes, put the leftover fish in the oven since we had no icebox, and heated enough water for a bath. I put the chamber pot under the leak so I could use the washpan for bathing, moved it behind the screen, and took off my fishy-smelling nightgown. I rinsed by standing in the pan and dripping water down me with the washrag Mama and I shared. Then, because I had forgotten to get my clean nightgown out of the drawer, I had to put the fishy one back on.

"Nearer My God to Thee," they sang, and the organ squeaked. Tears came into my eyes, it was so beautiful.

I took the old quilt and a sheet and started into the kitchen to make myself a pallet on the floor. "Good night, Mama. Good night, Rev'rend."

I went over and kissed her. She was damp and shiny from the pumping and singing, but she hugged me to her breast. "Good night, baby." She gave off a wonderful spirit of warmth and love and the pure flavor of home. When I lay down on my pallet, even though I could hear her singing and laughing in the other room with the Reverend, I felt lonely and missed her.

They sang off and on for an hour and I began to doze. Then I was aware that they had blown out the lamp and were talking quietly in the dark. I became wide awake and my ears pricked up. They were whispering and I couldn't make out a word except the Reverend saying, "She don't have no call to . . ." and Mama replying, "Shhh." Then they were real quiet except for a little scraping and rattling.

I felt my stomach lurch and my face start burning. I jabbed my fingers in my ears, squinched up my eyes, and scrooched into a ball under the sheet.

I've often wondered since if Mama would have let the Reverend stay so long on Saturday nights if she had known then that he had a wife and six head of children somewhere up in Halifax County.

CHAPTER TWO

*S*unday *morning I woke up and stretched. I could hear* Mama bumping around in the other room making up the bed, and I knew she was running late. It was fourth, or church Sunday. She would cook breakfast for the folks, fry a chicken for their dinner, and get off early.

"Ophelia, get up, child!" she called. "Merciful Jesus! What you done to your shoes?" She was looking them over. "Wet and stinking. Well, you ain't going to church in these today."

"Can't I put them in the oven awhile, Mama?"

She glared at me. "You might forget and eat 'em for breakfast. No, you going to keep the chillen for Carrie and let her go to church with me. 'Course Miss Lou 'specting you to wash up after supper tonight."

Mama was combing her hair. It was wiry and unmanageable, but she tied it down with a green handkerchief and hurried out the door.

"Here's the Rev'rend's watch on the table," I called. I held up the gold pocket watch. It glistened in a ray of sunshine, and the words *golden time* came in my mind.

She came back and took it from me, muttering, and put it back on the table. "Leave it be. I'll fetch it to church for him."

"Mama, please let me go to church." There was somebody I wanted to see there.

"Next time keep your shoes clean and maybe I will."

I watched her ease down our rickety front steps and pull heavily up the road to the Big House. I was thinking how Mama had walked that road all her life, hundreds of times. And how many had walked it before her?

Ginger Hill had been part of an old plantation that had be-

11

longed from the beginning of time to the Farthingales. But through the years it had been divided up into separate parts among numerous descendants. Mr. David Farthingale was the last of his family to own Ginger Hill, and he got in debt over his head. Folks said he wasn't raised to cope with business matters, only to race horses and live high. After he lost his land he couldn't see a reason in the world for living, so he shot himself with a silver-handled pistol. All this happened a long time before I was born, but everybody in Choanoke County knows these important things. His son, Mr. Philip Farthingale, lived in Attamac, the county seat, and had a hardware store and two children, David and Katie. Mr. Jim Lockwood bought the farm when it was sold for debts.

It was a ten-horse farm and provided a living even during the depression. There were three families to farm it, not counting Mr. Lockwood—Mr. Deiter, the white foreman, with his son Jed, and Joe Batts and Willie Jones, colored tenants with their big families. Each family had a tenant house. Mama and I had the smallest one because we didn't need much room, and we were the closest to the Big House where Mama cooked for the family. Joe and his wife Carrie lived half a mile from us down the road by the first tobacco field. They had seven head of children and more coming along all the time, looked like. The four oldest were boys, then there was a girl three, a boy two, and another baby girl, little Ethelene. Willie and Bea lived over by the second field, and they had five head, Bucky, sixteen, Sue, my best friend, fourteen, and Monk, Almalee, and Sonny, all younger.

This was the entire world to me and it was full of excitement.

I stopped my daydreaming and went back in the house to heat up some grits and a piece of leftover fish for breakfast, along with some stale coffee, strong and bitter. Then I fed the chickens and walked over to Carrie and Joe's, glad that the rain had stopped.

I found things there in their usual state. The four older boys were outside playing, all covered with mud. Frank and Sammy were in the umbrella tree chunking "cheeny balls" at Scooter and the chickens. Bobcat was sitting in the mud making a ditch. There wasn't a blade of grass anywhere around the unpainted house that sat on the edge of the tobacco field, and most of the window lights had been knocked out. Mr. Lockwood would give the tenants new panes to put in, but I guess Joe never had time, and those young'uns would break them out so fast it didn't seem any use anyway. In the winter the wind just whistled in, but they'd chink up the holes with cardboard or newspapers, and no one died of freezing or even pneumonia.

Flea, the two-year-old, came to the door crying. He had on a shirt but no pants, and both sides of his nose were running green. He was fuzzy-headed, big-eyed, and cute.

"What's a matter, Flea, honey?" I asked.

In answer he howled louder and louder. Then I saw Geraldine, his three-year-old sister, hiding behind the door. She had her hand behind her and a mean look on her face.

"Let me see now, Geraldine," I said.

She drew her hand back further. "Let me see!" She squealed as I very firmly took her little paw and prized it open. Inside was a cocklebur which she had been applying to Flea's little brown bottom.

"Where'd you get that?" I asked.

"Off'n the dog," she replied sullenly.

"Don't you know better than that?"

"Naw." She poked out her bottom lip and glared at me for spoiling her fun.

"Where's your mama?"

13

She pointed to a closed door.

"Go get her," I said, rubbing Flea's wounds with the palm of my hand and trying to get him quiet.

"She got the chair on the door," she replied saucily.

A big yellow dog with huge muddy feet came in, jumped up on the old brown sofa, and curled up. Geraldine leaped on top of him, hugging his neck ferociously until he snarled.

"That your dog, Geraldine?"

"Naw, he just live here."

"That dog'll bite you," I told her.

She continued to choke him, and I walked out on the porch to wait for Carrie to appear. I shooed a stuck-up-looking rooster out of the porch chair and sat down. "Go get your mama for me, Frank," I said. Frank was the oldest and biggest boy and was perched on the highest branch in the umbrella tree that would hold him.

"She say I bother her, she skin me," he told me, hanging by his knees on the little branch that was bending dangerously.

"Where's your pa?"

"He in there too. They sure had a big fight last night."

"Fight?"

"They fit awhile, then Mama bash his head with a 'bacco stick. Now they gettin' their rest." He skinned the cat.

Flea crawled up in my lap. I took the corner of his shirt and wiped his nose clean.

"You chillen had breakfast?"

"Yeah, corn flakes and 'densed milk," Scooter replied, rolling his pink tongue over his mouth in approval.

"I et a snake," said Bobcat from the mud.

I laughed. "Bobcat, you didn't eat no snake."

I took Flea and went in the kitchen, which was back of the front room. The corn flake bowls were sitting on the table with a trillion flies enjoying the leftovers and glued over the condensed milk can like it was flypaper. Flea crawled up on the table, brushed off the flies, and sticking his finger in the can, began licking the gooey drops of milk. I went out on the back porch, primed the pump, and brought in some water. There was no fire, so I rinsed off the dishes in cold water, using a little hard lye soap. It was a lot better than nothing.

As I was finishing the dishes, here came Carrie sort of dreamy-eyed in her old blue-flowered robe. Her eyeballs were yellow as a baby chick around her big, plum-black pupils, and her large mouth hung open. She was holding little baby Ethelene, a sweet, furry-headed thing, straight in front of her so the baby could nurse. Carrie had the robe hanging open with her full, big breasts out, and Ethelene would go from side to side squeezing as she went. I hope mine won't get that big, I thought. Even with a nursing baby, Carrie's stomach was already sticking out with another one inside. She sat down heavily in a chair.

"How you, Ophelia?" She didn't even notice I had washed her dishes, just gazed out the door at the field.

"Fine, Miss Carrie. You want to go to church? I'll keep the chillen."

"Yeah, I'd really like to. Ouch!" She slapped Ethelene on the ear, and the baby screwed up her face and bawled. "Get down, Flea! Stop that there!" He was holding the can to his mouth, letting the sticky milk drop in. She grabbed him by one arm and swung him to the floor. He began to bellow and in his exertion sprayed his mama and the floor. "Look what you done! Get out o' here!" She shoved him toward the back door, and he went out squalling. The baby resumed her rooting.

"Yeah," Carrie said, "I'd sure like to go to church. Joe! We goin' to church," she called.

15

In a minute Joe came in wearing his pajama pants and a ragged, sleeveless undershirt. He had a big, pleasant, dark face with an oversized mouth. In contrast to his bigness, his voice was thin and reedy. I always felt like Carrie was his mother.

"Hiya, Ophelia. How Miss Cassie?" he asked.

You have to remember that Mama had a very special status in the world due to her position in the Big House and her organ playing and good sense.

"Fine. This is fourth Sunday. I'll keep the chillen for y'all to go to meeting if you want."

"Go get ready, Joe," Carrie ordered.

"Ain't you got no coffee, Carrie? I got to get waked up."

"Man, I ain't makin' no fire today; it's too hot."

He stood in a kitchen chair, reached up to a loose board in the ceiling, and brought out a bottle of grape pop. He grinned at me, bit the top off with his teeth, and took a big gulp.

"Gimme a sip," Carrie demanded. He let her taste it and she strangled, coughed, and upset Ethelene, who was shaken away from her breakfast. "Don't choke me, man!" Carrie gasped.

Joe wandered out to the pump on the back porch, where he washed his face and finished his pop, while staring out across the tobacco rows. "That tobacco goin' to flop if this rain keep up," he announced. "Guess I ought to shave if we goin' to church," he added. That's one advantage of a colored man—he doesn't have to shave every day.

Somewhere in all that confusion they found their Sunday clothes. Carrie wore her red straw hat and Joe his blue starched shirt and yellow striped necktie. Then he hitched up the mule to the cart and away they rode, Carrie sitting on the cross board holding her pink umbrella over her head very grandly. The children waved good-by, and Bobcat stuck out his tongue at them. I held Ethelene, who kept rooting around in my dress for something, but it wasn't there, of course. I put her in her crib, gave her a big drumstick bone to suck on, and she was happy.

Before he left, Joe had killed us a chicken, wrung her neck off. I made up the fire in the cookstove, boiled water, and dipped the old hen in it to loosen her feathers. The ugly, strong smell of wet feathers floated all over the house and out in the yard as well. I made Frank and Sammy help me pick her and singe the pinfeathers off with a burning paper sack. The children gathered round while I cut her open with the butcher knife and pulled out the stinking goozles, all yellow and slick. I put them on a board and told the boys to take them to the pigs in the wallow by the woods. They started off grand, but they hadn't gone far before they tilted the board and all the innards fell in the mud. With sheepish grins they turned to see if I was looking. The old yellow dog went flying down to eat up what he could, so nothing was wasted. Then the boys picked at the leavings with sticks, the devils.

I cooked chicken and dumplings. About three o'clock they were ready, and so were the children. I never did care much for a fresh-killed chicken, but it wasn't bad. The sun came in and out of the clouds all afternoon, and the mud got a glossy look. After we cleaned up, I boiled the bones out of the chicken neck and we used them to play jacks on the porch. In those days everything was worth something and everything seemed like fun.

We heard a lot of noise, and here came a big old open, black car with yellow-spoke wheels splashing down the road like crazy. All the young'uns ran out to see who it might be. The road came right by the house, too close, and I called the boys out of the way, the car was going so fast. It flew past us, then braked up with a screech and backed to where we were standing wide-eyed. In it were four slicked-up colored boys, and they thought they were pretty cute, you could tell. Each one had on a necktie, and the driver had a little thin mustache and wore a purple cap. The car radiator, decorated with a fluffy squirrel tail, was steaming and hissing as though it might explode, and pasted on the windshield was a faded yellow pennant that said *Peanut Festival*. They were sporting, all right.

"This your place, honey?" the driver asked me in a Norfolk Yankee accent.

"I'm keeping these chillen," I told him like a fool.

"We need some water," he said, pronouncing it "worter."

"The pump's in back," I answered, picking up Flea, who never had found any pants to put on.

"I'll show you!" shouted Frank, delighted to have such highfalutin company.

The colored boys all piled out of the car, and I should have been suspicious then. Bobcat and Scooter jumped on the running board and blew the horn.

"Cut it out, kid!" one of them snarled, as Scooter took his turn. The boy backhanded Scooter so hard he fell on the ground; then he knocked Bobcat down.

"You be careful how you hit those chillen!" I shouted wildly. But the driver took my arm and shoved me into the house, took Flea out of my arms without asking, and put him in the crib in the bedroom with Ethelene.

"Now how about a little kiss, baby," he said in an oily voice, grabbing me in his bearlike arms. I tried to beat him off while the other boys stood looking and snickering on the porch.

"Let me go!" I hollered, pulling and tugging with all my might. He was breaking my back. I had to fall in his arms, and he was smearing his big lips all over mine. He pulled me toward the bed. Instinctively I knew it was the worst thing that could happen to me, and I fought hard all the way. The baby and Flea watched with great interest as we struggled across the room. The boy threw me across the bed, and I shoved my knee in his groin as hard as I could. He yelped. "Bitch!" he shouted.

He was on me again and I bit him on the shoulder so hard the blood came. He yelled louder, then let out a horrible guttural sound. I saw blood everywhere, and he was reaching to his back where a butcher knife was stuck into him. Oh, Jesus! Frank was backed against the wall with his eyes as big as black plates, cowering in terror, while that nigger pulled out the knife and screamed, "I'm killed! Help me, Winfield, help! Oh, lordy, I'm dyin'!"

He lurched into the other room, leaving a trail of blood, and I stumbled to the door. His friends were gone. I looked outside and saw them chasing the little boys, who were running hard, each armed with a long knife, and Geraldine, who had an ice pick.

My attacker was still screaming that he was dying when his friends finally got to him. Don't die here, don't die here, I was thinking. They got him in the car and drove away hurriedly, the old car giving off explosions like gun blasts.

"I stuck the tires," Geraldine said triumphantly, testing the needle end of the ice pick with her finger.

I called all the boys to me and comforted Frank, who was crying. He'd never stuck anybody before and was all to pieces. I told him he had saved my life and was the bravest eight-year-old I had ever seen, and he felt better. Then I collected the knives and the ice pick and washed them off. We got the blood in the bedroom up before it dried and made a spot forever. Only a little blood got on the bed, and I was glad of that. Finally we settled down for another game of jacks, and Bobcat lay down in the mud and let a caterpillar crawl on his bare stomach.

"Bet they're some of those Turkey Neck bootlegger niggers," I said to Frank. "How come they had such a big car and neckties?"

"You think I killed him, Ophelia?" he asked eagerly.

"I don't rightly know. You could have. It may come out in the newspapers."

Frank's eyes popped wide open.

If it did, we never saw it, because we never saw newspapers, and we never heard of that bunch again. I guess Frank has gone through life wondering if he killed a man and maybe believing he did. He has always had a sense of great importance, anyway.

CHAPTER THREE

*A*fter the afternoon meeting, Joe and Carrie came home, leaving Mama to play the organ for the night service. I walked down the lane to the Big House, looking at the sky which was filled with fluffy pink clouds, the kind you see after a summer rain. The world seemed alive, living green, breathing, and the air smelled good and fresh. Two bobwhites were calling alarms from the bushes beside the field, and the nighthawks were skimming over the ditch. Little frogs jumped about everywhere, and big hidden ones were chirrumping.

> Where you going, little frog?
> Your jumping is so spry,
> You packing all you can in life
> Before you got to die?

Suddenly, shuddering, I thought of the boy who got me down on the bed. What would Mama say? Jesus, you were good to me today, I thought. The feeling of those big stranger lips on my mouth rushed over me and made my stomach rise.

I looked out at the river flowing so peacefully and felt better. The clouds reflected on it in a perfect pink path, and straight down the path, with its motor purring, I saw one of those big rich people's cabin boats, skimming along like it really knew the way.

The Big House loomed up before me on the little hill, its white sides tinged with pink from the sunset. It was an old, square, wood house built a long time ago by the slaves, so folks said. It had porches on the front and back with pretty banisters and rails, and there were green shutters at every window. The house stood up on high brick foundations, which were hidden

21

all around by latticework, some of it broken out through the years. Surrounding the house were enormous old boxwoods, and in the yard were four giant oak trees and a magnolia. The lane leading from the road to the house was lined with pecan trees.

Inside the house a wide hall went from the back door to the front, which faced the river, and a large parlor was on the right and a smaller living room on the left. The staircase with its shiny banister went up from the front hall. On its south side, the parlor had a large fireplace with brass andirons of lions' heads sitting in it, as if they were guarding it. Over it was the prettiest wooden mantel you could ever imagine with carved flower garlands at the top and fat angel heads at each side. Brass candlesticks stood at each end of the mantel, and in the center sat a beautiful wood-and-gold clock that ticked with such a deep and dignified sound it must have made every second feel very important. Every time I heard the old clock chime the hour a tingle would run through my body and I would feel like praying.

The parlor was filled with fragile-looking antique furniture, polished to a shine and smelling of wax, and it gave me a fright even to think of using it.

On the left of the back hall was the bedroom that Mr. Lockwood's mother, Miss Emmy, had slept in and, in fact, died in. Miss Emmy's white crocheted counterpane was still on the bed, and her hairbrush and silver hand mirror were on the tall dresser. This room was generally unused and saved for company, but it was dusted every week.

The large dining room on the right just inside the back door and a lavatory made from an old pantry under the stairs were the only other rooms downstairs. Upstairs were a hall, a regular bathroom with a tub—constructed in recent years from the old nursery—and three large bedrooms.

The walls were of white plaster, a little cracked, but fascinating to see after our unpainted, slatted ones. And there were pictures, some hand painted in gold frames, hanging in every room on long wires strung from the molding.

The house hadn't been painted in a good long time, but even with the white paint chipping off and the shutters faded to a moldy green, it was still grand. Chipped paint was a lot better than none. It was the only white folks' house I had ever been in, and when I tipped through it I felt strange, like an intruder.

This night there was an extra car there. The folks had eaten early, so I went toward the dining room to get up the dishes. Reaching the door, I saw a flash of blue dress and quickly backed up. Then I heard them.

"Janet, I love you." It was David Farthingale and Janet, who had come into the dining room to neck. I froze in a shadow. I could hear them kissing, then Janet giggling and saying kind of breathless, "Stop it! You're hurting my arm. We've got to go back on the porch."

I darted out the back door before they saw me and waited until I heard them go to the front porch. I listened long enough to know that Katie had come along with her brother to visit— come to see Leighton, rather, and who could blame her?

By the time I had finished the dishes, the moon was up. It was a glorious early summer moon, the kind that tugs on your insides trying to say something to you. I could hear Janet and David and Katie and Leighton talking and laughing on the front porch. Then I did a wicked thing: I slipped behind the boxwoods and peeped at them. Janet was sitting on the railing with her long, pale yellow hair shining in the moonlight. David was trying to get near her, first on one side, then on the other. If he sat still for a minute, she would tangle his hair with her fingers, keeping him stirred up, then throw her head back, arch her neck, and laugh. "Oh, David," she giggled, "you idiot."

I guess David was a sort of idiot, but there weren't many boys who could resist Janet's devilment. She was pretty, with those big blue eyes, dainty features, and long, silver-gold hair. Besides all that, she had the knack for using her charms, and David was no match for her wiles.

David and Katie looked a lot alike, with wavy auburn hair, freckles, and brownish-gray eyes. David was a good athlete, and Katie was a tomboy. She was a little square-looking without being fat, and she knew more about rowing a boat and riding a horse than she did about trading small talk with a boy. But they were Farthingales. This meant they were the best of folks in Attamac, and they belonged with the Lockwoods, just like sterling silver belongs with French china.

I really wanted to see what Leighton was doing and had to put my head over the porch to get a look. I would have died if they had caught me. He and Katie were sitting in the swing gliding softly back and forth, and he was holding her hand nervously, as though he was almost scared to, or maybe didn't want to and thought she expected it.

The pale silver light made the house shine whiter than ever, and they were like people in a storybook, half in and half out of the shadows and so beautiful. I could see a fleck of Katie's red hair when they swayed from the shadow into the moonlight, and then Leighton's handsome profile as he turned to her. She was staring back in a sort of trance. My heart pounded so loud I knew they could hear it.

Then suddenly Leighton kicked the floor, jerking the swing into a frenzy, and they spun around crazily with dots of light reflecting every which way. Katie squealed, and they went into spasms of loud, nervous laughter.

"Tommy Dorsey comes on in ten minutes," Janet announced, tuning the battery radio which she had propped on the steps. "This old amateur hour is sad."

"A girl from Pineville that I know got on it and won," Katie said with importance, stopping the jiggling swing with her feet.

"A soprano, I'll bet," Janet sneered.

"Well, yes, she was," Katie admitted.

"I would absolutely rather die than be or hear a soprano."

"You don't have a thing to worry about," put in Leighton. Then he began to sing in a high falsetto voice.

"Oh, dry up," Janet commanded. "Let's go to Macy's Cross for a Coca-Cola."

They ran through the moonlit yard, piled in the Farthingales' car, and drove away, all but Janet singing loudly in false soprano voices, "Over the summer sea,/With light hearts gay and free . . . ."

I kept quietly behind the boxwood until the singing died away in the summer night, then walked slowly on home.

CHAPTER FOUR

*he last week in June turned sunny and hot, and the to-
bacco grew tall, each plant spraying out like a fountain
with the large, pointed green leaves that would soon be
ripe for picking. We watched the fields with pleasure and
pride, every day saying to each other what a beautiful crop it
was this year. A good crop meant new patent leather shoes,
white organdy dresses, and plenty of coffee and sugar. Mr.
Lockwood told us on a Sunday night that we would start
barning the next day.

Mama and I felt a keen excitement early Monday morning
when we went to the Big House to cook breakfast. Mama put
on some collards and fatback for their dinner while I quickly
washed the dishes. Miss Lou would manage some way the rest
of the day while we went to help with the barning.

"Hurry, child, no time to lose," Mama exclaimed. There was
an urgency in the air as we walked briskly down the lane in
the hot July sunshine with our big straw hats on. Not a bird
was singing or a frog croaking; not even a breath of air was
stirring in the morning heat. Sweat poured off Mama's face
onto the front of her dress as we hurried along.

We went to help at Joe and Carrie's barn since most of their
children were too small to work. They had to bring the children along with them, however, and everybody helped mind
them. The old log barn was at the edge of the pine woods, and
Flea and baby Ethelene were put in an improvised playpen
under a shade tree nearby, while Bobcat and Scooter, barefooted and eager, were sent to scrounge dead branches for
the furnace with a warning to look out for rattlesnakes. Geraldine trailed after her brothers, her bottom lip poked out. It

was all great fun for them at first, but after a while they grew tired and cross. Finally Flea cried so hard Carrie let him out of the pen, and, wearing an old dress of Geraldine's with no pants under it, he wandered about happily, playing with the ax and a broken tobacco stick. Frank was big enough to hand tobacco, and Sammy drove the mule cart through the fields for the croppers to pile the leaves on.

I was excited because I would see Sue and Bucky, who would also be helping at the barn. In fact, during tobacco season we had to pitch in together with all our might.

Over near the woods I saw Sue helping her mother pick some chickens to put in the big iron pot over a fire to cook for the hands' dinner. I waved to her and she waved back, but there was no time for visiting. In a minute up rode Bucky in a mule cart full of tobacco sticks and began to unload them.

"Sure hot," he called to me by way of greeting.

"Sure is," I called back. "You going to crop?"

"Naw, hang."

Just then Mr. Lockwood drove up in the pickup with five extra hands, three men and two women, in the back, hired to help barn. One of these was shriveled, gray-headed old Granny Mosher, who lived on a houseboat on Chinquapin Crick and claimed to be ninety-three years old. Once last summer Sue and I had walked down to see her and, sure enough, found the boat, with Granny sitting out on the rickety little back deck, wearing a big straw hat and catfishing. She let us come aboard, put her pipe down, and spat a mouthful of snuff juice in the crick. By gosh, she was dipping and smoking at the same time, living on a boat, and had caught herself a big old cat to boot. She must have been the happiest person on earth. And what's more, she could still loop tobacco. It was good to see her back this year spry as ever.

27

Soon we were getting in line to begin the rites. Frank and I were assigned to "hand" the tobacco brought in by the croppers to the loopers, who tied it in bundles and put it on sticks that were placed in the barn for curing. We began eagerly, hands flying, straightening the sticky, yellowing leaves for the loopers.

"When you going to start hanging, Frank?" I asked him.

There was danger in standing up on the high rafters in the barn to hang the sticks of tobacco on the tier poles that crisscrossed the eaves.

"Next year," he boasted.

I knew he didn't want to hand because it was mainly women's work.

"You ever seen a barn burn up, Ophelia?" he asked.

"No, but I've seen one that had burned up the day before and was still smoking. Have you?"

"Yeah, on the farm where we lived before we come here. It 'sploded like a cannonball. I ain't never seen nothin' like it."

"Was it night?"

"Yeah, the flues busted. Looked like all hell broke loose."

I glanced at him in surprise. "And all that tobacco gone?"

"That's why we come here. Pa couldn't pay off."

I cringed. If a barn caught fire it went up with a blast that blotted out a lot of the year's work. It was a fear we all lived with, and the reason why once the furnace was fired to start the curing, somebody had to watch it day and night.

The first few days we finished early because the lugs were the only leaves ripe enough to pick, but by the middle of July we were working from early morning to sunset, always hoping the weather would stay dry enough to finish the barning.

One afternoon a thunderstorm came up with a sudden boiling wind. Rumbles of thunder began way across the river, followed by a cracking flash of lightning that sent the croppers scurrying for shelter. Carrie lumbered to the woods to gather the children, and we hovered together under the lean-to shed of the barn, anxiously watching the black clouds swirl across the sky with quick, bright forks of electricity darting toward the hot earth. I felt breathless; my heart beat fast as a torrent of rain crashed on the tin roof of the shed and a pine tree not a hundred feet away was hit by a bolt of lightning that split it in half with a sizzle and a thunderburst that stunned us. We gasped, the children screamed, and even Mama uttered a cry. Lightning was the one thing on earth she feared besides the devil. She had had an aunt who was struck and killed at a to-bacco barn long ago, and I had heard the story so often I felt I had seen her myself, with the long white sear from her head right down her body and out one foot. I saw Mama squint her eyes and move her lips in silent prayer as we jostled around nervously, sweating and terrified.

The squall soon moved away to the east, but not before the fields were flooded, making it impossible for the cart to get through the furrows. Mr. Lockwood sent us home for the day. I could see the worried look on his face as he glanced at the sky. If the rain continued for several days, the tobacco, which was exactly right for picking, might shrivel up, flop, and die. But fortunately the sun was out the next morning and quickly dried the fields.

Mama and I took turns with Sue and her mother boiling the pot for dinner. We had pork and corn meal dumplings, chicken pastry, brunswick stew, and sometimes fried fish. Everything out of that pot tasted more delicious than what they serve in the finest restaurants in Washington, D.C., or New York City.

After working so hard all day, how wonderful to eat, all of us together, like a picnic. Appetizing odors made you forget your aching feet and blistered fingers.

> Tobacco, you are green, then gold.
> Will I turn too when I am old?
> Tobacco, some say you're a sin,
> But we're living off you, friend.

I laughed when I thought that up. I was handing, handing the sticky leaves, drenched with sweat and shifting from one bare foot to the other.

"What's so funny?" asked Carrie, who was looping surprisingly fast for her. Her stomach was bigger than last month, and she was wearing a Mother Hubbard, the best maternity dress of all. Her eyeballs were pure yellow, and for once her mouth was closed, with a big bulge of snuff in her cheek.

"Nothing, just thinking about tobacco, how preachers say it's so sinful and nearabout all of them smoke it."

"They ain't always right," she answered in a muffled voice.

Suddenly little Flea let out a horrible yelp from the woodpile. Carrie loped over to him in her heavy gait. Blood was spurting from his foot, and he was screaming in pain and terror.

"Jesus!" Carrie cried. "Oh, Jesus, he done cut his toe off! Oh, lordy, help! Help!"

We all went flying to them, even Granny Mosher.

"I told you not to play with that ax," Carrie wailed at Flea, as she grabbed him up with his little toe dangling and the blood dripping.

"Wrap a piece of 'bacco round it; it'll staunch the bleedin'," screeched Granny Mosher, and somebody ran for a leaf. We gaped in horror as the blood stained the woodpile.

Carrie wrapped the tobacco around the hanging, bloody little toe and held it tightly while chanting, "Oh, lordy, lordy, help me, help me." I never saw Carrie so to pieces before.

"The boy needs to go to the doctor," said Mama sensibly, and Carrie moaned all the louder because in those days going to the doctor was a case of real extremity. Luckily, as the Good Lord would have it, at that moment up drove Mr. Lockwood in the pickup and took them to Attamac, twelve miles away, to the doctor. Away they went down the road in a cloud of dust. Mr. Lockwood would have taken that boy to the doctor if his whole crop of tobacco had been wiped out. He was just that kind of man.

When Joe, who had been cropping, came back to the barn, we told him what had happened.

"Well, I be damn!" he exclaimed in his reedy voice. "Gone to the doctor. I be damn." He shook his head unbelievingly and started unloading the cart. He wasn't a bit worried about paying the doctor, because he knew either Mr. Lockwood would pay the bill or the doctor would charge it and never expect to be paid.

CHAPTER FIVE

he rain held off, and we got the tobacco cured and graded. Mr. Lockwood and Mr. Deiter had charge of taking it to market. Our job was done.

It was hot and dusty and suffocating by the middle of August. I walked over to see Sue on a Saturday afternoon while the rest of her family had gone to Attamac. Their house was not too far from the woods and was much nicer than Carrie's. For one thing, they had only five head of children, and they were older and could help around the house more.

"Hey, Sue!" I called.

"Come on in, Ophelia. I got this here doggone ironin' to do. Sit down and talk while I finish. We got behind durin' tobacco."

Sue was a pretty girl with darting, unquiet eyes and very dark skin. Her mouth had a nice shape, and there was something attractive about the way she moved around and held her head. She was fourteen, her body was plump and pretty, her breasts had come out in cute mounds, and the boys liked her. Sue knew a lot of things that she didn't mind telling me, and I never got tired of listening.

She was sweating over an overstarched, blue, man's shirt spread over the ironing board. The board was set up in the front room, where they had a sofa, only busted a tiny bit, an old Victrola that wouldn't play but looked good and shiny, some chairs with straw bottoms, one iron bed, and above all, a radio. It was their pride and joy, and it was playing.

"What you listening at?" I asked.

"Opras."

"What's that?"

"I don't 'xactly know. Some queer kind of stuff that come on from a record, the man said. Listen!"

The batteries were getting weak, and a soprano was faintly trilling between blasts of static. We bent double giggling. Sue gave an imitation, and we laughed until we were crying. "Oh, lordy," I shouted. "Must be something new they've thought up."

The iron had become cold, and when Sue looked in the stove, the fire was out. "Fire's out, dammit," she muttered. "I'm too hot to build it up. Let's go to the woods. I know where some grapes are ripe."

Barefooted and still giggling, we walked down the dusty path toward the woods.

"You know that Maggie Lamb, don't you?" Sue asked.

"Yeah, the high-yellow gal on the Neck road."

"You know who her pa is?"

"No, who?"

"Old man Deiter."

I gasped and covered my mouth with my hand. "You reckon Mr. Lockwood knows it?"

"Sure he do. Everybody do."

"And he don't fire him?"

"Listen, dummy, things like that happen every day. Jed Deiter's ast me to."

I gasped again. "You didn't?" I cried eagerly.

"I ain't studyin' him. I told him where to go." Her nostrils flared.

"Sue," I asked fearfully, "you ever done it?"

She walked along quietly for a moment. "Once," she answered, tossing her head.

I looked at her aghast. "Who with?" I whispered.

"Bucky."

I stopped dead still. This came as a terrible shock. I thought an awful lot of Bucky. "Your brother! It couldn't of been much . . . . I mean, how come you picked your brother?"

"I didn't 'xactly. You don't know boys; you ain't got no brothers. Ophelia, boys are mighty different from girls. They got their mind in their britches nearabout all the time. You'll find out one day."

I shuddered at the tantalizing thought. "Where'd . . . ?"

"Oh, at home one day when Ma and Pa were gone. He tried it some. I didn't like it and made him quit. I don't know what they see in it. It ain't nothin', believe me." She was smooth, wise.

"Maybe it's different to everybody," I remarked, and she cut her knowing black eyes at me and squinted.

"Here's the grapevine," she whispered. "Let's slip under it."

"This here's Mr. Deiter's vine!"

"Shhh! Ripe grapes belong to anybody whose tongue is set for 'em, and my mouth is pure waterin'."

We left the path and slipped under the immense scuppernong vine which was loaded with the greenish-gray grapes, their winey aroma casting us under a spell. How heavenly they tasted on the hot August afternoon. The vine covered an area the size of a small house, and the sunshine never penetrated the thick branches. Deep shadows hid our brown arms and fingers as they wove in and out of the coils, busily picking the grapes. We placed the tiny mouths of the grapes on our lips, gave a hard squeeze, and the squirt of delicious juice and pulp rolled about on our tongues. We were careful not to bite the seeds, which were bitter and could ruin the whole taste. It was endless joy; each grape called for another. Suddenly Sue screamed.

"A snake! A little green one right up there!"

He was the color and shape of the vines.

"He won't hurt you, Sue," I said, getting a better look.

But the shadows were deepening, and we didn't quite have the nerve to put our hands up into the coiled vine again. So reluctantly we left, almost, but not quite satisfied with the luscious grapes.

We got back to Sue's in time to see the family coming down the lane in the mule-drawn Hoover cart. Willie and Bea sat in front with packages piled between them, and the four head of children were in the back. I waited to speak to them, but I couldn't look at Bucky—I kept thinking of what Sue had told me. He called to me and asked if he could walk home with me. I didn't say no, and we walked along quietly. I couldn't think of a thing to say.

Bucky was a tall, big-boned boy with a large, honest mouth and a short, flat nose. Almost always he had a serious expression, often pursing his lips and frowning as though his thoughts perplexed him. He had on a new shirt and tie, probably bought that day, and when we were out of sight of the others, he pulled out some Wing cigarettes.

"Bucky!" I blurted, forgetting that other thing. "You're not smoking?"

"Sure I am. Make my own money on tobacco now." He jerked the pack open with his teeth and awkwardly got out a cigarette. A good part of the tobacco in it fell out, but he gamely put the limp remains in his mouth and struck a match. He sucked in and coughed, a little embarrassed. I knew he hadn't had a chance to practice up. He took the cigarette from his mouth, placed it between his second and third fingers, and puffed again more carefully.

"Let me have one," I begged.

He pulled a cigarette from the pack, gave it to me, and lighted it. I drew in and out and quickly got the knack of it. We smoked all the way home. I felt so grown up smoking, and with a boyfriend, an *experienced* boyfriend, wearing a white shirt and a brown checked necktie.

Suddenly, with no warning, my head started spinning and my stomach heaved with a throbbing convulsion. The grapes rose up together in a great wave; my brain went pop, pop, pop, and I ran for the privy, where I hung my head over the smelly hole. After I lost everything, my head rolled around and I noticed the half-smoked cigarette still burning on the floor. I picked it up and threw it down the hole and it went pshhh.

I was too embarrassed to come out and face Bucky, so I stayed in there a long time. When I came out, he was gone, and I slunk in the house and lay on the bed, sweating.

I couldn't go to the Big House to help Mama that night. I lay there and thought of those beautiful grapes that were all wasted and how my walk with Bucky had been ruined. Why? Because I had sinned, sinned, sinned. Even though we grew tobacco, smoking cigarettes was a sin. That's what Mama always told me. And you can't get away from sin: you've got to suffer for it.

Mama told me a lot about sin; in fact, I was raised hearing about it. Reverend Halleck never let up on it—every Sunday he preached that sin, suffering, and forgiveness all went together in a row. Sin was real to Mama like a person, like the Devil himself. Mama suffered for her sins and she did it joyfully, she said. When her bad tooth ached, she was paying a debt she owed. She got something out of everything. She took her burden of suffering so gladly she made a real pleasure of it. This confused me. If you enjoyed something, it didn't seem like suffering.

There was something to do with my father that Mama made out to be connected with sin, and she told me how much she suffered for that and how I would suffer in my life for it, too, because of the Commandment about the sins of the fathers visiting the third and fourth generations, although I was only the second. I often wondered what my punishment would be and asked Mama about it. She said she couldn't tell, but when it came I'd know it.

Maybe I'd get typhoid fever or more likely the leprosy that sounded so horrible in the Bible. A star might fall on me, or my sweetheart leave me. I wondered a whole lot about the suffering that would come to me because of my father. What had he done? Killed somebody? Stolen things? Mama wouldn't tell me. He remained an exciting, mysterious shadow. But I had a feeling for him, a sort of longing, especially when I looked at my wavy brown hair and my creamy skin and knew I was the embodiment of part of him. Then I wanted the suffering to come so that I could receive something from him, do something for him, whoever he was, wherever he might be.

CHAPTER SIX

I *always loved the river so much. It had as many moods as* a person, and to me it seemed a living thing with its own thoughts and plans as it went running, dipping, churning toward the sea as though it was searching for home. Some nights in August Sue and I went down to bathe in it. They were hot, still nights, lavish in mosquitoes, millions of them, with their sickening drone sounding faintly against the loud blare of the katydids. We slipped through the edge of Miss Lou's lawn, the grass soft and furry under our hot feet. Grass was a luxury like a real carpet.

We crept past Leighton's old rowboat to the shore. The water was lapping timidly on the narrow, sandy beach as though it hated to make any noise at all, but was only whispering a little secret. Even though there was no moon, we could see where we were going. The little waves shimmered and gurgled. A few cypress trees grew just off the shore with their big, gnarled roots looking like spooks and dwarfs. We stayed away from them because of snakes.

We didn't have any bathing suits, never did as children. Whispering in low voices, we took off our clothes, put them carefully over a bush, and, giggling, waded into the river. We were the color of the night and of the quivering water that soothed our bodies with warm caresses. The river was like fresh tea with sugar in it. I had brought a tiny piece of soap to scrub with, and it was a sheer delight washing clean in the river. Then we were fish and boats and frogs. We didn't know about mermaids. We forgot we were growing up; the river made us feel like children. I ducked my head, but Sue wouldn't.

But she could float on her back for a few seconds with her plump, round breasts pointing up to heaven. We couldn't swim a lick.

Suddenly Sue hissed at me. She pointed to something white coming down the lawn to the beach, somebody walking to the shore in a white dress, drifting along like a fairy. We were quiet as ghosts in our nakedness. Miss Lou never told us not to bathe here, but we didn't want to get caught.

The figure went silently down the beach for a long way, and after a while we saw a match struck to light a cigarette.

"It's Janet," I whispered, "smoking."

We very quietly left the water and crept to the bush to put our clothes on, feeling refreshed and excited.

"Let's see where she's gone," Sue suggested, full of curiosity. "Ouch! These pesky mosquitoes!"

They seemed to bite Sue more than me. Maybe her meat was sweeter.

We sneaked down the beach, dashing quietly from bush to bush until we saw Janet. She was sitting cross-legged, hunched on the sand Indian style, her head back, smoking. She was a self-possessed thing, cocksure of everything she did. She was sitting there like she owned the world, smoking like a movie star. For some reason it irritated me.

Then, someone tall was approaching. We held our breath. It was Jed Deiter! We could make out his handsome, sun-burned face and his head of slicked-down black hair. He had on white duck pants rolled up to his knees and a sweat shirt. He was barefooted, walking with quick, jerky steps as though in a hurry.

Janet didn't even look around, just puffed nonchalantly on her cigarette. Staring at the dark river, she said something in a low voice, but we couldn't hear what. We sneaked up closer.

"What happened last night?" he asked gruffly, sitting down beside her. She turned her head toward him slightly.

"I couldn't make it." She flipped her cigarette into the river.

"I waited an hour," he said, angry.

He stretched out quickly, propping up on one elbow and putting his other arm around her. She kept gazing at the stars with her neck in a long curve, her blonde hair flowing loosely down her back.

Jed pulled her down to his face and kissed her. She stayed stiff and indifferent. Then he grabbed her, threw her all the way on her back, and kissed her wildly, leaning on her, holding her roughly. Sue's mouth popped open and she put her hand over it. We could hear them panting.

"I love you, love you, love you," Jed muttered in a hoarse, low voice, kissing her between words. "Someday I'm going to . . ."

"What?" she whispered.

"Have you. Take you. Rape you."

As we watched, Janet laughed and sat up, brushing the sand out of her hair and fluffing it.

"What do you feel, Janet? You've got to feel something to let me do this."

"What do you want me to feel?" She touched his face.

"Like I do," he said huskily, drawing her closer to him.

"What would Mother say?" She giggled.

"What would she say if I ast you to the movies?"

"She wouldn't let me. You're too old for me."

"No, I'm the tenant farmer's son," he said bitterly.

"You're nice," she soothed.

"I'm not good enough for no nice girl."

"Am I a nice girl?"

40

He had her down again, kissing her in a new clinch. "No," he muttered.

This time they went on a long time. They were real kisses. He had her pasted all over him and he was all over her. His hands were busy on her white dress, and she kept pushing them away. They didn't talk, just struggled and kissed and rolled over and over and breathed hard, he cussing her and her arm around his neck. Sue and I were fascinated, google-eyed. Then he was pulling up her dress.

"You're not!" she hollered, sitting up and panting wildly, her hair every which way.

"You've got to!" he rasped, and plastered her to him again on the sand. But she held onto his arms somehow and in between kisses gasped, "I'll never come again if you don't behave."

Finally he let go and she pulled away from him, leaning back on her elbows again, her chin up. "Real starry tonight," she said softly. He walked to the water's edge, waded in, and threw water over his head and neck. Then he came back to her, sat down again, and put his arm loosely around her waist.

"Want to cross the river tomorrow night?"

"How?"

"I know where I can borrow a boat."

"Motorboat?"

"Yeah."

"Hm . . . I'll try to think of something to tell Mother."

"Be here at eight?"

"I might." She rubbed her nose on his cheek.

"You're going to drive me out of my mind, Janet."

"You'll get used to it," she teased.

An owl hooted from a pine above the beach.

He kissed her again, his hand on her waist, gently caressing.

41

She snuggled into his arms. I thought they would never get enough of kissing and loving, but he seemed calmer and more controlled. It was on her terms now. We waited them out. It took a long time, and I began to feel wrung out. I wondered how Janet felt. Finally she pulled herself away. "I've got to go. It's late. Daddy'll be out looking for me."

"I'd like to walk you home."

"No, you can't."

"Be here tomorrow night?"

"I might."

She walked away without turning around, her white dress floating down the pale beach. The waves leaped on the sand with more force. A breeze had sprung up and there was sheet lightning at intervals. Jed stood there, alone with his passion, watching Janet fade away. We could almost smell him as the breeze cooled him off. He watched her disappear, hunched his shoulders, and walked rapidly away in the opposite direction, his dark head bent down.

"He done told the truth about one thing," Sue said when we were alone.

"What's that?"

"He sure fixin' to rape her."

"Maybe she wants him to." I giggled.

"She ain't got no business with that toad-frog."

"Her ma's going to skin her alive one day."

"She ain't nothin' but trouble and fixin' to get in more."

"Mama said she's got wild blood like a gypsy," I agreed.

"And her brother got tame blood," Sue added.

I started to take up for Leighton, but kept quiet and felt the blood running hot in my head.

"We'd better go now," I said.

Mama was sitting on the porch fanning the mosquitoes and

waiting for us. "How come you so late?" she asked. "You been up to something?"

"No ma'am," I answered. "It was nice and cool by the river." We giggled.

The wind increased and the lightning flashed brightly. Sue ran for home through the windy shadows. Mama and I went in the house, took out the sticks that propped up the windows, and let them down. It began to pour. When we got in bed and blew out the lamp, the wind whistled in the cracks, and I pulled the sheet over my head. Through the storm I thought of Jed Deiter and Janet. With each cracking flash of lightning I could see them plastered together on the beach with her white dress crumpled in the sand. And with the terrible bombardment of the thunder, I crept deeper into the bed nearer Mama, my heart pounding wildly, trembling at the naked emotions of the night.

CHAPTER SEVEN

ollowing the rainstorm we had a vanilla day, pure and shiny. I went to the Big House to do the breakfast dishes and a little light washing. Janet had washed her hair and was sitting outside on the back steps drying it and writing a letter. She had on shorts and sat with one leg propped up on the rail. She didn't look up at me.

"Hey, Janet," I muttered to her as I went up the steps.

"Ophelia, I've got a blouse for you upstairs. Come up and get it before you leave."

"Thank you." Her manner made me mad, but I wanted the blouse. It might be silk.

When I had finished the dishes and was on my way to Janet's room I met Miss Lou in the hall. "Here's something for you, Ophelia." She gave me a quarter. It was a lot of money.

"Thank you, ma'am," I said happily. She didn't have to pay me. It was her house we lived in. "Janet said come get a blouse," I added.

"Go on up there. She's in her room. And, oh, Ophelia, have you seen a little blue vase with butterflies painted on it? My Aunt Jessica made it, oh . . . fifty years ago at the Seminary. I seem to have misplaced it."

"No, ma'am, I ain't seen it." Miss Lou was always losing things.

I went upstairs, tiptoeing. The Big House always had a mysterious odor of something like old wood and paper. When I smelled it, my heart started dancing, maybe because I was in another, finer world. When I smell that odor today, my heart beats fast in the same way and I get the same elated feeling.

I had to pass Leighton's bedroom. I tried not to look in, but

44

I couldn't keep my eyes from turning. He was lying on his stomach on the bed, propped up on his elbows, looking at a magazine. I quickly tipped on to Janet's room and knocked on the door frame. She was in her slip putting on fingernail polish and holding up her hand to dry.

"Over there on the chair," she waved to me.

It was a white rayon blouse with a little torn place near the bottom and a button off in the back. I loved it.

"Thank you," I said and started to leave.

"Did you get my panties and stuff washed?" she asked.

"Yeah."

"Good. And Ophelia, you want a movie magazine?"

Janet was surely in a good humor.

"Yeah," I said.

"That one under the table."

I took it. On the cover was Jean Harlow with her platinum blonde hair. "Thanks!" I said warmly.

I went quietly back down the hall. Leighton was still lying on the bed, but now the magazine was put aside and he was on his side looking at the wall, the back of his blond head turned to the door. I flew downstairs, my heart pounding.

After dinner, when I was sweating over the dishes in the kitchen, Leighton came in. He was tall and slender with a large, handsome face topped with wavy, golden hair that he tried to slick back, but that bulged over his forehead in a pompadour. His eyes were as blue as cornflowers, like his daddy's, and his skin was so fair it was pink with a few freckles dotting his long, straight nose and his cheeks. He had Miss Lou's wide, thin mouth. When he talked he would raise his eyebrows and wrinkle his forehead, which gave him a little-boy air. Today he was wearing khaki pants rolled up to his knees, a light blue shirt, and tennis shoes.

45

"How about helping me tar the boat this afternoon, Ophelia?" he asked.

I wiped my face with my arm, hating for him to see me so sweaty. "Okay!" My insides sparkled.

"Bring some old tin cans, will you?"

"All right." I hurried to get the dishes done.

The rowboat was turned upside down near the boat dock in the scorching two-o'clock sun. Leighton had a little fire of driftwood going and over it teetered a pot of boiling tar that smelled strong and exciting.

"You're going to turn over the tar," I warned him.

"Go get me some bricks," he ordered, and I ran back to the house and spotted some under the porch. I found a place where the latticework was rotten and loose and climbed through. My dress got hung on a nail, which ripped a long gash and left a regular train dangling in the back. I thought, Mama will kill me. I had to tear the piece all the way off, a good three inches all around, leaving me a very short skirt. Leighton, being a gentleman, didn't seem to notice.

We got the tar pot on the bricks and I gathered more driftwood to burn. Then with long sticks we dabbed the boat seams with the hot, gooey tar. It was a long, sweltering job. Leighton's face got redder and redder and the sweat poured off both of us.

"You're about to blister," I told him.

He had a perspiration mustache. "How about some water?" he said, wiping his face with his sleeve.

I ran for the water bucket that sat on the back porch and brought it with the dipper. He flung some dipperfuls over his head and neck and then drank and drank. I was as thirsty as I had ever been, but naturally I couldn't drink from the dipper,

46

as it was improper. So after he'd had plenty, I found a mussel shell on the beach and poured myself some drinks in it.

As we worked, we talked some, but not much, mainly about the boat and him telling me what crack to fill next. It was a happy afternoon.

"That's about it," he said finally. "Thanks, Ophelia. You're real good help." I swelled with pride. "Guess I'll go get a bath now." He laughed and walked slowly up the incline to the house, his face a brilliant pink against the green lawn.

"He's going to hurt tonight," I said to myself. Then I waded into the river to cool off my feet and splash my hot face. I had tar all over me, pulling on the skin of my arms and legs. I rubbed sand on it, but it stuck like only tar can. I sat down to work some off my feet where the coal-black spots were the worst.

"I ain't as black as tar," I thought happily. "I'm lots, lots lighter. Why, I look real white beside tar." I scraped until my fingernails were loaded, sitting on the sand with my spotted feet stuck in the edge of the timid little waves, watching the clouds change from orange to pink as the sun began to set. A poem invaded my brain.

> Pink is a feeling,
> Pink is a mood,
> I love pink dresses,
> I like pink food.
> Pink is the way
> I feel when I'm proud,
> And I'd like to live
> On that little pink cloud.

And I was right on that pink cloud as I walked home in my

47

torn dress, looking like a leopard with tar spots. But Mama didn't say much because it was Saturday night and Reverend Halleck was coming and they would be having a grand time as usual.

About eight o'clock, after a delicious catfish supper, I decided to walk over to Sue's. The sky was dark, the pink clouds were gone, but the air was still balmy and I felt wonderful. A toad-frog jumped over my ankle and I scooted down the lane like a scared mouse. Lightning bugs flickered all about, and the dryflies were blaring out their rasping song that reminds you of summer coming to its end. The whole world was pulsating like a motor, humming, buzzing, and glimmering.

Sue was sitting under the umbrella tree cooling off when I got there. Sonny, Monk, and Almalee were running around squealing and catching lightning bugs, and Bucky, too old for such messing, sat hunched on the edge of the porch chewing on a straw and slapping mosquitoes. Willie and Bea were inside working the radio that was giving out a variety of static. I sat down on a board beside Sue, picked a piece of sour grass, and sucked the stem.

"How you doin'?" she asked with a yawn.

"Okay." I told her how Janet had given me the silk blouse and the movie magazine, but I didn't tell her about tarring the boat.

"How come you didn't bring it?" she asked, referring to the magazine.

"Didn't think of it."

Bucky walked over and joined us. "How you doin'?" he asked. It was the first time I had seen him since the cigarette smoking, and I could feel my face prickle.

"Fine. How're you?" Our conversations were never very fluent.

"Okay."

"Lookee, Sis!" Monk screamed at Sue, sticking a glass bottle of lightning bugs under her nose.

"Yeah. Ouuu! They stink!" Sue hollered, to his great delight. The bugs obliged by cutting their taillights off and on. They never ceased to fascinate us.

"How come they never lights up in the day?" asked Almalee, holding one in her fingers.

"Ain't nothin' fool enough to light lamps in the daytime," Sue told her.

"Wonder could I light up if I et one?" Monk asked with scientific imagination. "Wonder what they tastes like?"

We laughed as he pondered over eating one that he held up gingerly in his fingers. Finding himself the center of attention, he put the bug in his mouth and bit it. Then with a yowl he began to spit and gag while we roared with laughter and rolled on the ground.

"You sure lit up," Bucky told him between side-splitting guffaws, and Monk, his spasm over, turned angrily on us.

"Niggers! Niggers! Goddamn niggers!" he screeched and went flying in the house, yelling that we had made him eat a bug.

When we got through with our laughing spell, I asked Sue if she was going to school this year.

"Naw. I'm goin' to help Ma."

"You going, Bucky?" He was supposed to graduate soon.

"Naw, me neither. I got to work."

It worried me to think they were no longer going to school. When you got through with school you were grown and ready to get married and go to work forever. It gave me a funny feeling to realize that they had finished with children things like school. Mama always said she wanted me to go on and

49

then to college to become a teacher. Hardly anyone went to college, especially colored people. I wasn't even sure what it meant. I had never known a soul, except some white folks, of course, who had gone, not even our schoolteacher. But Mama wanted me to go. Just wanting to, just talking about it, made me different from almost everybody else I knew, whether I ever went or not.

As I was mulling over these disturbing things, we heard the sound of a motorboat from the river, loud and clear. The strained, roaring drone reached every inch of the farm, filled the air for miles. Sue and I looked at each other and I clapped my hand over my mouth. We knew what it was. Janet was getting ready to cross the river with Jed Deiter!

CHAPTER EIGHT

*S*chool started the middle of August. Then, in peanut harvest time, it would let out a couple of weeks while the colored children helped with the crop. At seven-thirty in the morning I walked past the Big House down the river road to the place where the old yellow school bus picked us up. There I saw Sonny, Almalee, and Frank Batts waiting, with their lunches in brown paper sacks. Monk had his wrapped in a greasy newspaper. All the boys were spick-and-span in starched shirts and overalls. Almalee had her hair in cute pigtails tied with pink ribbons and wore her pink organdy Sunday dress. The first day of school was always a big occasion.

We all felt butterflies in our stomachs, especially Frank, who had never been to school before, although he was eight years old. He was clutching a certificate from the health department that stated he had had a smallpox vaccination, and he felt real important flashing it around. Sonny jerked it away from him and pretended to tear it up until Frank cried and I had to get them settled down. We were fascinated with Frank's vaccination, which was taking in the worst way. It was as big as an egg and oozing. In fact, it looked a lot like a fried egg, but with the white in the middle and the yellow around the edge.

"Don't it hurt?" asked Almalee with maternal concern.

Frank sniffed. "Some."

"Godamighty!" exclaimed Monk, his eyes wide in admiration.

"Ain't you never had one?" Frank asked.

"Naw."

"How you get in school?"

"When they asts me I say I had it."

"Cain't they prove you ain't?"

"Naw. They just goes on to somebody else."

The yellow bus approached and we boarded it. There were plenty of old friends on it, and we shouted and laughed all the way to school. The driver was a big boy named Perry and he always let us have all the fun we wanted to. Sometimes the little boys got in a fight and the big ones egged them on, but I guess that was a part of their education. To me school always was fun from start to finish.

Our teacher was Miss Lovey. She was plump, with grayish hair, a nice face, and freckles under her light skin. What Miss Lovey lacked in education she made up for in authority. She knew how to whip those boys in line and she was a good teacher. She had six head of children herself, all grown, and she used to tell us how they were doing up in New York and Philadelphia. One was in Washington, D.C. Then once she cried right in school and told us her oldest boy, John Henry, had been killed up in New York City. The police had written her a letter saying he had been stabbed, but she never found out how it happened or who did it or why. And they buried him up there at the city's expense because Miss Lovey didn't get the message in time to have his body sent home, and she wouldn't have had enough money anyway. But the next summer she rode to New York on the bus, went to his grave and took some flowers, and she felt a lot better.

After that, at recess, the boys used to play a game they called "Who Killed John Henry?" One boy would close his eyes and another pretended to stab him with a stick. Then the one who was knifed would run after the others, accusing each one in turn until the guilty one confessed, if he ever would. Even though it didn't have much point, it was an exciting game because it was based on a real murder. Miss Lovey would smile sadly when they played it, but she never told them not to. Maybe she felt it was a sort of honor to have her son's death commemorated in this manner, and I wouldn't be surprised if the little boys along the Chilliwan aren't still playing "Who Killed John Henry?" though few now remember who John Henry was.

We went to an old one-room school set on a rise in the woods in one of the prettiest places I've ever seen. In the spring the dogwood trees bloomed all around it, and we got our drinking water from a spring that bubbled right out of the ground. What delicious, cool water. Sometimes I think of that water with a great longing.

Miss Lovey had her hands full teaching everybody everything. Some days we had over forty head in school, and other days, just fifteen or twenty. Almost everybody was irregular. There were first-graders to seniors, and it was up to Miss Lovey to say who belonged where. She had everyone pegged just right. Some of the big girls and boys helped with the smaller ones. After you graduated you could still go another year or two if you wanted to, but when you became sixteen you usually graduated or quit without graduating if you had been just impossible.

The little children learned reading, writing, and arithmetic and colored a lot with little bits of crayons on rough yellow tablets. We older ones studied some history and geography. The day started with singing "America." Then we said the Lord's Prayer. There was one little first-grader named Santo who had a weak bladder, or maybe praying made him nervous. Every morning when we got to "Forgive us our trespasses" we heard a little noise. Santo had had another accident.

"Amen. Get the mop, Ophelia," Miss Lovey would say. She was always kind. We tried not to notice him.

Finally, when the weather got cold, Miss Lovey said one day, "Santo will stand outside the door while we pray." It was a sensible solution, for I was tired of mopping up every day. Santo never made another mistake. He had perfect control after that, even on those bitter cold mornings before the stove could heat up and we stood in our coats shivering and praying.

My favorite subject was geography. Such exciting places were pictured in *The Book of Many Lands*. We went across the oceans to China and Jay-pan and the South Sea Islands. We traveled to India, where we saw a picture of a holy man with a terrible snake in front of him and a king riding on an elephant. How I wished we had such exciting things in our country— emperors, kings, sultans, sheiks, Chinamen, temples, jungles, deserts, caravans. And Africa!

"Did we really come from Africa?" we asked with big eyes. In the book all the Africans were tall and wore such beautiful headdresses.

"Do they kill you with poison darts?" "Will crocodiles eat you?" "What are baboons?" "Do lions tear you apart?" "Do we have kinfolks there?"

Miss Lovey painted a colorful picture of the mysterious continent that fired our imagination. She told us about the chiefs, the tribal wars, the voodoo medicine men, the jungles filled with lions, savage animals, and big snakes, and the boom-ing drums. We could hear those drums; they were real and thrilling. She made Africa seem like the fountain of life and mystery, and she gave us an exciting reason for our color and racial differences. She made us happy and proud we came from such a strange, rich land. We were Africans! From the land of the lion, giraffe, and elephant. When she got through

I felt embarrassed about having part West Indian blood. I wrote a poem on Africa.

> Africa, the sunny place
> With lions and tigers on your face,
> Jungles growing on your head,
> Warriors sleeping in your bed.
> I can smell your strange dark mud
> And feel your drums beat in my blood.

I showed this poem to Miss Lovey. She thought it was lovely and was excited to think she had a pupil who wrote it. She wanted to send it in to a newspaper, but she never did.

Then she told us about the cannibals, the terrible savages who ate you. Our eyes bulged in horror, and we weren't sure we wanted to visit Africa after all. Bad people, she said, are everywhere, even in sunny Africa. But they were honest cannibals who ate your body for food. They didn't have any pigs or chickens and they were hungry. The word of the Lord hadn't reached them. I wondered if the word of the Lord could make them less hungry. I thought of Jesus, how He said to eat His body. What did it mean? Were Christians supposed to act like cannibals?

We spent a lot of time studying Abraham Lincoln, the funny-looking man with the long beard like God's in the Bible Story Book, only Mr. Lincoln was taller than God. He was everybody's hero. What made him so nice was that he used to live on a farm and outdoors in the woods like all of us. He had to cut down trees and split wood and kill chickens. We could understand Mr. Lincoln. Then, of course, he freed the slaves, just like Moses freeing the chosen people in the Bible. We learned about the Emancipation Proclamation—big words for a big job, but known to every child in school, even the beginners. When Miss Lovey told us they shot Mr. Lincoln, she cried and we felt tingles on our spine. "When they write a new book of the Bible," she said through her tears, "Mr. Lincoln will be in it." On his birthday we had a party—grape pop and flycakes with lots of raisins.

Once we had a storybook about the Greek gods and goddesses. We had heard of idols, but we didn't know a thing about gods. They weren't idols or images, Miss Lovey told us, but like beautiful people, only spirits, who had come down to earth to mess around. They had wavy yellow hair and were magical, flying about eating and talking and getting mad. One was named Apollo. I said it over and over. It had a foreign sound, a magic flavor. Apollo. I thought about Leighton, the way he looked the day we tarred the boat. Apollo looked just like Leighton.

There was a fire tower down the road from the schoolhouse, a steel frame with narrow steps and handrails. The sign said it was ninety feet high. Sometimes we used to walk over to it at lunch time and eat our lunch around it. Miss Lovey always warned us not to climb it, but she knew we would if the forest fire man wasn't there. It was more fun than a carnival, especially since we had never been to a carnival.

I remember that it was scary and dizzy to go up. If you looked straight down you might fall. Our stomachs would go funny and we'd holler and pretend to faint. You were a yellow-bellied, chicken-livered scaredy-cat if you didn't get your nerve up and climb to the top, but some of the girls just wouldn't go. Once a girl named Elvira got sick and threw up near the top. The ones on the ground caught some of the fly, and they had some things to tell her. She inched down, sweating and gray with fright, crying, "Oh, Jesus, help me, help me!" But most of us could go up and down without going to pieces, and we felt we had done something grand. It was fun to spit from the top or let your handkerchief float down. One time Sonny hung by his knees from the top rail and we girls swooned and begged him to quit. Then he hung by his arms and finally by one arm. We got down pretty fast when we saw the forest man coming in his truck, but not before he saw us and told us he would have something to say to Miss Lovey. She grounded us for a month.

But I can still remember how the world looked from the fire tower. We could see for miles around—the Big House like a white castle standing high on its knoll, our little gray houses looking fragile against the brown fields, the slate-blue river winding out to the shiny sound, the neat-looking fields and patches of pasture, the woods in different shades of green, a toy mule pulling a tiny cart on the clay road. If God sees the world from here, I thought, He must think it is very beautiful and neat. He can't see the mud or the ruts in the road from up here.

It was fun to see the world from a different angle.

CHAPTER NINE

*W*hen *I got home one day soon after school started, I* found Mama in bed moaning. Her bad tooth was acting up again.

"Ophelia, fix me a poultice," she muttered between clenched teeth.

I quickly got flour, vinegar, mustard, and hog grease, wet them down, and packed them in a rag to put on Mama's swollen jaw. Her forehead was wet with sweat and her eyes looked like pitch-black pools of swamp water. I unbuttoned her dress and put some cool towels on her head. She moaned freely.

"My sins are coming down on me," she panted. "Oh, Jesus, teach me to endure my pain!"

"I'm going to ask Miss Lou for some aspirin," I interrupted.

I ran to the Big House and knocked at the back door. Miss Lou was coming downstairs from her nap. Her hair was all smooth, and I could see fresh powder on her nose under her rimless glasses.

"Ophelia, what is it?" she asked.

"It's Mama. She's got a bad toothache. Can I borrow some aspirin for her?"

"Of course. Step in here and I'll get it."

She went back upstairs and came down with the tablets wrapped in a tissue. "Tell her to take two now and two more later. If she doesn't get better, let me know." I knew Miss Lou hoped Mama could fry her chicken for supper.

"Thank you ma'am," I said and turned to go.

"Oh, Ophelia!" she called. "Have you seen my yellow sweater?"

"No ma'am, I ain't."

"I don't know where on earth it could be. It's the one my brother and his wife gave me two Christmases ago." She sat down with a sigh at the card table in the sitting room to play solitaire. From where she sat she could see the river and shore, looking so peaceful and serene. Miss Lou loved to play solitaire. She would pop the cards with her long, shiny fingernails, and I know she never cheated because I had seen her pick them all up before she'd hardly played a one, then click and shuffle them again for a new game. Sometimes she'd study them for a long time before she picked them up, her head held over to one side. Miss Lou did everything the same way—calmly, quietly, prissily. I never could understand how she had a daughter like Janet.

I hurried back to Mama. The poultice hadn't helped much and she was still moaning. When I gave her the aspirin, she took three. Then I sat by her, waving away the buzzing flies that came in through the broken screens. Mama was real hot now. I rewet the poultice and the towels on her head.

"Sing to me," she said.

I sang "Swing Low, Sweet Chariot," keeping time with the fan.

Later I had to go back to the Big House to tell Miss Lou that Mama couldn't cook supper that night because she was worse. Miss Lou gave me some ice and a big pink pill for her and asked me if I'd run by Bea's to ask her to come help with supper. It was convenient that Miss Lou had someone else to call on.

The ice and pink pill helped Mama some, but it was a hard night. The swelling got worse and we hardly slept any at all. In the early morning I had to go tell Miss Lou that Mama would have to go to the dentist. Miss Lou said Leighton could take her right after breakfast and for me to go with her. Leighton didn't have a thing to do that day, she said. I ran back home excited. We didn't go to Attamac often. I tied my money, a dollar and seventy-three cents, left from working in tobacco, in a handkerchief.

Mama crawled in the back of the old Chevrolet coach, her face tied up in a blue bandanna, and I got in beside her. Janet was going too. It was the earliest I'd seen her up that summer. The white children's school hadn't started yet.

The drive to town was fun. We passed the children on the road waiting for the school bus, and I waved excitedly. They looked at me with open mouths.

When we were a mile down the road, Janet lighted up a cigarette. Leighton glanced at her disapprovingly, and Mama frowned.

"Want one?" she asked Leighton snippily.

He didn't answer.

"When you get off to school you'll find that boys do smoke," she told him. He still didn't answer. She went on, "And I guess you'll be going in another month."

This was the first I'd heard of Leighton going off to school. He had one more year in high school.

"We don't know whether I can get in yet," he replied.

I found out later they were sending him off to a military school where he'd wear a soldier suit.

When we got to town, Janet got off at Katie's, and Leighton took us uptown and parked in front of the dentist's office, which wasn't open yet. Leighton went to the hardware store and we sat in the car waiting. It was a bright, hot morning and I loved to watch the cars drive by and the people going to work. The merchants were opening their stores, letting down their awnings, and calling and joking back and forth. One man crawled into his front window and put up a penciled sign that said "Sale," and an invisible hand turned the card on the door from "Closed" to "Open." Two men came out of the drugstore and sat down in chairs with a checkerboard between them. Attamac had only eight hundred people, a dozen stores, a movie, a doctor, a dentist, and the courthouse, but it was everything we needed and more. There was such excitement in the town air. A colored man came down the street pushing a can on wheels and shoveling up trash with a rasping noise, cars kept whizzing by, and the dryflies were singing in the background, filling up any gaps that might have been quiet.

At nine o'clock Dr. Hoke, the dentist, came slowly down the street in his black coupe and parked beside us. We got out and Mama told him her trouble, then went to the curbing to spit.

"Come on in, Cassie," he said kindly. He was tall and thin and wore shiny, rimless glasses of the finest kind. I sat in the tiny colored waiting room on a dirty chair while he looked at Mama's tooth. Her cheek was terribly swollen. Dr. Hoke told her there was nothing to do but nurse it till it got better and then he could take the tooth out. He gave her a prescription for some pills to ease the pain and told her to stay in bed and apply cold cloths—just what we had been doing. Mama thanked him and offered to pay. He wouldn't let her, thank heavens. I wanted a new dress.

"The Lord wants me to suffer," Mama mumbled as we went out. "I'll do it gladly. It's mortifying the evil in me."

"Ain't you going to get those pills, Mama?"

She sighed. "I guess so. Can't work a good horse to death." I suppose she wanted to save some of the tooth's power for worse sins and stronger evils.

We walked to the drugstore, got the pills from the druggist, and Mama took one. They cost forty-five cents—a lot of money —but some things are essential. I wondered what they did in

Africa with no drugstores and no pills. Maybe they took ground-up bugs and tobacco like Granny Mosher, who had certain secrets filling up her brains.

I begged Mama for a new dress, and it seemed to cheer her up to go shopping in Crenshaw's Corner Store. Mr. Crenshaw knew just what to show you, which things you could afford and which you wanted to see. He showed me a red-and-blue plaid school dress with long sleeves in a fuzzy material. It was beautiful and cost three ninety-eight. I offered to spend some of my own money, but Mama paid for it. I felt like a princess. With my money I planned to buy some rayon stockings; I had never had any before. I picked out the pair I wanted, but when I reached in my pocket for my handkerchief with my money tied in it, it wasn't there. I searched and searched. I must have left it at Dr. Hoke's. Mr. Crenshaw was sympathetic, especially when he saw the tears in my eyes. "I'll keep them right here till you can go look," he said.

I flew back around to the office, but there was no red hand-kerchief. I went to look in the car, but it was gone; Leighton had gone off somewhere. I wiped my eyes and went back to tell Mr. Crenshaw my bad luck. "Well, you've bought a dress," he said. "I'll let you have these until you can find your money." They cost twenty-five cents. Mama shook her head and we left.

When we got outside, Mama shook me. "Why you got to be so careless!" she muttered while I cried. "Bad luck comes to everybody," she admitted, remorseful, "and then good luck. Hush up now."

We walked around to the courthouse, where there were benches to sit on, an artesian well to drink from, cool shade trees, and colored folks to talk to. We sat down and pretty soon Mama was talking to a real dark, skinny lady with a hooked nose, who grinned all the time. She was complaining about hard times and how somebody named Mrs. Rightmeyer had skinned her out of a job. "I aimed to get that place and told her so, and she done gone and got it that night," she said with a grin.

"Some folks'll do *any*thing for a red cent," Mama said with spirit, forgetting her tooth.

"*Any*thing," her friend agreed.

"The world's full of them kind," Mama went on.

"Ain't it?"

They seemed proud of their shrewd talk. I drank some water from the well and watched two sparrows fighting over an apple core. I was downcast over losing my money. I had hoped to buy some gloves, too. I wanted to walk into church with my new dress and stockings on, wearing my gloves, and go straight up the aisle with a holy look on my face and forgiveness in my heart for everybody in the world. It wouldn't be the same without stockings and gloves. I tore the wrapping paper on the package and touched my new dress. It comforted me some.

Leighton drove up and told us he'd like to stay until afternoon if Mama was all right. We said we'd meet him at the well at four o'clock. The pill had made Mama feel a lot better and she was enjoying being in town.

"We'll go out to Miss Em's and eat dinner," she said cheerfully. Miss Em was an old family friend. So we walked out the dusty road to the Gumberry section a mile away.

Miss Em's house was always neatly whitewashed and had a white picket fence around it. It sat high up on a bank above the road, and each year the bank caved in a little more so that part of the fence was out in space. But above the eroded part grass grew in the yard and there were different flower bushes and some red-spiked cannas blooming.

Miss Em was a busy, energetic soul, always doing something. Her house was neat and clean as she could keep it with the cars flying down the dirt road kicking up dust all the time. She lived alone and took in washing. She was a grand washer and ironer and took great pains with her work. When we got to the door we could see the baskets of neatly done clothes waiting in the hall to be called for by the best families in Attamac. Mama hollered for her and she finally answered from the back, where she was sweeping chicken droppings off the bare part of the yard with a bundle of broomstraw. She always wore her skirts down to her ankles, and when she went outside, a man's old felt hat.

"Cassie! Glad to see you! How are you? And Ophelia!" Miss Em was real folks. It was wonderful to have such a friend.

I listened while Mama told her all about her tooth and how it had put her down. Miss Em invited us to dinner, as we knew she would. She was boiling the pot, and it smelled good. I was hungry. White potatoes, turnip salad, side meat and dumplings—what could be better, especially when you've been up since dawn and lost all your money? We didn't have any dessert because Miss Em didn't like sweets. Mama always said that was the reason Miss Em kept such a smooth, creamy-looking face and that nobody would ever guess she was sixty-eight years old. I washed the dishes.

Later on Miss Em called over a neighbor girl named Crystal to visit with me. Crystal was dark-skinned, low and chubby, and wore lipstick. Her family was new in the neighborhood; they came from up north. Mama gave us ten cents to walk to the filling station to get drinks, a real treat.

"You been here long?" I asked Crystal.

"No, we moved in from New York," she answered in a northern accent. My eyes popped out. A real city person taking up time with me? I noticed she turned her shoes over on the sides and they were completely out of shape.

"You go to school?" I asked with a gulp.

She laughed. "No. I got a baby."

My mouth fell open. "You married?" It slipped out.

"My husband and I're separated," she said as though it was the finest thing in the world. "I live with my mother."

"How old is your baby?"

"Six months. A cute little fellow."

"How old're you?"

"Sweet sixteen and been kissed and then some!" She gave a tinkling laugh at the thought.

I couldn't think of anything else to ask, so we just walked along while she sang "That's the Story of Love." When we got to the filling station and bought our pop, she said to me through her teeth, "God, I wish it was beer!"

I never saw Crystal again. I found out the next time we went out to Miss Em's that her family had moved back to New York.

On the way home that night I asked Leighton and Janet if they had seen a red handkerchief.

Janet said, "Yes, I thought it was a filthy rag and threw it out the window."

I wanted to cry. I kept my eyes glued to the road all the way home, looking for a sign of it, but I never saw it. I pondered over it, knowing if Janet had picked the handkerchief up she was bound to have felt the silver money in it. Would a white girl with a mother like Miss Lou tell a lie? I couldn't believe it, but my money was gone. I hated Janet that night.

CHAPTER TEN

*W*hen Mama's tooth 'suaged down, she took a new lease on life and never did have it pulled out. She felt like she'd suffered and been delivered and that to go have it pulled when it wasn't hurting was like digging up snakes just to kill them. She was in fine shape for the Quarterly Meeting at our Zion Bethlehem Baptist Church the last of August. One Saturday she went to town with Bea and Willie in their Hoover cart and got herself a new maroon outfit, size forty-four, a black hat with a veil, and tan gloves. She looked like a fashion book.

The meetings started on Thursday night with a rally and prayer service. Miss Lou always let Mama off for three nights at this time, and we went every night. Miss Lou asked Bea and Sue to help her during this emergency since they didn't go to our church, but to Pentecostal Rose of Sharon Church on the Neck road.

Zion Bethlehem, which held about a hundred head, was filled to the brim. Although small, the church was pretty inside with windows of frosted white glass bordered with red, blue, and yellow rectangles, only two of them broken. Over the altar there was a round stained glass window with a white dove, its wings outspread, on a sky-blue background. On the preaching stage were two stands, one for the big, gold-edged Bible and one for sermons. The organ sat on the right, and the choir, in small, straw-bottomed chairs, on the left. For the meeting the women had decorated the platform with baskets of myrtle boughs and goldenrod.

Reverend Halleck, his face shining with sweat and intensity

of feeling, converted twenty-odd head. Some who had been converted the year before and had fallen by the wayside were reconverted. They found the Spirit anew, and it was a glorious time. There was a swollen silence in the church when the Reverend whispered, "It ain't the sin that counts, brother, but the forgiveness." (There were fervent cries of *Amen! Amen!*) Then the Reverend in his great, melodious, shaking voice would say, "You got to repent. You got to ask the Lord to *forgive* you." (Cries of *Amen.*) "You got to forgive *each other.*" (*Amen, Amen!*) "And lastly" (with a great pause), "you got to forgive your*selves.*" (A tremulous murmur of *Amen*s.)

It was a sermon we never tired of. After it was over, we felt like a hundred pounds of sins had been wafted away and we forgave everybody as the Lord forgave us. How happy we were as Mama pumped the old organ and everyone sang "Gonna See Jordan in the Morning."

Then the Widow Frizelle, who led the choir, sang a solo, "Oh, Where's My Sweet Lord?" She was dressed all in pink from head to toe, and it was worth going to church just to hear her sing. The men thought it was worth going just to see her. She was neither old nor young, but in between, and had that soft-voiced, intimate quality that made them feel extra-special no matter what their age. I saw Joe Batts looking at her with his mouth in a foolish grin. Carrie saw it too and nudged him.

"Shut your mouth before a fly light in it," she whispered with a little hiss. I was surprised Carrie noticed.

There were feasts every night after the service out in the churchyard on long wooden tables lighted by kerosene lamps. We had chicken stews, roasted pigs, delicious cakes, iced tea, and homemade wine. Everyone laughed and talked in happy, free voices and couples disappeared into the woods. Mama and Reverend Halleck went back in the church to plan the music for the meeting the next night. When Mrs. Frizelle started to go with them, Mama told her to go on eating, they didn't need her.

A good-looking boy named James Odell, who lived on the other side of the river, sidled up to me. I knew him from school, but he had stopped going two years before. He was lighter-skinned than Bucky and not as tall and had black eyes that constantly sparkled, dimpled cheeks, and a fetching grin. He wore a dark green suit with wide lapels and bulging shoulder pads, a checked yellow shirt, and a black-and-orange-striped tie. He looked grand.

"Heydy-o, Ophelia." He grinned. I wondered if he had been drinking.

"Heyo, James Odell." I studied my iced tea and picked out a bug that had fallen in it.

"Let's go walkin', honey." I felt sure he had been drinking when he called me honey.

"Why?"

"Why not?" He shook his head foolishly and I couldn't help but laugh.

"Everybody's doin' it," he added with another shake of the head, seeing the first one went over so well.

I knew better, but I felt so fine I went with him anyway. After all, there were dozens of couples around, behind every tree, bush, and tombstone.

"Ophelia, honey, you sure gettin' plump and purty. Mmmm," he remarked as we walked toward a big cedar tree at the edge of the graveyard.

I laughed again. Compliments are fun.

"And you sure are getting sweet-talking, James Odell."

"Let's sit on this here fellow's tombstone and do some light courtin'." No one had ever talked to me this way before.

"He might come up and object."

"Naw, if he do we'll just say, 'Go on back down there—.'" He tried to read the name on the head-marker, struck a match, and read, "Abraham Joseph Burns. Well, we know where he's at to start with."

I nearly died laughing. I never knew James Odell had such a witty personality.

We sat down on the grass and leaned up against Abraham's marker, which shielded us from the lights of the church. James Odell brought a little bottle out of his pocket. "Want somethin' to make you feel good?" he asked with a grin.

"I feel good anyway," I told him as growny as I could.

He set the bottle down. "Let me see how you feel," he said, quick and masterful, and grabbed me, threw me back, and gave me a kiss. Oh, sweet Jesus! It was my first real kiss and so quick and unexpected I could hardly get my breath. I thought briefly of the bootlegger with his big lips smeared on mine and how different James Odell's lips felt. Then came the second and third kisses, and the fourth and fifth. I was getting the hang of it mighty easily. It was unbelievable—me, Ophelia, getting kissed! I was new and different, a brand new person, looking back on the old one with wonder.

Soon he was putting his arms around me, and I felt I had strings in me that were humming and the vibrations were tingling up and down. Then he was pressing against me and it felt better than anything I had ever touched before, even better than bathing naked in the river at night. If I had been a lightning bug I would have lighted up as bright as the full moon.

When he started unbuttoning things, I drew back. I could hear him breathing hard and I smelled the liquor on his breath.

"James Odell, you ain't!" I said quickly. "You ain't." I took hold of his hands. He fumbled around, but I held him off. He laid his hot, dark cheek on Abraham Burns's cool, white tombstone. "Well, kiss me then," he said, and I went back in his arms and did.

I had always thought Bucky would be the first boy I kissed, but I found out you never know, never know what branch on the path will brush your face in the dark or when a twig you step on will fly up and hit your head. I only know that from then on James Odell and I kissed every chance we had. And ever afterwards I was different, grown-up, no longer contained in my own body but reaching out, longing, needing. It was part of the Lord's plan, I guess.

On Saturday afternoon we had baptizing at the river. There were fourteen girls and ten boys to be baptized. The girls wore white dresses, and the boys blue overalls and white shirts. The congregation formed a long parade from the church and marched to the river singing "Sweet River of Life." Those to be baptized then stood in a semicircle while choir number one sang "Lead Me to Zion," which was sort of their theme song, and choir number two responded with "Roll, Jordan, Roll." Then Reverend Halleck in his white duck baptizing suit led them down to the river and they waded in waist-deep. They took hands while he prayed and the two choirs hummed softly on the bank. He then took each child in turn, held his nose, and dipped him under, baptizing in the name of the Father, Son, and Holy Spirit.

The clouds were rosy in the sky in the late afternoon, and the children were happy and excited as they came dripping out of the river to their mothers, who had towels and dry clothes waiting. I had been baptized two years before and have never forgotten how I felt afterwards, as though I truly belonged to the Lord. I could tell by their eyes that these children felt the same way, except for one little girl who was crying because she had been scared to death to duck her head.

Sunday afternoon was the last meeting we had, and the treasurer made his report. Then we had the final roll call when each person rose and pledged himself anew for Jesus and it was marked down in a black notebook. This was something Reverend Halleck had thought up, and it made a big impression on everyone to rise and say, "I do," and get checked off. The children just answered "Yessuh." Afterwards we sang a last hymn, "Onward, Christian Soldiers," and filed out, ready once more to combat the sinful world and the weaknesses of the flesh.

I looked around for James Odell in the churchyard, but there was no time for kissing. Mama had to hurry home to help Miss Lou with a supper party. We got a ride home in Joe's cart, changed into working clothes, and hurried to the Big House.

When we got to the kitchen we saw Miss Lou confronting Sue, who was sobbing and looking down at the floor. We quickly retreated to the back porch for we knew something was wrong, but we couldn't help hearing. I also peeped through the window.

"It was in your sweater pocket, Sue," Miss Lou was saying in an icy-cold voice and holding out a rag of a handkerchief.

"I found it on the ground," Sue mumbled.

"Where?"

"On the path near the clothesline." Sue never looked up a time.

"This special handkerchief never goes to the clothesline, Sue."

"I found it."

"It was my favorite handkerchief, brought to me from Brussels by Dr. Caldwell."

Sue stood waiting, her head bent over and her fingers twisting.

"Now you've ruined it." It had been used, you could tell that. Naturally Miss Lou wouldn't want it after Sue had blown her nose on it.

Sue sobbed, shook, and waited, her shoulders drooping.

Miss Lou's eyes narrowed. "You stole my handkerchief, Sue," she pronounced. "And now you've lied about it. You go straight home and tell your mother."

Sue ran out the door and down the path like a rabbit. We watched, very embarrassed. I knew she wouldn't tell her mama. I saw Miss Lou throw the handkerchief, which she held warily by a corner, into the garbage bucket, her mouth twisted to one side. Then she washed her hands at the sink, called Mama, and told her what to fix for supper.

"There's a boiled hen in the icebox," she said. "We'll have chicken salad and sliced tomatoes. I made a coconut cake for dessert." She told me to peel the tomatoes and put on about two dozen eggs for deviling.

"Yessum." Mama seemed kind of quiet. We were both suffering inside for Sue. My stomach felt all puckered up and I wanted to cry.

After Miss Lou left, I blurted, "S'pose she did find it on the path?"

Mama sighed. "Miss Lou thinks she stole it. If somebody thinks you've done something, you might as well of done it." She sighed again.

"What do *you* think, Mama?" I couldn't, wouldn't think Sue would steal Miss Lou's handkerchief.

"I don't rightly know, Ophelia. Sue ain't a bad girl. Maybe she's just weak. We're all weak. You know what the Rev'rend says about forgiveness."

"But, Mama, I don't believe she did it! I don't!" I cried.

She put her arms around me and comforted me. "Hush, hush! We got work to do. Ten head coming for supper. Get out that chicken and let's get to cutting. And get some kindling to build up this fire. We got to boil eggs."

That was the trouble. There were always eggs to boil and white people to feed. All the world seemed like one big boiling egg, getting its insides cooked hard as a stone. I knew how Sue might want that handkerchief. I had seen it, too, with its soft linen middle and the frilly lace around the edge like a Valentine. But stealing was a sin and Sue was my best friend. It was like doing it myself to think she might do it. I had an ugly feeling for Miss Lou that night. No one is ever guilty alone, I found out. You have to hide other people's sins to be decent yourself, and Miss Lou should have known it.

It sort of rubbed out all the joy of the Quarterly Meeting.

CHAPTER ELEVEN

*T*he Farthingales, Hollingses, and Thompsons came to supper at the Big House. I used to wonder how the Farthingales felt about coming out to Ginger Hill, their ancestral home. Mr. Philip was only a little boy when his father lost it and shot himself, but old homes are terribly important in a community like Attamac, almost more important than anything, because they last longer and don't change as much as people. They give people something to cling to, to steady themselves with like an anchor. Old houses transcend life itself and go on forever, unless, of course, they burn up. They furnish a purpose and meaning for their families to live by; they are solid measures for judging people. An attachment for a house is no fickle romance that fades and dies, but a deep love from the soul, growing all the time.

Even though his father had lost Ginger Hill, Mr. Farthingale would always be an "aristocrat" because he was born there, but I can't say how long his family rating will last—until people forget, I guess, and memories are pretty long in Attamac. Mr. and Mrs. Lockwood were not quite as fine folks as the Farthingales, but ownership of Ginger Hill over the past twenty-five years had increased their standing, especially since Miss Lou was a Hollings from Twelve Elms, an old home in the Indian Hills section. Unfortunately that had burned when Miss Lou was a young girl and most of the family heirlooms with it, but it was still an outstanding landmark in the minds of all the important people around Attamac. A drawing of Twelve Elms hung over the mantelpiece in the parlor of Ginger Hill.

I used to look at Mr. Farthingale when he came. He was tall

and thin, with graying hair and sad eyes. People said he was a bright student and wanted to study medicine, but his mother couldn't afford to send him to college. So he went in the hardware business with his wife's father.

Mrs. Farthingale was a plump, faded blonde with a turned-up nose. She was born looking like things didn't smell just right to her, and when she came to Ginger Hill they apparently smelled worst of all. Once I saw her point out to her husband an old armchair when nobody was looking and shake her head as if to say she wouldn't have had such a thing there if she were the mistress of Ginger Hill. But I felt sorry for them having to see the old place gone from them forever, with the family ghosts making up to strangers and the private graveyard out behind the weeping willows full of Farthingales, including Mr. David with the bullet still in him. I know how I would have felt if Miss Lou had put Mama and me out and somebody else had gotten our little house.

But that evening they seemed to be having a grand time. I could hear the ladies laughing on the front porch and the gentlemen talking more than men usually talk. The men were smoking cigars and were wearing rich-looking, bluish-gray summer suits, all but Mr. Lockwood, who had on his white linen church suit and a blue striped necktie. They all kept their coats on in respect for the ladies. Luckily a good breeze sprang up. The river began to show whitecaps and to look real perky, even foamy, and the waves broke on the shore with their beautiful swishing sound. It was a good afternoon for a party.

David and Katie had come with their parents to see Leighton and Janet, and the four of them walked down to the green yard chairs near the old boat dock to get away from the elders. From the cut-glass punch bowl on the porch I carried them some cups of fruit punch. I served Katie first.

"Thank you," she said politely. Katie looked pretty in her tomboyish way, but as usual she was half tongue-tied around Leighton.

"Punch, punch, punch," said Janet with disgust. "*De*licious old punch. Wonder what happened to those mint juleps we hear so much about from the good old days. I've never even seen a mint julep. Here's to the mint julep, wherever it went to." She raised her punch cup.

"Oh, they went out to Kentucky," David explained. "The bluegrass country. They give them to the horses out there. That's why they win so many races."

"We still have plenty of mint," Katie remarked. "Mama puts it in the iced tea. You know, it grows under the dining room window, David."

"Come to think of it, we have some too," said Janet, beginning to get an idea. "And whiskey. Daddy keeps it upstairs in the wardrobe . . . a bottle of Rock and Rye."

"How do you know?" Leighton asked.

"Haven't you ever explored around? Good Lord, you probably haven't. You wouldn't. Oh, I've tasted it. Burns like the very devil. Listen! Why don't we . . ."

I had lingered and loitered as long as I dared, and a cold glare from Janet sent me scampering up the sloping, fresh-cut lawn to the kitchen to help Mama get the supper ready.

After supper the young people went off in the Farthingales' car, promising to be home in an hour. The company had such a good time on the cool front porch they didn't notice the car wasn't back until they got ready to leave about ten o'clock, which was the standard hour of departure in those days. Mama and I were still washing up, taking great pains as Miss Lou had used her best antique dishes. Then we heard Mrs. Farthingale ask, "Why, where are the children?" She had had a real good time that night and she looked like everything had smelled better than usual.

"They said they'd be right back," Miss Lou remembered.

"I hope they haven't had an accident," Mr. Farthingale put in quietly. It was his car they had gone off in, and I guess he was doubly worried.

"We'll check up at Macy's Cross on our way," said Mr. Hollings, Miss Lou's brother. Just as the folks were all leaving and calling to each other, "You all come, now," "Come to see us," "You all be sure to come!" we saw the car flying down the road toward us. It stopped about fifty yards away to let someone out, then came on to the house. David quickly hopped into the back seat with Katie. Janet got out the other side with a lurch. "Sorry we're late." She giggled and stumbled into the house.

No one paid too much attention to her in the spirited good-bys and you-all-come's yet to be said to the Farthingales. When the company had driven away, Miss Lou told us to leave the rest of the cleaning up until tomorrow. She and Mr. Lockwood turned back toward the parlor talking about what a good time the guests had had.

Then I heard Mr. Lockwood say, "Fred told me Claud Hicks was indicted for embezzling."

"For the land's sake!" Miss Lou gasped. "Claud Hicks? I can't believe it."

In Attamac everybody is like cousins, but some are once or twice removed. An indictment for anything was a blow to the whole town as well as vast excitement. Mr. Hicks had some kind of bank job and was a good friend of Mr. and Mrs. Lockwood. The town must have been buzzing with the news that night. I wondered what embezzling meant. Was it drinking? Or messing around with women? It sort of sounded like both. In the white folks' world everything was worse. In our world wrongdoings were more apt to be overlooked and forgiven, or at least understood.

I was thinking these thoughts as Mama and I walked down the lane toward home. We were tired and quiet, each brooding over her own worries. I thought of Sue and her humiliation, of Janet staggering drunkenly into the house, and now somebody caught embezzling. When we passed the old ramshackle smokehouse, which was now grown up in cockleburs and honeysuckle, we heard an unmistakable sound: someone throwing up. The noise was dreadful, as though the heaving came from the depths of the body and could find no relief. We stopped and listened. I felt a sympathetic knot in my throat at the violent dry heaves.

"Somebody sure sick," Mama muttered. Then we saw a figure leaning on the corner of the smokehouse, his white face glimmering in the shadows. It was Leighton. He was moaning and trying to vomit.

"Leighton! Leighton! That you, boy?" Mama called, walking towards him. The poor boy bolted like a colt and ran as fast as he could toward the river. "What's the matter with him?" Mama asked. "Ain't like him to be out here sick. Always did like his Mama's finest attention when he was ailing."

I didn't say anything. Mama would never guess about Janet and the whiskey.

"I wonder . . ." Mama stopped, pondering Leighton's strange behavior. She took a dip of her Tube Rose snuff. Shaking her head, she walked on and I followed mutely, humiliated that she should have seen him like that. This was worse than Sue's trouble. I wished I could go back and help him, but I guess nobody could have helped him just then.

After I got in bed I could imagine Leighton stealing in the

Big House and up the stairs, his face as white as clabber. A first time. Suffering from going too far, the mortified feeling, and swearing to God never to do it again. I remembered my first cigarette and the scuppernong grapes.

I wondered if Miss Lou was lying quietly in bed waiting, knowing. Would she accuse him, like Sue, or use better sense? Did she want him to be a perfect angel clothed in feathers instead of a body? Probably. Miss Lou most likely couldn't even imagine him doing anything but what was right, and that in the manner of a gentleman. Suddenly I was glad Leighton had gotten drunk, and I hoped it would make him feel different toward Katie, like James Odell and me in the graveyard. I listened to the waves breaking on the shore, the brief moment of silence as they drew back, followed by the eager tumbling splash. The rhythm soothed me to sleep, and I dreamed of kissing somebody who first grinned devilishly like James Odell, then looked sick and pale and sad, like Leighton.

The next morning the Lockwoods were a mighty quiet family at breakfast, not talking at all. It seemed as though they were the ones who had been drunk. Miss Lou sipped her coffee with her mouth in a straight line and didn't even eat an egg. Her husband looked redder than usual around the collar and stared at the faded roses in the centerpiece. Then he excused himself and went off in the car before Miss Lou could closet him for a talk. At the time I assumed it was all because of what the children had done. I didn't know that Mr. Lockwood was concerned with money difficulties that had to do with the embezzlement.

Leighton and Janet straggled down about noon. I saw her pointing her finger at him and laughing silently when he started down the stairs with a haggard look and shoulders hunched up. He escaped by going down to his boat until dinnertime. Janet fixed herself a glass of Coca-Cola with ice and went into the pantry to drink it and smoke a cigarette without her mama knowing it. She always knew what to do.

You all are free as birds, I thought, when I went upstairs to make up beds. I got that funny little feeling when I went in Leighton's room. I picked up his soiled, smelly clothes from the floor, where he had thrown them the night before, and put them in the clothes hamper. His bed was a mess, the sheets stained and crumpled into a knot, the bedspread on the floor. He had slept on two pillows that smelled faintly of whiskey, and the dent his head had made was still there. I touched it before I fluffed up the pillows, and when I smoothed the sheets I did it gently as though this would help him rest well the next night.

Then I made Janet's bed that, strangely enough, smelled like cologne, washed her underwear and hung it on a little rod in the bathroom, and went down to fix the tea for dinner.

CHAPTER TWELVE

*T*he middle of September Leighton went away to a Georgia military school. There were three trips to Norfolk to get him ready, although he was to wear uniforms all the time. I guess Miss Lou wanted to make sure he had all the right underwear and bed sheets. On a Wednesday, Joe Batts came up to the house and brought the new, shiny steamer trunk out on the back porch and then put it in the back of the car for them. At breakfast they kept telling Leighton things to do and not to do. Even Janet got up in time to see him leave.

"Please get a handsome roommate, one with a lot of money," was her advice. "It'll be good for us both."

"How about one with a good-looking sister?" Mr. Lockwood added.

"Son, be sure to keep up with your work," Miss Lou told him, her voice thin like she was taking cold. She was just sick because her baby boy was leaving; I knew that.

"Now, hush, Mother, he'll do fine," Mr. Lockwood said, annoyed. He was feeling the sadness too. I felt funny myself like the last day of Leighton's boyhood had come before its time.

"Only ninety-two days till I get back," I heard Leighton say and try to laugh.

It sounded like forever. None of us were ready for him to go, not even Leighton himself. But I guess they wanted him to have the best they could give him and this was the best as they saw it, or maybe they thought military school would keep him away from drinking, smoking, and bad girls.

They had to take him to Pineville fifty miles away to catch the train, and in a few minutes they were piling in the car to go.

" 'Bye, Leighton," I said with a weak wave of the hand.

We stood in the yard watching and trying to smile as they drove away, and Leighton waved back to us. "He'll be Mr. Leighton when he gets home in that soldier uniform," Mama announced. "He'll be grown up." I felt sad—I didn't want him to be Mr. Leighton.

The white folks' school started and Janet had to go. She never rode the bus like other country people; her papa took her to Attamac every day. She was glad when school started because it gave her something to do. Movie magazines are fun and smoking in corners and meeting Jed Deiter on the sly, but after four months of it, Janet became bored, except for meeting Jed. I doubt if she ever got bored with that. She was cagey, though; her parents never found her out. Nights in September, when the sun began to set a little earlier, she could hardly finish her supper before she'd be excusing herself for a walk down the beach. I knew why, but I never saw her with Jed again except once.

We had a long dry spell that September, and even after Leighton left it was as hot as July. One Friday afternoon I was walking home from school down the dusty lane with that little feeling of homesickness for the beautiful, passing summer. The dryflies were buzzing and there was something in the air, something different that means fall is coming, and it stirs your stomach up. I was kicking a pine cone in front of me, wondering what Leighton was doing in his new school and if I would see James Odell at church on the fourth Sunday. A bobwhite soared off from the bushes and I watched it fly to a pine thicket. That's when I saw them, Janet and Jed, going in the direction of Jed's house. That was strange; it puzzled me. Janet would never, never go to his house. Jed didn't have a mother. People said she had run off a long time ago. Maybe she had a reason; maybe Mr. Deiter beat her. Anyway, it was just the two of them, father and son, and it seems sad when a boy doesn't have a mother or a man doesn't have any woman to keep his house. Bea used to clean up for them and wash their clothes.

When I got home, Mama was lying on the bed.

"What's the matter, Mama?" I asked, alarmed. "It ain't your tooth?" Mama never rested without cause.

"Naw, honey, the air seems heavy and give me a headache. Seem like it's pressuring me."

I rubbed her head. "It does seem hard to breathe," I agreed. "How's school?"

"Fine. I made a hundred on spelling."

I killed some flies that were buzzing around Mama and got her a fresh drink of water from the pump. The sky looked scalded and shimmery. "It's just a queer day," I said. "Don't look like rain, but it don't look right."

"Weather going to change," Mama predicted. "I feel it in my bones."

"If you're all right I think I'll walk over to Sue's. She wants to hear about school."

When I got there, Bea told me Sue had gone to clean up for Mr. Deiter and for me to go get her. I walked down the path by the woods, past the grapevine, and on to Mr. Deiter's tenant house, which sat in a clearing across from the woods and was painted gray. Mr. Deiter kept it looking neat. He and Jed both were hard workers. They just weren't a high class of folks, compared to the Lockwoods. I wondered why. Was it the way they talked, or Mrs. Deiter's running off, or because he worked for Mr. Lockwood? Working for somebody wasn't bad, was it? What exactly made the difference, I wondered. Of course Mr. Deiter hadn't been to college, but neither had lots of white folks, even Mr. Farthingale. It might have been Mr. Deiter's furniture. It was old and didn't look much better than ours.

When I got to the door, Mr. Deiter himself came out, tightening his belt. "Heyo, Ophelia," he said. "You doin' okay?" He was always polite.

I stammered, "Yessuh. Is Sue here?"

"She's inside." He went down the porch steps, got in the truck, and drove away. He was a tall, lean, handsome man with dusky-red skin like an Indian's and a big hooked nose that made him look like he meant business. People said he was mean in a fight.

I went in and found Sue making up the bed and straightening things.

"Hiya, Ophelia," she said, surprised. "Be through in a minute." She shook out the tablecloth on the floor. "Well, how's school? Miss Lovey still shoutin' and poundin'?" She laughed.

"School's fine. You ought to be going."

She swept a little pile of sand under the straw rug, picked up a dollar bill from the table, and put it in her blouse.

"A dollar!" I cried. "You get a dollar for this?"

"Well, I been here since noon. Let's go." She cut her eyes at me, and we went out the door. No one ever locked up; all the houses were wide open.

"It sure feels funny out here, don't it?" Sue asked.

"I can tell you something even funnier. I saw Janet and Jed go in the woods over yonder."

"When?"

"Right after I came home from school."

"You sure?"

"Yeah."

"They didn't come to the house. Least I don't think so." She frowned.

"Wonder where they went?"

"There's an old shack back in the woods."

I grinned. "Let's go see," I whispered with devilment.

"Naw, let's don't. Who cares what them two do?" She shrugged.

My face fell; I felt let down. Sue always cared what they did before. "You reckon he raped her yet?" I persisted, eager for spicy talk.

"Ha! He don't have to, girl. Believe me, that Janet is full of it."

"What would Miss Lou say?"

"She wouldn't believe it if Janet swole up. She'd claim it happened like Jesus Christ and the Virgin Mary. If she saw it happen, she'd claim they were pickin' daisies and she'd seen the daisies. Miss Lou believe what she want to believe, either the worst or the best, dependin'. And if it's her folks it's nacherly the best, and if it's other folks, it's the worst."

I thought about the stolen handkerchief. "Miss Lou seems nice to me, Sue, but nobody is pure perfect and I know what you mean."

"You'd see good in the devil himself, Ophelia."

"I'd sure hate to see the devil." I giggled.

"Chances are you'll see him one day, but he'll take another form, a real pretty form. Oh, he's sly. He's in yourself even, down in your own guts. But you don't know it till it's too late."

"Sue, you know what you're saying?"

She tossed her head. "What I hear about you and some guy

at the Quarterly Meetin'? Bucky was good and sore when he heard it."

I felt myself flushing. "I got me a fellow."

"Did you do anything? Come on now, tell me!" She stopped and held my arms, grinning in my face.

I hung my head and giggled. "Aw, Sue. You know I didn't."

"Did you kiss him?"

"Yeah." I giggled again.

"Was it fun?"

I nodded.

"Did he feel you?"

I blushed. "He tried some, but I stopped him."

"Uhuh. Bucky'll want to hear about all this."

"No, Sue, you can't .... Sue, please ... don't tell him or I cross my heart and hope to die if I don't never speak to you again." I was pleading with her as she hurried on down the lane. Finally I begged so hard she gave in.

"All right. I was teasin'. I'll just tell him you have a fellow."

"I don't even know that I do, to tell the truth."

"Now you been kissed, you're on your way to the devil." Sue laughed. "The more you do, the better it feels."

"Sue, you seem to know everything. How?"

"I was born knowin' stuff. And I know where some persimmons are ripe. Want some?"

Ripe persimmons are mighty good, and I followed her into the woods. Suddenly the world became cloudy and the pine trees began to whistle and jump in the air. We were caught in gusts of sand and pine straw that the fresh wind picked up.

"Storm coming," I said. "Maybe we'd best go home."

"It ain't far. I got my mouth set for a good, yellow persimmon. I just got to have one."

We ran, ran through the little wood. In the middle of a thick clump of beeches we found the persimmon tree, which was loaded with fruit, but there wasn't a branch we could reach. Sue tried to shinny up the trunk, but about two yards up she got stuck. I put my hands under her to give her some support.

"Sue!" I cried indignantly. "You ain't got no bloomers on!" Her buttocks were warm and soft and squashy on my hands.

"Well, ain't you never been bare-bottomed, Miss Prisspot? S'pose I ain't got no bloomers to wear?" She clung to the tree like a monkey, her dress hiked up and the wind blowing like the devil. She couldn't move up or down.

"Do somethin'!" she screamed. All I could do was support her bare behind.

"You gals havin' trouble?" said a voice behind us.

I turned Sue loose and she let go the tree and fell on me. We tumbled to the ground, trying to get Sue's dress down good, because there was Jed Deiter looking and grinning with his elbow propped on a tree. How long had he been there?

"We're going!" I cried. "Come on, Sue."

"I might could get you some persimmons," Jed said, still grinning, his black eyes flashing with devilment.

"Naw. Come on, Sue." I wanted to run.

"How you goin' to reach them?" Sue asked, ignoring me.

"Climb the tree."

I think he wanted to show off. It was a real tall tree.

"Let's see you," Sue said. She must have really wanted those persimmons.

Jed climbed the tree. He had on rubber-soled shoes and he went up like a squirrel, threw us some fruit, and was down in a flash. Sue picked out the biggest persimmon of the bunch.

"Thanks, Jed. You're real smart on climbin'." Sue couldn't help flirting with anything that wore pants, even Jed Deiter, a white boy.

She put the persimmon to her mouth and took a bite. In a split second she was puckering up and spitting and Jed was laughing like a demon.

"Dammit, damn you!" she sputtered, as he bent over giggling and pointing at her. "They're bitter as hell."

"Ain't my fault. You ast for 'em. Go on, eat some more."

"You knew they were bitter, Jed Deiter. You done it on purpose. You tricked me!" Sue's eyes flashed and she spit at him.

"You tricked yourself," he bellowed, "you funny, fuzzy little nigger."

He leaned down and grinned right into her face, and I think he would have kissed her if I hadn't pulled her as hard as I could. We ran for home without looking back, and just as we reached the clearing a fierce rain started.

CHAPTER THIRTEEN

efore we could reach Sue's we were almost swept away by the attacking wind, which blew in with a roar and drove the cold rain into us unmercifully, stabbing us all over. Sue's dress kept flying up over her bare behind until it became soaked and plastered down around her hips. Our heads were drenched; our breath made painful knots in our throats as we ran. Branches of trees and crazy loose objects swirled everywhere around us, and great flocks of birds flew past us going inland into the gale, crying in hundreds of voices. We could see black, angry clouds through the sheets of rain; the world was dark and strange and moaning in the wind, which was cracking trees like splinters under its force. Everything anchored to the earth was straining to get free and join the racing wind.

When we reached Sue's we were unable to open the front door against the gale, so we beat frantically on the back door, which they had barricaded with a heavy table. Finally Bea heard us and Willie opened the door. Sue and I burst into tears as soon as we were inside.

The family was gathered together in a little knot, and the children, their eyes big with fright, began to cry.

"Is the world endin'?" Almalee screamed. She knew her Bible.

"Naw, baby," Bea said, holding the three smallest children in her lap the best she could, but unable to keep the fear out of her own eyes.

"We goin' to blow away," cried Monk, terror-stricken.

A great thump shook the house as a large tree limb hit the

roof and rain began to pour in from the eaves. We wailed with fright, praying out loud to the Lord to save us.

"Get yourselves together," said Willie hoarsely, trying to do the same for himself. "It's a goddamn cyclone, that's what it is, and the mules ain't tied up." He looked with concern toward the dilapidated barn. We could see the barn door flapping in the wind and shingles sailing off the old gray roof like pieces of paper.

"I got to get home to Mama," I screamed. "She's all by herself."

"Godamighty, Ophelia, you cain't go out there," Bucky shouted to me, peeping through the window at the fury outside.

"Let me go, I got to!" I cried, pushing the table away from the door, which crashed open in the force of the ninety-mile-an-hour wind. I bolted for home as fast as I could, holding my head with my arms to keep it from blowing off. The wind was from behind, pushing me so fast I stumbled and fell. As I glanced up I saw a huge black thing flying over me. It was the barn roof, I found out later. It didn't come down at all, just blew on toward the river.

With the force of the wind behind me and the drenching rain beating me, I went stumbling on, grabbing trees and bushes to steady myself. Tree limbs, pieces of houses, cans, dead birds, everything on earth movable, went flying over me through the air. The world was noisier than I had ever heard it, moaning, creaking, whistling, crying.

Nearing home, I saw the front porch roof was gone. I banged on the door, shouting to Mama. When she opened it, I was swept inside so fast I hit the opposite wall. We had a terrible time closing the door, but we finally managed it. Then we clung together shaking, with the wind rattling the house until it was doing a regular dance on its foundations and we knew the end had come. At least we were together.

"Oh, merciful Jesus, my baby, I thought you were killed!" Mama wailed, holding me in a death grip.

"Me and Sue were in the woods when it hit," I said through sobs. "We ran to her house. I think their roof's blown off."

"It's the end of us!" cried Mama. "Jesus, Jesus, save us." Her senses began to come back. "Baby, you got to dry off." She found a towel and wiped my head and gave me some dry clothes. I put them on with quivering hands.

We put pots and pans under the worst leaks, but water kept blowing in everywhere. Suddenly, with a crash of glass, a pine branch blew through a window, and towels, pictures off the walls, and papers began to blow around the room in the wind. It was now pitch-black dark and we couldn't get the kerosene lamp lighted. Every match was blown out before it touched the wick. Finally, in a corner of the kitchen, we managed to fix a candle in a jar and light it.

Luckily there were some cooked sweet potatoes and a piece of side meat left in the oven. We ate a few bites of what we thought was our last meal and said how much we loved each other.

The wind increased, though we didn't see how it could, and the house continued its frantic dance. We put a quilt under the bed and crawled onto it, pulling another quilt over our heads. We heard the chimney blow away and the terrified squawk of the chickens as the old hen house went off in the wind.

Two other window panes crashed with explosions, one broken by a dead seagull, whose crushed body landed suddenly beside me. I screamed, for it was an omen of death; I was sure of it. Mama crawled from under the bed, bravely took it by a broken wing, and carried it to the back door, which she opened, letting the bird into the stream of air. Then she crept back under the bed to cling to me in a sweaty embrace.

Without any warning, about midnight the wind ceased; the world became unbelievably silent. The sudden quiet seemed queerer than the din of the storm.

"It's quit! Mama, it's quit!" I gasped, throwing off the protective quilt and feeling the cool air on my slick skin. I crawled from under the bed and opened the front door. I could see nothing but blackness. From outside there was the funny smell of raw life, the odor of broken trees and plants with the green stuff cut and bleeding. I had smelled it before in lesser degree after summer windstorms, the odor of things uprooted from the ground, broken loose, their hidden decay set free and the rot blown about the world. There were dead animals out there, too, I thought suddenly. And maybe people.

Mama and I lighted the lamp and went outside. Our porch was completely gone, and we saw all kinds of broken things scattered everywhere. Dead birds of all kinds were strewn about crazily with wings and necks bent in curious angles.

"We're saved!" cried Mama, choked up, "and we got to give thanks."

We went back inside and Mama prayed a good long prayer to the merciful Lord, reminding Him she was depending on Him to have saved everybody else we knew. Near the end of the prayer we heard somebody crying, "Cassie, oh, Miss Cassie."

Without saying amen we dashed back to the door. Here came Joe Batts out of the night soaking wet from head to toe. He climbed inside, leaving puddles of water wherever he stood.

"Joe, are we glad to see you!" Mama exclaimed. "How's your family?"

"Miss Cassie, Carrie's gettin' ready to drap the baby. She got took by the storm. She 'bout to die. Cain't you come help her?"

Mama grabbed her coat and some newspapers to go over our heads, since it was still drizzling, took the lamp, and started out.

"Miss Cassie, ain't you got somethin' to eat? I ain't had no supper."

Lord, how could he think of eating at a time like this? Mama quickly got him two sweet potatoes from the kitchen.

"Ain't the chillen had anything?" she asked.

"The storm got us so worked up we couldn't do nothin'," Joe muttered, his mouth full of potato.

Mama grabbed up a pan of eggs, and we went out into the dark night.

"You ain't seen the river, is you?" Joe asked, peeling the last potato and plopping it into his mouth.

"We ain't seen nothing but wind and rain."

"Well, the river rose up to the road in places. Ain't no tellin' what drownded in it."

It was a strange and fearful world we saw by the feeble light of Mama's lamp. Everything was pounded to pieces or drowned or flattened, as though a monster with a giant hammer had worked over every inch of earth. We made our way down the lane very slowly, wading through puddles that were three feet deep in places. I saw something slithering behind Mama in one regular lake.

"Ouuuu!" I screamed. "Ouee, snakes, snakes!"

Panic-stricken, we rushed, fell down, tried to get through the puddle, like trying to run in a nightmare when your legs won't move.

Finally we were out. I kept screaming; I knew I was bitten, but I couldn't find any place and they made me go on, shivering and crying. We climbed over fallen trees that lay in the path like traps. Joe found a dead hog floating in a puddle and tried to pick it up, but it was far too heavy even for him.

"That there hog sure was brained." He whistled, examining it with curiosity. "Hit by a brick, look like. Godamighty, weren't it awful? Our kitchen roof done blew off."

"Terrible," Mama agreed. "We better get to Carrie, Joe." He left the hog carcass and we went on doggedly.

Suddenly the air showed a keen little upsweep, making us gasp. Then, before we knew what was happening, the wind swooped back down on us, propelling us along like paper dolls. We clung together as things went sailing past us once again, this time blowing in the opposite direction, back to the sea, as though the wind was trying to undo all it had done.

"Jesus, oh, lordy!" Mama cried. We never got used to that wind. I felt myself lifted off the ground more than once. Our coats were like wet, flapping wings and we could hardly breathe.

Somehow we got to the house, which was shaking so in the wind it seemed to have a hard chill. We went inside and hardly felt any safer than we had on the outside. We never knew where the pan of eggs went.

Joe had brought all the children downstairs for fear the roof would go, and it was as sensible as anything I had ever known him to do, for the house was old and battered to start with. There on a quilt in the front room lay Scooter, Bobcat, Geraldine, and Flea, all sound asleep, their little dark arms enmeshed.

Frank and Sammy, old enough to be aware of things, sat quietly on the old sofa with sleepy, scared eyes. The front door flew open and a blast of wind scoured the whole house. There was a crash as the lamp blew over, broke into splinters, and went out. In the darkness, over the noise of the rushing wind, we heard Carrie in the bedroom moaning. Joe struggled to get the front door closed and found a candle for Mama, who went in to Carrie without even taking off her drenched clothes. Joe followed her, and I sat down beside Frank and Scooter, taking their hands in mine for comfort.

"She hollered all the time Papa was gone," Frank told me in a hoarse little voice. "I took her a drink of water and she drinked it."

"That was a good boy, Frank. Now put your head on my lap and sleep."

"Is she fixin' to die, Ophelia?" he asked.

"No. Just spawning a baby. Don't you remember when Ethelene was born?"

"Naw, but I 'member when Sammy was borned."

"Naw you don't," said Sammy, insulted. "You was a baby too, then. Babies cain't 'member nothin'."

"I 'member when you come out," Frank said. "You had lumps on you."

I laughed, even with the world crazy with fury and Carrie hollering with pain. "Hush up, boys. Try and get some sleep."

The wind blew and the house quivered, but finally the little boys slept on my lap. During the long, stormy hours I could hear Mama telling Carrie to push, push, push, and Carrie groaning and crying. My neck felt stiff and I had goose pimples on my legs and arms. Carrie was caught, just like we were caught in the storm. She had no choice; there was just one way out, to endure it.

"Push! Push!" I can hear Mama now. "Come on, Carrie, be a good girl. Push it down." I was, through it all, never sure the house wasn't going to blow down. I almost hoped it would, putting an end to Carrie's struggle and Mama's pleading.

Joe left them to their misery and slipped upstairs to sleep.

All during the night, in between the whistling of the wind and Carrie's groans, I could hear his loud snoring. Joe had the gift of sleeping. I guess he felt in the way downstairs and decided to take his chances on the roof blowing away.

Toward morning the wind began to die down and finally the house stood still, released from its ague. Mama called me and I went to the door of Carrie's room. Mama had Carrie propped on the slop jar, her massive frame wavering precariously. "Help me to hold her," Mama directed me, and I braced her on one side.

"The baby coming rump first. That's bad. The water trying to leak out," Mama explained.

I felt something slippery on the floor with my bare feet. In the dim light of the lamp I saw it was black and thick—blood! I gagged, but held onto Carrie, who kept crying, "Oh, Jesus, Jesus, let me die, let me die."

"You ain't dying," said Mama calmly. "Keep pushing."

"I'm dyin'," Carrie whimpered faintly. Then she had a contraction that lasted for long minutes. At the height of it she screamed in a guttural voice loud enough to wake the dead, or even Joe, and held onto my arm so tightly that her fingernails cut into my skin.

"Come on, Carrie. That's a girl. Again. Again," Mama urged her.

"Let me die!" Carrie screamed through her tears. "I cain't stand no more." She gasped like she was losing her breath.

"Get down on your knees, Carrie. This baby got to break through," Mama told her, pulling her arm. But Carrie only sat on the jar moaning and weaving about crazily. I marveled that the slop jar didn't break with her. It must have been made of the finest, strongest porcelain.

There was a little light coming in the window now, and the

world was strangely quiet except for Carrie's cries. It made me wish for the darkness of the night and the violence of the storm to come back to blot out this pain.

Carrie sat on the slop jar through several more contractions, each longer and harder than the last. She screamed like a tortured animal, panting and begging the Lord for mercy. I can never, never have a baby, I thought wildly. If this is the end of that thing people do that's supposed to be such pleasure—why, it's a trick! A trick of pleasure that gets you into unbearable pain.

Now Carrie gave a piercing scream, she was writhing, she was senseless in her agony. I was sweating and tasting something salty in my mouth. I had bitten my tongue and the blood was trickling down my throat.

"Mama, don't she have any aspirin she could take?" I cried.

"Naw, nothing. Go get Joe," Mama commanded, holding onto the wild woman on the slop jar.

I flew upstairs shouting for him. He lay sprawled over a bed sleeping like a baby, but noisier.

"Joe! Joe! Get up! Come quick!" I hollered, shaking him good and hard.

"Hm? Hm?" he mumbled, then frowned and yawned.

"Joe, come on and help us. Carrie's about to die." I really believed it. She had to die after what she'd been through.

He snorted. "Be right down," he muttered. "Go on."

I ran down the steps and heard him raise the window and relieve himself out of it before he came down.

It was getting lighter every minute now. In some way Mama had Carrie up and walking around. I looked in the crib. Baby Ethelene was sleeping as soundly as if the night had not been filled with unearthly sounds and awful things. Life was full of marvels. I wondered if Carrie's breasts had ever dried up.

97

Now she began another hard contraction and I felt my spine prickle.

"Down, down on your knees," Mama cried. "This baby want to get out. Help me get her down, Joe."

"Get down, Carrie," Joe said calmly in his reedy voice, but it reached her. She got down on all fours on the gritty floor. The pain seized her full force.

"Spread your legs," Mama commanded. "Hand me the towel, Ophelia."

Carrie sprawled on her knees and elbows, screaming with hoarse, frayed vocal chords. Mama pulled up her blood-stained gown and felt for the baby.

"The buttocks are bulging out, Carrie. Push, girl! Push it out. We can't do it for you."

"Carrie, push it out," Joe repeated sleepily.

The pain subsided and Carrie crouched there like an animal, crying hysterically. We waited for the next pain with hope and horror. It came, welling up with the fury of the storm we had just passed through. At its climax Carrie uttered short, repeated cries. Mama worked under her, pulling at those tiny buttocks. Joe helped hold her steady. I stood ready with the towel, blood flowing in my mouth.

"It's through! It's coming out!" Mama shouted. "Hold the towel here."

I tried to do as she told me, putting the towel under Carrie. There was a squirting sound as the baby shot out part way and blood flowed everywhere.

"Hold it, hold it!" Mama cried. "The head is stuck now."

She worked it gently around and it came forth, long and wrinkled and bloody. Mama caught it with the towel that she snatched from me, then shoved a pan she had ready under Carrie to catch the blood. Before it all subsided, Mama had the baby upside down in the air, patting those little buttocks that had caused so much trouble that night. Serves it right to get spanked first thing, I thought crazily.

The baby gasped, filled its lungs with air, and cried with little dry cries. It breathed, and the dreadful miracle of life was complete.

"It's a boy!" Mama announced, and Joe laughed.

Mama told Joe to move Ethelene. He took her out of the crib still sound asleep and put her carefully on the quilt in the other room with the four other sleeping children.

Mama put the baby in the crib, the long snaky cord still attached. I could hardly look. She had string and a long kitchen knife. I wondered if it was the one that Frank had stabbed the bootlegger with. Mama tied the cord, then cut off the end and covered the baby with a blanket. Joe had lifted Carrie onto the bed, where she lay quietly, bulkily, her eyes glazed. Mama examined her. The bleeding had almost stopped and Mama put clean towels on her.

"Think you could wash the baby off?" she asked me.

Standing over the baby, Joe was giggling and poking him in the stomach. "Hiya, boy. Hiya, boy," he said.

I went to the kitchen, stepping over the five sleeping children in the front room. Day was breaking now, and though it was still cloudy, the rain had stopped and the wind had died to a whisper. The kitchen was bright and wet—there was no roof over it. I looked up and saw three pelicans flying overhead, crying pitifully as though lost. I touched my finger to my tongue and it was red. Stepping out on the back porch, I vomited over the rail.

When my spell was over, I looked out over the field, which was one large lake with only the highest rows showing above the water. Everywhere were tree limbs and trash and white, dead birds floating. We had passed into another world, terrible and unforeseen. I felt like some queer, disembodied creature, uprooted from all I had held to the day before.

I took the washpan and pumped some water into it. For a miracle the pump worked the first time without priming. I found a piece of cloth attached to the kitchen clothesline that hadn't even blown away and went to wash off the baby. The little fellow cried when the cold rag touched him, but I cleaned all the white stuff and blood from his creamy skin and he looked a lot better. Mama turned him over on his stomach and told me to go upstairs and sleep. She lay down beside Carrie.

Upstairs I found Joe lying on one of the beds with his arms under his head.

"Ophelia, come here and talk a minute," he said in his sweet voice.

"Joe, I'm too tired," I said. I could hardly feel my arms or legs.

Joe seemed happy that the baby was there. "Help me think up a name for him," he said.

"Let me go to sleep, Joe. Mama'll help you think of one later."

"Come here, Ophelia." He grinned.

I foolishly walked over to him.

"What you want, Joe?"

He grabbed my arm and threw me down beside him, running his hand down inside my blouse and smiling like an idiot while he squeezed my breast hard. I hollered, which seemed to surprise him.

"Shhhh," he whispered, letting go his pinch. "Don't you want to?"

"You must be crazy, plum crazy!" I shouted, pulling away.

"Come on, Ophelia. I'll show you some fun." He held my wrist and tried to get me down on the bed again.

"You damn fool!" I cried, and he let me go.

I ran downstairs, lay down beside the children, and slept.

CHAPTER FOURTEEN

J slept on the floor until midmorning with the children all around me, poking at me and giggling, but I kept dozing, I was so tired. Finally, I became conscious of Mama telling Joe to bury something.

"Where?" he asked.

"Anywhere," she answered with impatience.

The voices woke me. Was the baby dead? After all we had gone through? Oh, no! Then I heard the cry of the newborn and felt better. I moved and found my muscles were sore and aching all over.

"Ain't he cute?" I heard Carrie ask with a tinkle of laughter. "Are you hungry, sugar?" I could hear a contented little sucking noise. My Lord, she's all over it, I thought wildly. *I* wasn't over it at all.

"What we goin' to name him, Carrie?" Joe was asking.

"You name him, Cassie. After seven head it ain't easy to think up a name," Carrie remarked.

"How about Franklin Delano Roosevelt?"

"That's Flea's name." Carrie laughed.

"Sure is," Joe agreed, as though he'd forgotten it.

Mama thought on it. "Well, this boy sure came in like a lion and on the wildest night I ever saw. He's got to be something special."

They all laughed and I could tell Joe and Carrie were proud.

"That was a herrikin we had last night," Mama informed them. She knew things like that. "I think you ought to name him Herry-Kane Batts."

"Yeah!" said Joe. "That's okay with me."

Carrie smiled. I stood in the door watching her hold little Herry-Kane. He had fallen asleep with his furry head drooping over.

The other children came in one by one with dazed expressions to see what the night had brought.

"When he get here?" asked Sammy sensibly.

"Last night," his mama told him.

"The roof's done gone," Frank informed us, taking more interest in the effects of the storm than in the new arrival.

"Did the bird drap the baby through the roof?" Scooter asked, trying to connect the events of the night into some sort of pattern. He had heard of the stork.

Joe laughed and slapped his thigh. "Yeah, that's just what happen, Scooter." Joe had a good sense of humor.

The children looked around in wonder at the open kitchen, the big wet world, and the dead birds floating in the shiny lake on the fields. Sammy found a mangled seagull behind the sofa. "Is this the bird that brung the baby?" he asked. Everyone laughed, the children joining in.

Baby Ethelene, on seeing her mother with her breasts exposed, climbed up on her lap, ignoring the baby on the other side. Carrie good-naturedly let her get a hold of one side and suck some. Then Flea began to howl because he was jealous. Carrie laughed and asked me to put the baby in the crib, and let him get up on the other side. Ethelene and Flea sucked away, glaring at each other, and Carrie lay back and closed her eyes.

"Hadn't you better see about the mules, Joe?" Mama asked him. "You reckon they're all right?"

"Sure had, Cassie. And we got to have some vittles too."

"I hungry," Bobcat wailed, realizing sadly he was past the point of nursing his mother. Geraldine was silently watching her mother with Ethelene and Flea. I knew something was coming, but before I could stop her, she had pinched Flea on his leg as hard as she could. He bit his mother, screamed, and upset everything. Carrie was mad and I had to take the seven hungry children out so she could get some rest for her nerves.

In some way Joe started a fire in the wet kitchen stove, using a few loose boards from a corner of the front room. He said it didn't matter, the whole place would have to be repaired anyway, and of course he knew he wouldn't have to pay for it. We boiled some fatback with sweet potatoes and white potatoes. It might not sound appetizing, but I never tasted a better meal. When you're hungry enough, I reckon green caterpillars would taste good.

Before we ate, Mama said we ought to say a thanks. "Sure should," Joe agreed. He felt good because both his mules were unharmed. Everyone bowed his head except Geraldine, who still had her mouth poked out. "Thank you, Lord, for saving us from the storm. Thank you for the baby living and Carrie too. Bless our food. Save us for heaven. Amen." I took Carrie a big serving and we all ate.

It took us a long time to get over the effects of the hurricane. Willie and Bea's house held up and no one was killed, but one of Willie's mules, old Bessie, was brained. It takes a lot to brain a mule. All the chicken houses and chickens were gone except one setting hen that had made a nest in Mr. Lockwood's garage. I guess she just sat right on those eggs through the storm. She reminded me of Carrie.

Mr. Lockwood was out first thing the next day checking on

everything and everybody, looking worried to death. So many things would have to be repaired, and that took money. I had the embarrassed feeling whenever I saw him in those days that he was troubled all the time about money. It gave me a bad, insecure feeling as though some dreadful doom was hovering over all of Ginger Hill, as I suppose it was. We were in it together, and Mr. Lockwood was the protecting father and only hope of us all. At least we had made a good tobacco crop, but everybody knew the price was too cheap. The depression was at its darkest time.

Gradually the water drained off the fields into the river, but the smell of rotting things lasted for weeks. Mr. Lockwood set Joe and Willie to gathering up the decayed birds and chickens and burying them. Joe found the dead hog, cooked a giant barbecue, and invited us all. Willie and his boys couldn't barbecue Bessie—they had to lug her to the middle of the woods with some ropes and leave her there to rot. Once Sue and I took the children on a picnic to the place so they could see her bones and part of her hide. They had really loved old Bessie.

One tobacco barn had blown down and another had lost its roof. And the trees—Miss Lou came out the next morning after the storm to look at the giant oaks that had fallen, with their roots all pulled up and showing, like huge snakes. She cried, took off her glasses, and put her nose in a handkerchief. Miss Lou was gentle-hearted about everything, especially anything to do with Ginger Hill. The trees had been there since the place was built, and losing them was almost like having the house blow down. They lay sprawled over the yard and there wasn't a way in the world to prop them up again. I always thought that oak trees were so sturdy they were like invincible kings, but that storm laid them over like toys. I guess nothing can stand up against the fury the Lord passels out sometimes, and we felt lucky to be alive. Everything has a purpose, Mama always said.

It made me feel like writing a poem. I wrote it on my school tablet and hid it under the mattress.

Wind, Wind, killing Wind,
Over the world and river,
Blowing down our friendly trees
And shaking up our liver,
You really took away our breath
And scared us all almost to death.

I read it over a lot and felt rewarded. I meant to write another verse about the dead seagulls, but I never did. They smelled so high after a few days I began to think they didn't belong in any poem.

Then I wondered about James Odell, if a tree trunk had hit him in the head or if the Good Lord had protected him from harm.

In a few weeks Mr. Lockwood had the kitchen roof put back on Joe and Carrie's house and all the window panes put back in. Carrie was really proud of the new glasses with the little papers stuck on them, but it wasn't long before the boys had knocked some out again. It just isn't easy with eight head of children, no matter if you're rich or poor. And little Herry-Kane had colic. Mama told Carrie it was because he was born on a stormy night. Carrie's eyes got yellower and yellower and she complained of the low blood. She hardly ever got Frank off to school any more.

When the men came to saw the fallen trees into stovewood, Miss Lou cried again. We could hear the saw buzzing away in the October afternoons. Then the wood was stored neatly in the woodhouse or outside it in cords. The Big House seemed naked after all the trees were moved. Standing there on the little knoll, it had an embarrassed look like a girl when her skirts blow up in the wind with nothing to shield her from open shame. This was the kind of change that shook Miss Lou's soul, and Mama and I hated it as much as she did. In a way it was worse than Leighton going off to school, because he would be back. When I thought of him, I could hardly wait to see him in his soldier suit.

PART TWO

14

CHAPTER FIFTEEN

he hurricane made a division in our lives. Afterwards, things were always before or after the "herrikin." There were not only changes in the looks of Ginger Hill, but changes in our lives. I had my birthday one Saturday in October—I was fourteen years old. Mama and I got a ride to town with Willie and Bea in the Hoover cart and Mama got me a new dress, red with navy blue trim on the collar. When we returned home, Mama asked Sue over to eat supper with me while she went to cook supper at the Big House. Sue and I had a whole fried chicken, even the breast, a real treat. She gave me a little picture of Jesus she had bought at the ten-cent store. I was pleased and stood it on my dresser. I still have that picture.

After supper Bucky came over and we gave him the chicken back and gizzard that were left over. When he finished them, he licked his fingers and took out his cigarettes and offered us one. I shook my head, remembering with embarrassment the last time, but Sue took one and they smoked like old hands. It made me feel grown-up to have two friends sitting around smoking cigarettes.

"Sue, you're sure getting grown," I said coyly. "Not going to school and now smoking. When you getting married?"

"I ain't never gettin' married," she said with a smirk. "I don't want to be saddled with no passel of young'uns."

"When you gettin' married, Ophelia?" Bucky asked, blowing smoke out at me and grinning. Bucky had nice white teeth.

"When somebody asks me, I guess," I answered boldly.

"Let's get married," he suggested. "You're fourteen now." He didn't mean it, but it made me feel grownier than ever. I

111

thought of James Odell and wished he'd say the same thing, even if he didn't mean it either.

After they finished their cigarettes and put them out in the slop jar, Sue said she had to mosey on home and Bucky said if I'd walk home with her, he'd walk back with me. So we went down the path in the night.

It was cool enough for a sweater, and the moon was out big and orange hanging over the water. The October moon is always the prettiest one in the year, something special, like red berries at Christmas. Mama called it the hunting moon, maybe because it made you feel inside like hunting for something, but you knew you couldn't find anything better than that moon. The way it hung there glowing with the river shining under it, a shimmery gold path of water leading to beautiful secret places! It gave us a magical feeling, a fairy-tale mood—the October moon mood. I thought of people in the cities and felt sorry for them, even the rich people with their fur coats and big automobiles, because they couldn't get the October moon mood like me and Sue and Bucky. We were lucky.

The breeze blew in our faces through the moonlit air, and I tingled with excitement. Here I was growing up, fourteen. Fourteen sounded so different from thirteen, which had a cricky sound. I felt like running up to meet fourteen, holding hands and skipping down lanes with it.

Sue seemed sort of quiet; maybe she was enjoying her mood to herself. Bucky walked up close behind me and touched my back.

"Snake on you!" he cried.

I screamed and grabbed my back. Bucky slapped his thigh and doubled up laughing.

"Bucky, don't you scare me like that," I told him.

"Gals are so scary." He laughed. It made him feel manly to

think so, and he kept picking at my shoulder and teasing me. Then he bragged some about how much money he was going to get from picking peanuts and hauling the sticks for the peanut vines to some other farms.

"Mr. Lockwood goin' to teach me to drive the truck," he added.

"Bucky, that's something!" I cried. You know how boys like to be admired.

We got to their house and Sue went in with hardly a word, just "Good night, lovebirds. I got to get up early tomorrow."

Bucky and I started back to my house, facing the moon, which was climbing higher and higher and losing its deep orange color.

"Moon fadin' out," he remarked.

"Sure is," I agreed with a tingle.

"I ain't fadin' out, are you?" he said, looking at me. These words seemed to have some secret meaning. I looked right back at him.

"No, I ain't fading out," I told him.

"Let's stop and watch it fade some," he suggested. I never dreamed Bucky could be romantic. I guess it's in everybody. He grinned at me, his white teeth shining in the moonlight. We sat down just off the path on a pine tree that the hurricane had blown down.

"Don't want no chiggers." I laughed.

We sat there a few minutes in silence, slapping at some mosquitoes. Bucky edged over to me and whispered in my ear, "Ophelia, how you feel about me?"

I was expecting it, yet it took me by surprise. "Bucky, I like you. You know that."

His strong arm stole around my waist, and he leaned over and put his lips on mine, drawing me up to him. His mouth was

113

damp and he didn't move his lips, just pressed them lifelessly on mine. Our eyes stayed open and we looked at each other with a magnified, blurry view, eye to eye, lips to lips, and our noses crushed up between. I thought to myself, this is stupid. But we just stayed there quietly, neither one knowing exactly what to do next. Finally, I drew back and Bucky stared on.

"We've kissed! Ophelia, we've kissed!" he exclaimed with awe.

It doesn't seem like it, I thought. But Bucky appeared to be in a sort of trance. He drew up for another go, pressing his face slam into mine and holding my waist tighter. I closed my eyes this time, thinking it might be better, but still it felt the same, like rubbing your face up against some fatback, only maybe not as lively. Then with his right hand he touched my left breast through my dress and flipped his middle finger back and forth on it. I took my hand and pushed his finger away and opened my eyes to stare once more into his dark ones open right against mine. Then gradually he drew back and was breathing hard. It surely didn't take much to impassion Bucky.

"Ophelia, let's lay on the ground," he suggested boldly.

I tossed my head back. "I ain't going to do that, Bucky. Not tonight or any night till I get married." I made up my mind right then, October moon mood or not. Besides, I didn't like the way Bucky flipped my breast like he was shooing off a fly.

"Aw, come on, Ophelia," he whined, trying to pull me down.

"Don't be so common, Bucky. It ain't like you."

"Look, Ophelia, a man got to . . ."

"You ain't got to do nothing but live till you die."

"Ophelia, I'll marry you soon as I can. I promise."

"I got to go to school. I ain't getting married any time soon."

114

I stood up and brushed my dress off. "But you're polite to ask," I assured him. I didn't want to lose his friendship.

He sat forlornly on the tree trunk digging in his ear with his little finger. I looked at the moon. "Moon sure has faded out," I remarked. "I got to get home now."

He got up to follow me and I stopped. "Why don't you go on back, Bucky? I'm nearly home and Mama'll be there."

"You ain't my kind, Ophelia," he said harshly. "It ain't right to let a man down."

"I ain't let you down. You let yourself down," I told him angrily. He wasn't going to make me feel bad just because I wouldn't lie on the ground with him.

"I got a birthday present for you," he admitted sadly.

"What is it?" Curiosity got the best of me.

"A ring." He dug in his pocket and brought it out. I took it. In the moonlight I saw it was shiny silver with a dark stone in the middle. "Gee, Bucky, it's pretty! I never had a ring before."

"Well, keep it. We can be engaged on it."

"Does that mean we'll get married?"

"Yeah, sure."

"Well, I don't know." I wanted that ring and I liked the sound of engaged.

"Suit yourself."

"I'll keep it." I put it on my finger. It was too big for all but the middle finger, so I wore it on that. Then, before he could say any more, I ran on home to Mama, scarcely looking at the moon, which had faded to kerosene lamp color. I wanted to see my ring in the light. I didn't care if it came from the ten-cent store—it was beautiful to me. The stone was dark blue. A boy had given me a ring and we were engaged!

Mama didn't do a thing but laugh when I showed it to her. She took it as child's play, but later when we were going to bed, she must have started thinking about it, because she reared up off her pillow suddenly and said, "Ophelia, don't you let Bucky do nothing to you. You ain't let him, have you?"

I was embarrassed, just as if I had. "No ma'am. You know I haven't, Mama."

"I ain't never told you much about boys, Ophelia, but you bound to know their urges. And you know what comes of it. I want you to go on to school and amount to something. Don't you let no young buck mess up your chances."

"I won't, Mama. I'll give him the ring back if you want me to." I could feel my face getting hotter and hotter.

"Just don't let that little old ten-cent ring bring you a thousand dollar's worth of trouble."

"I won't, Mama. It really doesn't mean anything at all."

She lay down and pulled up the covers. Soon she started to snore, so I knew she wasn't too worried. I lay quiet a long time, twisting the ring around my finger and thinking, but somehow I wasn't as thrilled about it as I had been at first. And Bucky's kisses weren't a thing like James Odell's. I could hear the waves lapping on the shore, calling to my mind the things of nature that no one can stop or help and the way that we're all like waves waiting to reach some shore and roll up on the sand. But then, I thought dismally, after the wave gets there and creeps up as far as it can, there's nothing left for it to do but go back in the river. Feeling sad and uncertain, I snuggled over close to Mama and finally went to sleep.

I went back to school when it was repaired from the hurricane damage, but the flue still smoked so much we had to keep the door and some windows open to breathe. The school

116

room was so cold we might as well not have had the heater going. Miss Lovey took advantage of the situation to teach us about Eskimo life. She told us about the igloos and how the whale-oil lamps were all they had for heat and light and how they smoked up the place just like our heater was doing. We felt very sympathetic toward the Eskimos, and the lesson made a deep impression on us, especially when we had a light snow around the first of December, which made us colder than ever. Finally Miss Lovey told us we needn't come back to school till after Christmas, and there was a big whoop and everyone was as joyful as could be. We popped corn and made snow cream with some sugar and milk Miss Lovey had very thoughtfully brought with her that day. It was such fun. Nobody could have been much happier than we were singing "Jingle Bells," wishing each other Merry Christmas, and then tramping home through the snow with our feet soaking wet because we had no boots.

Those days before Christmas I tried to avoid Bucky all I could. I wasn't anxious to let him get the habit of pressing his mouth all over my face and trying other things, and I was afraid he might ask me to give the ring back. As a result I didn't go over to Sue's for a long time, and I noticed she didn't come over to our house either. Then one cold night, coming home from helping Mama at the Big House, I felt my ring. The stone was gone! I hurried in our house, lighted the lamp, and looked. It was true. I searched all over the house, but I knew I'd never find it.

I sat down and cried, because with the beautiful blue stone gone, so was my engagement. It was a sure sign I wasn't supposed to marry Bucky, but I didn't tell him, not for a long time. I examined the empty metal band left around my finger and saw it was green with tarnish. I jerked it from my finger and threw it in the wood bin, feeling cheated, yet relieved at the same time.

When Mama came huffing and puffing in from the Big House, I didn't mention it. She was quiet too. It might have been because Reverend Halleck had gone to Halifax County for a revival, so he told her.

We ate our supper of sausage, hominy, and rutabagas in silence, each lonesome in her own way.

CHAPTER SIXTEEN

he days before Christmas always pass so slowly for chil-dren, and that year they crept by slower than ever. If I had known what was going to happen during the holidays, I might not have felt so impatient, but luckily I didn't know. I was dreaming every day of getting new shoes, of the wonderful Christmas feeling I was going to have, and of the excitement of putting beautiful holly branches in the house in glass pickle jars and the little red cellophane wreaths in the two front windows. I went around singing "Silent Night" and "O Little Town of Bethlehem." If Mama felt like it at night when she came home, she would play the organ and we would sing carols together. Can anything ever equal those times? The tingles would go up and down my backbone and creep all over my stomach when Mama pumped that little organ, making the sweetest music since the angels sang on the hillside the first Christmas Eve.

Then too we were all waiting impatiently for Leighton to come home. Miss Lou went around with a primped mouth at the thought, and we were all busy cutting up the fruit for the fruitcakes she always made. It took three days to finish the fruit and pick out the nuts, then another morning to stir the batter with the huge wooden spoons, and the whole afternoon to bake the cakes in steaming pans of water to keep them moist. And the spicy smell! It drifted through every part of your body, making you squirm with joy.

Everybody was thinking about Christmas except Janet. She caught the grippe and lay in bed for nearly a week. She vomited a lot, and I had to carry out the slop jar and empty it. Then I'd dash back to the kitchen to smell the fruitcakes baking. I never

119

saw Janet so down and out. She lay there in bed white as a sheet, crying like a baby. I even felt sorry for her.

"Ophelia, get out of here!" she screamed at me. "You smell!"

I knew I smelled like the kitchen; my clothes were full of that good odor, but Janet couldn't stand it. Finally her mama called Dr. Perkins. He came driving up in his little gray coupe and came in with his black bag and his clothes smelling like disinfectant, that scary odor that sets your heart beating fast because it reminds you of getting vaccinated. Dr. Perkins took her temperature, felt her pulse, and looked at her tongue. He told Miss Lou she would be all right soon, ate a slice of cake, along with a glass of homemade grape wine, and drove away. But Janet kept lying in bed, vomiting and crying, probably to get out of going to school. She didn't even go with her parents to meet Leighton's train in Pineville.

Oh, Jesus! He looked handsome like a man and a soldier when he got out of the car. He had grown taller and thinner, and his blond hair was clipped close to his head so that hardly a curl showed under his military cap. His uniform was gray with big brass buttons in double rows down his chest. Mama and I stood out in the yard all smiles, waiting for him to speak to us, as thrilled as if he had been an angel come to announce glad tidings. Mama grinned from ear to ear, showing her gold tooth and nervously clutching a dish towel.

Leighton jumped out of the car and came running over to us, took Mama's arm, and gave her a big hug like always. "How're you, Cassie?" he laughed. With me he was more awkward. He didn't know whether to shake my hand or what, but finally he gave my arm a little touch. "Hey, Ophelia, how you doing?" I was struck dumb and grinned stupidly.

Then he busied himself with the suitcase his daddy was getting out of the car trunk and said, "It sure is good to be home.

Look out for me at supper, Cassie. Haven't had any good home cooking since I left." He was really glad to get home, you could tell. He dashed to the house. "Got to see that ailing sister of mine," he called. We looked up and saw Janet waiting for him at the door, looking pale as a ghost. When he threw his arms around her, she burst into tears and cried all over his beautiful uniform.

Miss Lou pushed them through the door. "You'll have a relapse, Janet. Go back inside. Is the fire going in the fireplace, Ophelia?"

"Yessum," I answered. I had been keeping it going and poking it all afternoon so it would look bright and cheerful for Leighton.

Supper was a happy meal. We had fried chicken, his favorite dish, hot rolls, and chocolate meringue pie. Mama and I were as happy as they were. Mr. Lockwood, however, seemed preoccupied and didn't talk much, although Miss Lou had the candles lighted and the silver and crystal goblets gleaming just like on Sundays. After all, her baby boy had come home, but I didn't think he was a baby boy any more. He looked more like a god than ever.

Janet came down to the table for the first time since her sickness, but she was quiet and in a kind of dream, not a bit like the old spicy Janet. Leighton kept telling them about his experiences at school, about how his roommate had put a rat trap in his underwear drawer and caught the inspecting officer's hand, and how they threw rotten oranges out the window at night at the teachers going by, things that boys like to brag about. Finally Janet was smiling.

"Aren't you going to ask me about my rich roommate?" he asked her.

She smiled. "Sure. How rich is he?"

"His old man owns a sock factory in South Carolina."

"Then he should never get cold feet," she responded and giggled hysterically.

"And he has a sister," Leighton added. "She came to visit him with his folks during Thanksgiving. I went out to dinner with them."

"Is she pretty, his sister?" Miss Lou asked, leaning forward, and I listened intently as I passed the hot rolls to Mr. Lockwood for the second time in a row.

"I could lie and say yes, but she really is fat, wears glasses, and has kinky black hair," Leighton admitted. I felt relieved.

"Sounds very attractive," Janet commented.

"She is nice, though," Leighton hurriedly added in the girl's defense. He was like that, always kind. Just as he was asking Janet about the local gossip and how Katie and David were, I had to go back to the kitchen. I had already filled the water glasses three times and the coffee cups twice.

There was a lot to be done before Christmas on Monday. For one thing, Miss Lou was having a party for Janet and Leighton on Friday night, inviting all the children of the nice families in Attamac. I was as excited as anyone over it all. We were having hot fruit punch, popcorn, nuts, and all kinds of cookies that Miss Lou specialized in. I kept swiping cookies in the kitchen until Mama threatened to send me home if I didn't stop it.

"You know Miss Lou going to give us some, she always do," Mama told me. "And Mr. Lockwood already give me the money to buy your new shoes with."

I was so happy over the prospect that I jumped up and down.

"Something ails that man," Mama added with a frown. "He just don't act peart for Christmas. Either his nerves are working on him or his blood is low." She shook her head. "Every evening he comes in here and fixes himself an eggnog, but it don't seem to taste right to him."

Immediately I thought of the embezzling, whatever it was, but I knew Mr. Lockwood was too good to do anything that sounded like that. I was to find out by accident Saturday morning what was wrinkling up his forehead.

The party Friday night was a big success, if mess on the rug was anything to go by. Popcorn, nuts, and drinks were spilled on everything, and the noise was terrible. The boys were all at that age when each one tried to brag the loudest, all but Leighton. He just wore his uniform and acted quiet. I know all the girls' hearts were humming. I kept watching Katie Farthingale when I took in fresh servings. She looked at him as if she could eat him alive, but she was quiet too and seemed content just to look at him. There was a little blonde flirt there named Jo-Ann something, who had just moved to town, and she took him right over, much to my disgust. She took hold of his arm and kept talking to him, blinking her eyes right into his, and punctuating her conversation with squeezes of his arm muscles. I don't know what kind of folks she came from. I thought to myself, he'll tell her where to get off. But he didn't. In fact, he seemed to like her a lot and even asked his daddy for the car the next night to go to town to see her, which must have pained poor Katie. The whole thing made me mad, how that Jo-Ann could fool him like that. Then I began thinking, was she fooling him? She was bound to like him; how could she help it? But it still puzzled me. It would have been different if he had been going to see Katie. Everybody around Attamac, white and black, knew that Katie Farthingale ought to end up with Leighton Lockwood.

I noticed that Janet didn't waste time in the living room with the others. She was intent on getting David off to herself. She had richer tastes than eating popcorn in the parlor. She took David into the dark corner of the dining room since it was too cold on the front porch. I heard some little clicking noises in there as I passed down the hall with a batch of cookies. They were necking pretty heavy. I couldn't help myself; I stopped quietly outside the door to listen. I didn't feel too bad about eavesdropping because I knew Janet would have done the same thing if someone else had been in there and she had been outside.

They were kissing all right, and I could hear David breathing.

"Good God, Janet, you've never let me . . ."

"You're so bashful and sweet, David," she purred. A silence followed while they struggled together in a clinch, David breathing harder all the time. Of course they could only go so far right there in the house, but I bet if those silver candlesticks could talk they'd have plenty to tell. I stood there afraid to move, not knowing whether to rush past the door and out to the kitchen or go back to the parlor for a fresh start.

Then I heard Janet say in a low tone, "Let's get married, David."

This stunned him into letting her go; I could hear her fall backward on a chair. "Janet, how can we? We have to go to school, crazy. But someday we can."

"I'll tell you what we can do," she murmured.

"What?"

"Go out in the car."

Luckily they took time to kiss again, and this gave me a chance to slip through the door. I ran to the kitchen, wondering if I should tell Mama. But I didn't say a word, just peeped out the window to see two figures creeping outside together and hurrying over to the parked cars. I felt I was in on the plot, yet I didn't know how to stop them. If it had been murder, I would have, I swear I really would. Still, a burden of guilt crept into my heart, dampening a lot of my Christmas spirit. And it died a little more when I found out about Mr. Lockwood's troubles the next morning and when Leighton went to see that Jo-Ann the next night. But even these things were nothing to compare with the dreadful things that were to transpire in the next few days. The stars were set wrong in the heavens that Christmas.

CHAPTER SEVENTEEN

*M*ama and I were going to Attamac early the next morning with Mr. Lockwood in the pickup when he went to get staples and Christmas presents for the hands. I went up to the Big House at six-thirty to start the fire in the range and was surprised to find Miss Lou messing around the kitchen. She had on her old, bright blue wrapper, and her hair was up in curlers with the toilet paper sticking out of them. She was sniveling.

"Miss Lou, I'll make the fire," I told her. "You go back to your room before you catch cold."

She gave me a sorrowful look over her glasses and said she thought she would. She didn't have the slightest inkling of Janet's wild actions the night before, I knew that, but she looked sadder than I had ever seen her. It seemed that neither her beautiful fruitcakes nor even Leighton coming home had brought on the Christmas spirit for her. Something was wrong or Miss Lou wouldn't have been in the kitchen at six-thirty on a Saturday morning.

I made up the fire and got it burning with a dash of kerosene. Mama came in and had the bacon sizzling in no time. When I went to set the table in the dining room, I heard Miss Lou talking in low tones to Mr. Lockwood in the downstairs washroom where he was shaving.

"What if you can't get the loan from the bank, Jim? What will we do?"

"Let me worry about it, Louise. I should never have borrowed from Claud personally, but he said the bank had extended me all it could. I gave him a demand note and now he's asking for payment. He's under indictment, and you must realize it makes me look guilty by association. Maybe the new man at the bank will let me have a loan. If we could just have one good year . . . . Ouch!"

"Oh, you're bleeding, Jim! Here, let me fix it."

"No, no, go on and get your orange juice, Louise. I never could shave and talk at the same time." I could tell that he was put out with her.

She came into the dining room as I went to fetch the bacon, eggs, and grits. I quickly told Mama what I'd heard. She grunted with worry and didn't even tell me I shouldn't have been listening. "He be in a real fix," she muttered. "I hope he don't lose the farm."

I had never thought of Mr. Lockwood losing the farm, and my heart flew into my throat. What if we should lose our home? Where would we go and what would we do? Mama might get a job as a cook in Attamac, but we'd never have enough money to rent a house on the three or four dollars a week she'd make. What would become of us if Mr. Lockwood didn't get that loan? I could hardly eat my breakfast for worrying about it. I couldn't even enjoy looking at the frosty fields along the road as we rode to Attamac or seeing the people's pretty Christmas wreaths on their doors.

But when we reached town and got out at the courthouse, I felt happier seeing the rows of colored lights strung across the street and the decorations in the store windows. Just looking in the windows at the little cotton snowmen and the tinsel draped over perfume bottles and boxes of bath powder gave me a rich feeling. Of course, I never thought of possessing them. Seeing them was enough.

We looked in the store windows until nine o'clock, which was opening time. Then I went to the ten-cent store to buy my Christmas presents with the quarter Mama had given me.

127

It may not seem like much, but this was during the depression. Of course, Mama's present was the most important, and I spent an hour looking for something for her. I first considered some perfume. There was a good-sized bottle for ten cents and I wanted it badly, but then I saw some beautiful Christmas tree ornaments. I was tempted to get Mama a lovely, fragile, blue-and-pink glass boat hung by spiral wire until I thought of where she would hang it. We never had a tree, and I couldn't imagine it hung on the holly in the pickle jar. I finally decided on a green glass pin which I knew would look nice on her maroon Sunday dress. I parted with ten cents.

Now I had fifteen cents left and Sue and Bucky to buy for. Should I spend ten cents on Sue and five on Bucky or the other way around? I spent another half hour wandering around the store until the white girls who worked there began to give me suspicious looks, as though I was planning to steal something. This made me nervous and I almost got in a panic trying to decide what to buy, but in the end I bought Sue five cents worth of hairpins and Bucky a ten-cent jar of black hair ointment. This I thought would pay him back for the ring. The decisions had taken a lot out of me, but I felt much better once they were made. I hadn't even thought of Mr. Lockwood down at the bank trying to get a loan so we could all keep our homes.

When I met Mama in front of Crenshaw's Corner Store like we had planned, I saw she had acquired a few mysterious bundles. Now I was to get my shoes, and Mr. Crenshaw himself fitted them. I wanted patent leather. Every pair I tried on hurt me somewhere, but I finally took the ones that hurt just on the heels. I was used to blisters there. I left the store feeling like a princess. I begged Mama to let me wear them right then, but she said no, I must wait for Christmas morning.

They lifted my spirits, and I thought about them so hard I hardly noticed Mr. Lockwood on the way home to see if he had a sad or happy look or if his neck was redder than usual.

Sunday night we went to church for the Christmas Eve service. When Mama pumped out "O Come, All Ye Faithful" on the organ and the congregation sang "Silent Night," chills went up and down my spine. Reverend Halleck was back from Halifax County and Mama's grin was bigger than the new moon I had seen over the trees on our way to the church with Joe and Carrie in the mule cart.

Everybody felt fine. The Christmas spirit was zooming around the church, making us happy we were born and living. Mrs. Frizelle sang a solo, "Away in a Manger." She closed her eyes, sucked in her nostrils, expanded her ample bosom, and sang out for glory, her contralto voice carrying through the church like angel chimes. She was dressed in royal purple and a red hat with long black feathers, and her light cheeks were tinted with pink. She added glamour; everybody could feel it. She was the classiest person in the Zion Bethlehem congregation and always smelled like attar of roses. When she sashayed down the aisle, the men nearly swooned.

And James Odell was there. He didn't see me at first, but when he did, he kept winking at me and grinning every time I looked back at him. Didn't he look sporting in a blue shirt and red polka-dot necktie? I was so filled with the Christmas spirit I could hardly breathe and only halfway heard Reverend Halleck preach on the love we ought to feel at this time of the year. The Reverend was all aglow, his gold tooth never shinier than when he read the Gospel passages that night about the angels on the hillside out from Bethlehem singing good will to men. He kept looking around at Mama and holding out his arms like they were wings. He must have had a successful revival in Halifax County, I thought happily.

When church was over, James Odell found me outside in the churchyard and whispered, "Ain't you givin' me a Christmas kiss?"

I was excited, but answered coolly, "Where you been all the fall?"

"Busy, honey," he answered. "Come on over here under the umbrella tree."

"It ain't raining," I replied.

He looked up at the sky full of stars. "Naw it ain't, but a star might fall on us," he said slyly and led me right away from the others.

And it seemed that stars in multitudes fell on us under that umbrella tree while he kissed me all he wanted to. It was the best Christmas present I ever had. I don't think Jesus would have minded us celebrating his birthday this way because we were enjoying something that didn't belong to anybody else and that would have been wasted if we hadn't. Mama always told me you weren't supposed to waste things in this world.

Then, too soon, he said, "Well, I got to go now. Willie Thomas is waitin' for me, and him and me got some business to 'tend to," and winked. I noticed then that he smelled like rose hair oil and moonshine liquor mixed together, but it was a delicious smell.

I didn't ask him what his business was; I felt too good from the kisses. He and Willie Thomas, whoever he was, left in an old Ford that had smoke pouring out of the exhaust pipe and a big, loud knock sounding in the engine. As they drove away they added to the holiday spirit by throwing out firecrackers. I watched them flying down the bumpy road, merrily knocking, smoking, and banging. Lord, I forgot to say Merry Christmas, I thought suddenly, and then, as an afterthought, Willie Thomas sure must be rich to have a car.

Turning around, I saw Joe Batts talking to the Widow Frizelle. Or rather she was talking to him. She had the knack of holding on to a man's arm or lapel and getting his undivided attention. And she was pretty in that red hat trimmed with the long, black waving feathers.

"Joe Batts, I haven't seen you in weeks. Where've you and Carrie been keeping yourselves?" she asked sweetly, just as though they might have been vacationing in Florida instead of home minding their eight head of children, plus the chickens and mules.

"Er . . . we been around," Joe giggled in his reedy voice that cracked even further under the strain.

"Joe, I've got a big old favor to ask of you," she continued, caressing his necktie like it was pure pleasure. "You know how it is with no man around, how us women are so helpless without a man." Joe just gawked and simpered while Carrie stood by the mule cart pouting. "This being Christmas Eve night, I need somebody to help me put up my Christmas tree, nail it on a stand, you know. Wouldn't take you but a few minutes if you'd do it for me." Her voice trailed up and she looked coyly into his eyes. Joe hemmed and hawed and tried to get some words out.

"You're not letting me down on Christmas Eve, are you, Joe?" she purred.

"No ma'am. Sure," he agreed. "Carrie, you all go on. I'll go fix Mrs. Frizelle's tree and be on home later." It was about two miles to the widow's house.

"I'll go help you," Carrie offered.

"Naw, honey, it ain't no need," Mrs. Frizelle assured her, putting her arm around Carrie's waist real sisterly. "You go on home and tend to the chillen."

"You ain't goin' to be late, are you, Joe?" Carrie asked.

"Naw, I'll be right on."

Joe went off in a trance with the widow, and silently we got in the cart and Carrie tisked to the mule. I knew she was mad by the way she whipped old Jenny. Our necks jerked and off we went down the road.

"Sure is good to have Rev'rend Halleck back," Mama remarked.

I knew he'd be over later and I'd be sleeping on the pallet, but I didn't mind.

We got off at our lane, said our thanks and Merry Christmas, and saw Carrie go jogging home down the lane in the night.

"She sure is peed off at Joe," Mama commented as we went in the house and lit the lamp. "He better not get to messing 'round with that Lida Frizelle, or he'll know it."

Reverend Halleck did come over later. Mama got out the cookies and cakes that Miss Lou had given us, made some coffee, and we had a real party. Reverend Halleck had a jar of some kind of spirits, and he and Mama had a good time laughing and talking. I thought they might sing some carols, but I guess they had had enough of them at church and just wanted to socialize.

Finally I hung my stocking on the wall over the stove and fixed my bed on the kitchen floor. I could hardly wait for the next morning when I'd get my slippers.

CHAPTER EIGHTEEN

I woke up with an excited, choking feeling. I ran in the other room shouting "Merry Christmas!" and fell on the bed kissing Mama all over the face. Laughing, she put her arms around me. Then I flew to get down my stocking, which was stuffed with nuts, raisins, an orange and an apple, and pieces of hard candy, just as on every Christmas morning. On the floor were the presents wrapped in brown paper because we didn't have any white tissue in those days. I tore open the biggest one, my slippers, put them on my bare feet, and danced around the cold room. Then I opened my other package. It contained the black gloves I had tried on the day I lost my money—exactly what I wanted.

"Oh, Mama!" I cried happily. "Now open yours."

I carried her two presents to the bed. She gasped with delight when she saw the green pin, and in the other package was a box of violet dusting powder from Reverend Halleck. We took deep whiffs of its fragrance. "Smells good," I declared.

Since Mama didn't have to go to the Big House until late on Christmas morning, I made up the fire in the kitchen stove and perked us some coffee.

"You're coming up for breakfast, ain't you?" she asked.

"I want to see Sue and Bucky first."

I went, wearing my new slippers. It was the first time I had gone in a long while. Almalee and Monk were already outside playing with their little red wagon which Santa Claus had brought them. Monk was sitting in it with his legs dragging on the ground, and Almalee was trying to pull him.

"Merry Christmas!" I called to them. They came flying to

see if I had brought them anything, and I plopped peppermint drops in each of their mouths.

"See our wagon?" Almalee asked proudly.

"It's mine," Monk insisted.

"Not all yours," she countered. "It's my turn now."

"Naw it ain't."

"I ain't pullin' you no more." She stuck out her tongue at him. He gave her a slap in the face and she burst out crying, gave the wagon a violent kick, and ran in the house to her mama.

"That's no way to act on Christmas," I told Monk, who ignored me and went to catch a big red hen and put her in the wagon for a ride. But the minute he started pulling her, she flapped her wings and flew out with a loud cackle.

"She don't like your wagon, Monk." I laughed and went on, leaving him chasing her for another try.

It didn't seem much like Christmas inside. Bea was cooking breakfast, and the pork she was frying had smoked up the house, which was cold and drafty due to several broken window panes. Bucky in his undershirt and overalls was on one of the unmade beds reading an old funny paper. Sonny was in a corner on the floor trying to play a game of checkers by himself, and Sue was hunched down in a green rocking chair with a blanket around her, studying her fingernails. Nobody noticed my new slippers.

"Merry Christmas, everybody," I said.

"Hiya, Ophelia," answered Bucky, swinging his legs down to the floor politely.

Sue just stared at me sourly. "Christmas gift," I remarked, laughing, and gave her her present.

"Thanks. Take a chair." She seemed strange.

I sat down in the corner and tried to get up the nerve to give Bucky his present. Finally I hopped up and took it over to him. "Something for you, Bucky."

"Thanks, Ophelia." He seemed grateful and opened it up. "I swigger now I can be a sport," he kidded, and unscrewing the top of the hair ointment, dabbled in it with his middle finger.

I took my chair again and tried to open up a conversation with Sue. "You folks go to church yesterday?"

"Naw, we didn't get there," Sue said.

"We shot firecrackers instead," Sonny explained.

Sue finally turned toward Bea and screamed, "Ain't that cookin' finished yet, Mama? That smoke pure makin' me sick!" She stood up, letting the blanket fall to the floor. "I got to get some fresh air." She headed for the door in her pajamas.

Oh, Jesus, I saw then. It struck me like a bolt of lightning: Sue's stomach was pooching way out. She was pregnant. My mouth hung open in horror as she flung the door back and stuck her head forward, closing her eyes and breathing deeply.

The thought jumped into my mind, was it Bucky? My Lord, her brother? I peeped at him. He had gone back to his funny paper and was running his finger slowly under some of the lines.

"Breakfast ready," Bea announced, opening a loaf of bread. "Won't you eat with us, Ophelia?" She acted just like nothing was wrong, as though she hadn't noticed Sue's stomach at all.

"No ma'am, I got to get up to the house." I rose to leave just as Sonny bobbed up, throwing his checkers wildly in the air, letting them fly in every direction. One hit me on the head.

"Sonny, you goin' to lose your checkers that way," Bea told him pleasantly.

135

He scooped up a few and threw them up again, shouting, "Merry Christmas! Merry Christmas!" in a false bass voice. Then he aimed one checker at Sue, hitting her neck. "Come on, Sis. Let's eat. You freezin' us out with that door open."

Casting a quick glance at Bucky, I said a hurried good-by and left.

"Bye, Ophelia," Sue said lamely.

"Your breakfast is ready, Monk," I told him as I hurried down the path. He was busy taking one of the wheels off the wagon and paid me no attention.

I was thinking so hard about Sue I don't remember walking up to the Big House. I intended telling Mama right away, for I knew she had to know sooner or later. I felt ashamed, as though I was pregnant, and I wanted to get the telling over with. But I didn't get to tell Mama the sad news because there was so much worse to come. Sometimes even now I wake up in the night and see it all over again.

Just as I walked into the kitchen and smelled the good bacon smell and saw Mama stacking up the hot cakes on the pretty plate with the silver dome top, we heard loud screams coming down the road. We looked out and here came Frank, Sammy, and Scooter running as hard as they could, flinging their arms around and wailing at the top of their lungs. A rattlesnake's bitten somebody, I thought quickly. Mama and I flew out to meet them. Frank fell into Mama's arms and Sammy and Scooter caught her dress, panting and crying, trying to say something but not able to get it out.

Mama tried to shush them down to hear what the trouble was, but they were hassling so hard they couldn't talk. She dried off their faces and eyes with her apron and held them all in her arms until Frank could swallow enough to speak. He was struck by terror, with tears streaming down his cheeks, his mouth open like a dying baby bird.

Finally he gasped, "Mama done hit Papa with the ax" (he stopped to screw up his face and wail) "and knocked all his brains out!" All three took to wailing again as we tried to take in what Frank had said. Mama came to first and whispered, "Holy Lord Jesus, you ain't telling the truth!"

Frank nodded dumbly without stopping his crying. Mama acted quickly. She flew in the Big House shouting for Mr. Lockwood as she went.

Almost immediately Mr. Lockwood came out running and calling directions. "Take these children in the kitchen, Louise," he shouted. Miss Lou came out behind him in her kimono, her hair streaming down, and Janet and Leighton followed excitedly, both in their bathrobes.

Mr. Lockwood and Mama jumped in the pickup and I slid in beside Mama. I wasn't going to be left behind. We dashed down the dirt road at top speed, bouncing on every rut, our hearts pounding. We ran over a hen that was strutting in the road and she flew up in the air, uttering a horrible death cackle and sending a shower of feathers everywhere. Nobody said anything. We hit a deep rut so hard I banged my head on the top of the cab and got a headache.

Mr. Lockwood stopped the truck near Joe and Carrie's house and we got out. There wasn't a sign of life outside, but we could hear a drum beating and children's voices coming from within. Mr. Lockwood hurried toward the barn and we followed.

We didn't have to look very far. Joe was lying on the ground between the house and the barn and oh, my God, it was horrible! His whole head was split open like a coconut with bloody, shining, gory gray stuff everywhere, as though ten chickens had been gutted there. Old Jenny, standing nearby, whinnied loudly as we drew closer, baring her teeth in a frightful sneer. The bloody ax lay on the ground beside Joe, the gray mess all over it. I would never have guessed that Joe had so many brains.

I felt spasms of nausea. I had seen many a hog brained, but never a human before. And what was so terrible, his mouth and eyes were still open and he was grinning. A rooster came strutting by, then started running off fast just like he knew.

I turned aside and closed my eyes. Mama didn't notice me; she was praying. "Oh, Jesus, come to aid us all. Help us, Jesus. Save us, save us." Then she saw me. "Get away, Ophelia! What you doing here? Didn't I tell you to stay put?"

Mr. Lockwood told us to go into the house; we had to find Carrie. She was in the front room sitting in a chair as though in a trance. The children were playing happily with their Christmas toys, but she wasn't paying any attention. I saw that Geraldine had undressed her new doll and was spanking it unmercifully. Bobcat was fervently beating his drum. Flea was running a toy car all over the room, making his own sound effects, and Ethelene was trying to climb into Carrie's lap, but Carrie just let her keep falling. We could hear the baby wailing in the bedroom.

"Carrie, did you do it?" Mr. Lockwood asked her in a low, strained voice.

She sat staring into space, her mouth hanging open.

"Carrie! Did you do it?" Mr. Lockwood repeated. We stood there waiting, searching her vacant, lost-looking face. Finally, without changing her stare, she spoke. "I done it, and I'm glad I done it," she mumbled, letting her shoulders sag until I thought she would fall out of the chair.

138

"Why did you do it?" Mr. Lockwood asked, as though the answer would undo everything.

"I done it, and I'm glad I done it," she repeated in a faraway tone.

She isn't even sorry, I thought wildly. She's glad!

"Get the children and Carrie in the truck," Mr. Lockwood directed us. I went in the bedroom, picked up little Herry-Kane, and wrapped him in a blanket. Mama rounded up the others and tried to find their wraps. She finally threw an old scarf around Geraldine, and we put all the children in the back of the pickup. Mr. Lockwood took a sheet off the bed and went back to the barn to spread it over Joe's carcass to hide him from the animals and the world. It was only right to cover up what was so terrible.

Mama and I sat in the back of the truck with the children to keep them from falling out, and Mr. Lockwood led Carrie to the cab. She stumbled inside, dumb and docile, still in her daze. The drive back to the house was slower than our trip over there. When we got to the place where the hen lay dead in the road, Mr. Lockwood stopped for me to pick her up. After all, there wasn't any sense in wasting a chicken. The children messed with her the rest of the way back. Flea ran his little car over her red feathers; Geraldine poked at her glassy eyes.

When we got to the house, all the folks came running out to see what had happened. Miss Lou looked like the end of the world had come, and Frank, Sammy, and Scooter ran out of the kitchen to greet their mama as though she could tell them it was only a bad dream and not real at all. She hardly noticed they were there, but they clung to her skirts and started crying again.

139

Mr. Lockwood whispered to Miss Lou and then to Leighton, who had gotten dressed, I noticed, and Janet, still in her night clothes, tried to muscle in on the whispering.

"Cassie, take them in the kitchen and feed them all," Mr. Lockwood said.

We rounded up the eight children, plus Carrie, who sat in a chair humped over dumbly. I put the baby in his mother's lap and he began to cry. Carrie automatically unbuttoned her dress and let him have what he wanted without saying a word. I felt I ought to cheer her up, but wasn't sure how to do it, so I just took the other children to play in a corner while Mama heated up the griddle for more hot cakes.

Miss Lou and Janet got themselves plates of breakfast and left for the dining room, Miss Lou throwing a perplexed look back at her kitchen so full of stray pickaninnies. Their Christmas had been ruined. In fact, we had forgotten all about Christmas. I looked down and saw that my new slippers were scratched up already and felt like crying. Then I saw Mr. Lockwood and Leighton drive away in the car, heading for Attamac. What in the name of the Lord was going to happen next?

The children all ate their breakfast except Frank, who was older and smarter than the others and realized that his pa was dead for sure. Mama urged a plate of hot cakes on Carrie, but she wouldn't eat.

"You got to keep up your strength, Carrie, no matter what," Mama told her.

"He didn't come home till eight o'clock this mornin' and it weren't the first time. The mule bellowin' for feedin' . . ." Carrie sobbed. "Cassie," she added in a faint voice, "it was Christmas."

"Here, Carrie, take a dip of snuff," Mama urged. But Carrie for once didn't show any interest. She just stared at the wall while the children shouted and played, happy to have full stomachs and a new place to explore. They thought it was a fine Christmas, all except Frank, who sat in the corner with big, frightened eyes. After all, he was now nine years old.

Hardly an hour later two cars and a sanitation truck came down the road. The Law had come. Mama was scalding the old hen that we had killed in the road, and the air was filled with the smell of wet chicken feathers. It was all enough to turn your stomach. Every time I thought of Joe lying there in the barnyard, I shuddered. The children played noisily, and I had my hands full keeping them from opening Miss Lou's grocery cabinets. Before I knew it, though, Geraldine had found the molasses syrup and was into it. She was licking it off her fingers and it was running down her sweater. I tried to get it away from her, wipe her off, and look out the window at the same time. She was yelling something awful.

I watched the two cars and the truck turn down the lane that led to Joe's house, making a little parade. The middle black coupe was marked *Sheriff*. I wanted to run over to Sue's and Bucky's to carry them the bad news, but I had to stay with the children.

It wasn't long before Mr. Lockwood and Mr. Bickford, the sheriff, came driving back to the house. They and another man got out of the cars and stood talking together; then they came to the kitchen. I was shaking with fright, but Mama went on picking the chicken, her face set in a scowl. Carrie just sat in her chair like a big lump, the baby still nursing.

Mr. Lockwood went over to her. "Carrie, you know what you've done. The sheriff has to talk to you." He spoke kindly. She stared at him with sad, yellow eyes.

The sheriff came up to her. "Carrie, did you murder your husband?" he asked.

"I done it," she mumbled, "and I'm glad I done it."

I was wishing she had left off that last part, but she had to say it.

"We'll have to take you in with us," the sheriff explained to her. The baby changed sides as though determined to get all he could while he could. Carrie looked at the man unbelieving.

"You'll have to come with us," he repeated.

She wiped her nose nervously with her hand, her eyes blinking. "Where you takin' me?" she asked in a scared voice.

"You'll have to go to jail until you can be tried, Carrie."

It was like Judgment Day and the blowing of Gabriel's trumpet. With an exploding sob I started crying. Carrie in jail, a common murderer! It was too horrible.

It was hard pulling little Herry-Kane away from Carrie, but Mama did it. He wailed and threw his arms out stiffly, but he was too little to know anything. Mama pulled out a drawer and fitted him in it covered by a blanket, fixed him a sugar tit, and he was asleep before the sheriff got Carrie in the car. She left in the same daze, without even saying good-by to the children. They didn't know where she was going, except Frank, who had listened to everything very carefully and was standing in the corner by the window. He watched quietly, breathing hard, as his mother was driven away by the Law.

Then the sanitation truck drove slowly by. I knew what was in it. I wondered if they had been able to scoop up all Joe's brains or if they just had to leave some lying around in the barnyard. Joe might have to be buried without all his brains. I thought of the funeral and Carrie going to jail and all those poor little children left alone. Who would take care of them?

Bobcat came over to me and said, "What's the matter, Ophelia? Didn't you get no Christmas present? You want to play with my drum? Here!" He gave a few loud beats to cheer me up and teach me how it was done. I pretended like I did want to beat it and tried to smile.

Mr. Lockwood was talking to Mama, and she was nodding her head. The whole thing was that somebody had to look after the children. Mama agreed to take care of them until some arrangements could be made, and naturally this meant that I would help too. We would have to move over to Carrie's, where all their things were. We hated to leave home, but it was the only thing to do. Mr. Lockwood said he'd ask Sue if she would help me keep them days while Mama cooked, because of course Miss Lou didn't want to give up her good cook. Mr. Lockwood would furnish us food.

We were too confused to go more than one step at a time. We didn't think about the future, just about the next few days. Mr. Lockwood told us to put the children back in the truck. Miss Lou said for Mama to take the rest of the day off to get them all straight. Then she gave Mama her Christmas present, two pairs of beautiful silk stockings, size eleven. Was Mama pleased! I could see Miss Lou opening her kitchen windows to air the place out as we were driving off in the truck.

We got a few things from our house, and Mr. Lockwood took us by Willie and Bea's to tell them the bad news and get their help. They were dumfounded and couldn't take it in that Joe was brained and stone dead. It was the biggest thing that had happened since the hurricane, and I guess it was as bad if not worse. They all set out at once to go and view the scene of the crime in the barnyard. They didn't find any brains left, but all of them saw the bloodstains. They kept shaking their heads in disbelief.

"I swigger, I just cain't believe she'd brain him," Willie remarked. "I swigger I never thought Carrie would kill him!"

Mama told them about Joe and Mrs. Frizelle and how Carrie said it wasn't the first time.

"She must have been eat up with jealousy," Bea said, shaking her head.

"You never know what's in a body's mind," Willie put in. "I swigger you don't."

"Lesson to you men to look out," Bea kidded.

"It ain't no goddamn joke," Willie snapped.

When their curiosity was satisfied, they went on home and Mama and I settled down in the house. We put clean sheets on Joe and Carrie's bed, and Mama got busy in the kitchen. Mr. Lockwood had given us the chicken that had been killed.

Black clouds came up, and it began to rain with a fierce wind driving it. It was bleak and scary, as though Joe's ghost might be restless and conjuring up the storm. I was glad he hadn't been killed in the house. We lighted lamps, and the children began to ask about their ma. We told them Carrie was sick and wouldn't be back for a long time. The main problem was the baby. Because we didn't have any bottles or nipples, we had to give him milk by the spoonful. At first he would gasp and choke, but he finally got the hang of it and learned to swallow it. Mama gave him some chicken gravy and he smacked his lips. Then he got a sugar tit and went to sleep.

Little Frank knew everything, and he worried. We told him his mama was all right and that we'd take him to see her in a day or two. We offered to let him sleep with us, but in his manful way he crawled in the bed upstairs with Scooter, Sammy, and Bobcat. They looked like four teddy bears all snuggled in together under the crazy quilt. Geraldine, Ethelene, and Flea slept together on a pallet in the front room. Geraldine hogged the cover, and when Flea said he was cold, she pinched

him, but we finally got them settled down and went to bed ourselves. It was then that I timidly asked Mama if she had noticed
Sue.

Mama snorted and said yes, she knew about it, that everybody did. I was hurt that I was the last one to know that Sue
was being talked about. Finally, I got up the nerve to ask Mama
the question in my mind. "Who did it?" came out in a weak,
quavery voice.

There are not many secrets in this world, and everybody
knew who the father of Sue's child was. Mama saw no reason
to keep me in the dark. "Mr. Deiter," she muttered with a
humph. "He cain't stop messing 'round to save his soul. Don't
you ever get near him, you hear me?"

I could feel myself getting hot. Suddenly I thought of the
day when he had given Sue a dollar. It had never dawned on
me what was going on. But I was so glad it wasn't Bucky. I
had the idea she might be put in jail if it was, because it was
against the law to do anything with your brother, or was that
in the Bible? "Don't you worry, Mama. I never go around
that man."

My mind was so in a whirl I couldn't sleep for a long time.
It flitted from Sue to Carrie to Joe like a fly buzzing between a
dead hog and a rotten fish. Then I tried to remember it was
Christmas night. It seemed ten years since I was kissing James
Odell under the umbrella tree the night before. Sleep finally
came and with it strange dreams of swimming naked in the
river, only it was winter and I was freezing.

CHAPTER NINETEEN

*W*e woke up to a cold world of ice. Everything was frozen up, the pump, the puddles, even the water in the kettle. The baby was crying and the children whimpering. There was plenty of work to do. I never knew how much effort it took for a family of eight head. First we built up the fire and got the children dressed. As soon as breakfast was over, it seemed it was time for lunch. Thank heaven for sweet potatoes and side meat. There was always plenty of that on the farm, and corn meal for bread.

Mama went on up to the Big House about noon to help Miss Lou, and I spent the day washing clothes, keeping the wood stove going, and preventing the children from burning themselves up. Sue never came over, but I hoped for her all day. The next day was the same, and the next. Finally Mama told Miss Lou that Sue wasn't coming and they sent her word again. She showed up the following day, sullen and pouty, and hardly did a lick of work, but at least having her there helped to break the monotony. I waited for her to mention her condition, but she never did, and I didn't either. She just lay back on the old sofa and daydreamed.

"Ain't you going to help me with this ironing, Sue?" I finally asked her. "These young'uns got to have clean clothes."

"Why?" she asked. "They don't know no difference."

I looked at her with real dislike. She'd find out, I thought to myself, and it would serve her right.

When Mama came at night, she would tell me what was happening at the Big House. I felt so disappointed not to be up there while Leighton was home to see him coming and going in his uniform and feel the excitement of the holiday. But somebody had to look after those children. They were pitiful, asking for their ma and pa, and neither one coming back to them, at least not so far as I could see.

Mama told me Leighton was courting that Jo-Ann every night and that Janet and David were going off together in the car every afternoon and night. Mama shook her head. She said Miss Lou looked worried to death and Mr. Lockwood was pale as a ghost. Most likely he didn't get his loan; it couldn't be anything else. Our very lives depended on that loan, and we knew it. But we were just trusting in Mr. Lockwood like he was a savior.

Of course he was worried about losing Joe, too, because Joe was a good, steady tenant, even if he had messed around with Mrs. Frizelle. She, Mama said, had been mighty upset about Joe getting killed and had had some very uncharitable things to say about Carrie. Mr. Lockwood was also concerned about the children and kept asking how they were and sending over groceries to us. Miss Lou came with him to see us one afternoon and brought two baby bottles, candy, flycakes, butter, and some old sheets and blankets.

Joe's funeral was held on Friday. Some people thought it was too soon, but because he was murdered, it was different from an ordinary death. We all braced ourselves for the sad occasion. Since he was killed on Christmas, a lot of people made him holly wreaths or just brought him the ones they had used on their doors. Mrs. Frizelle sent three red carnations, which everybody thought was a nice gesture, for she really helped cause his death. She also sang a solo, "O Sweet Departed," her voice ringing out like a woman lamenting her lover. We all cried.

147

Mama and I took every one of the children to the funeral. Different ones in the congregation helped with them while Mama played the organ. I held the baby, who did fine until Mrs. Frizelle started to sing, then wailed so loud I had to carry him to the back pew.

Mr. Lockwood saw to it that Joe had a decent coffin, and he and Miss Lou came to the funeral. The usher seated them down front on the first row, which was ordinarily saved for the family.

Reverend Halleck preached a wonderful sermon about how the excesses and powerful emotions of life cause us humans such misery, but he added forgiveness is necessary even in extreme cases. He never mentioned that Joe was murdered, and some folks were disappointed since they were hoping for something special. Reverend Halleck went on to say how fruitful Joe had been in helping to populate the earth and, believe me, nobody could argue with that. He said that being a father was one of the highest callings of all and praised Joe for his good disposition and hard work and congenial personality. I could see Mrs. Frizelle, who took it on herself to act as first mourner, sobbing into her silk handkerchief. Nobody could object, for Carrie was still in jail and they wouldn't let her out to come to the funeral, although Mr. Lockwood had asked the sheriff about it. The sheriff said he couldn't do it and doubted that she wanted to come anyway, since she was sticking to her story that she was glad she had done it.

We laid Joe to rest in the churchyard covered in holly wreaths and the three carnations. Then everybody made a lot of the children, saying how pitiful they were and trying to make them feel good. I will say to Mrs. Frizelle's credit that she offered to take two or three head of them home with her to look after, and I was all for letting her, but Mr. Lockwood thought we ought to keep them together until after the grand jury met.

The next day, Saturday, Mr. Lockwood drove us all to Attamac to see Carrie. We got the children ready, even the baby, and left at nine o'clock. It was a cold ride in the back of the pickup, but we had some quilts to bundle up in. Mama sat in the cab with Mr. Lockwood and held the baby. Leighton didn't go and I was disappointed. It looked as if I was never going to see him again.

Mr. Lockwood carried us straight to the red brick jail. All the children were big-eyed and excited. Some of them had never been to Attamac before, and it was like a dream to them to see so many pretty houses and buildings, all painted, one after the other.

When we parked in front of the jail, Scooter said with awe, "Ain't it pretty?"

A colored man was sweeping up out front. As we walked past him, Geraldine told him with a grand air, "My mama live here." He scratched his head and nodded sadly.

Mr. Lockwood left us after speaking to the fat jailer, who let us go right into the cell with Carrie. She was lying on her cot, but got up with a big smile when she saw us. Her cell was in a corner away from the others, which, I guess, were for men. Carrie had it all to herself, and it was very neat with the cot, a chair, and a little bench on which was a tray that held the remains of her breakfast. There was a water toilet and a wash basin in an alcove, hidden by a green curtain. I thought it was really nice.

All ten of us crowded into the cell; the jailer took out the breakfast tray, and then he locked the barred door. This gave me a funny feeling. "Half an hour," he said and disappeared down the hall.

The children began to hug their mama, who was glad to see us. I saw tears in her eyes. She took the baby, unbuttoned her dress, and nursed him. Luckily the milk hadn't dried up.

"How you doing, Carrie?" Mama asked.

"Right spry," she answered. "I been sleepin' mostly."

I guess it was the first real rest Carrie had ever had.

The children were poking around, jumping on the cot, and running the water in the basin. Bobcat, Flea, and Ethelene had never seen a flush toilet before, and I showed them how to use it. They were amazed. When Geraldine's turn came, she wouldn't get off. She loved it. She flushed it so much it wouldn't flush any more, but she kept pulling the chain and listening to it strain. She had never before had so much fun.

Mama sat in the chair and talked to Carrie, trying to cheer her up, but we soon found out she was in good spirits. "They bring the vittles on a tray," she explained, "regular, three times a day. They ain't bad and I get coffee every meal."

I guess Carrie had never had anyone to cook for her before, not since she was a baby anyway.

"And look here," she went on, bringing out a newspaper from under her mattress. She held it out to us. There was her picture big as life and above it the words *Axes Husband, Held for Murder*. "They come and took my pitcher," she said proudly. "It ain't bad, is it?"

"It's the spitting image of you," Mama said, clucking softly. We had never known anyone, colored or white, who had gotten in the newspaper. Carrie was famous. Of course we had sense enough to know that getting in jail wasn't the best way to get famous.

The children were most impressed. Here was their ma with a private room, electric lights, and a water toilet, being waited on by a white man, and her picture in the paper. Well, you couldn't blame them.

Carrie wanted to know every detail of Joe's funeral, and we told her who was there, about the holly wreaths and Mrs. Frizelle singing and sending the carnations. At that she made a humphing noise and got a sullen look on her face. When we mentioned how the widow had offered to keep some of the children, she said, "She ain't keepin' none of my chillen and you can tell her so." We said we didn't blame her.

Then Mama changed the subject and asked her what they gave her to eat, and she spent the rest of the half hour telling us what she had had for every meal. She ended up by saying they put salt in the corn bread, which ruined it. We nodded sympathetically.

Then the jailer came and said five more minutes. The children all took turns again at the toilet and washing their hands in the basin. We changed the baby's diaper on the cot. Mama brought out her Bible from her pocketbook and gave it to Carrie. "I'm lending it to you," she said. "It's the only one I got, but I want you to have it while you're here."

Carrie took it, about to cry. "You know I ain't much on readin', Miss Cassie," she said, "but I'd like to hold it sometimes." We knew then that Carrie wasn't glad she had done it, at least not all the time. And when she started getting sorry, the Good Lord would start forgiving her.

At the last minute Carrie grabbed Mama by the arm. "Miss Cassie, what they goin' to do to me?"

Mama patted her. It was a question we hadn't discussed. "Now don't you worry, Carrie. They'll take care of you all right. You just read the Bible and pray and we'll pray for you, too."

I wondered if Carrie would read the part of the Bible where it says you shall do no murder.

"Miss Cassie," Carrie added, "I'm in a family way."

I don't know why this surprised us so. It was her usual condition.

"Why, Carrie, honey, that's grand!" Mama sputtered consolingly. "That'll favor you with the Law. How many times you missed?"

"Two."

"That'll make it come in the summer, the best time."

"What they goin' to do to me, Miss Cassie?"

"You'll get tried in court, they say. It ain't nothing to worry about. Now you just get your rest, honey. Tell your mama good-by, chillen. We'll be back to see you."

The children hovered around Carrie, kissing her and saying good-by. Geraldine went back to the toilet for a last drop and flush. Then the fat white jailer unlocked the door, and we left Carrie holding onto the bars and watching us go down the hall.

To get their minds off their ma, we walked the children up the street and let them look in the store windows. They were seeing things they had never seen before, the pretty Christmas decorations and lighted trees everywhere. They quickly forgot their ma, left back in the jailhouse, when we bought them ice cream cones at the drugstore with a half dollar Mr. Lockwood had given us. Of course, we didn't take all eight children inside, but just Frank and Sammy to help carry the cones out. There was a licking good time.

We hung around the courthouse until Mr. Lockwood came to pick us up. He had been by the jail to speak to Carrie, and his forehead was in deep furrows, as though the whole world was turning against him. I felt sorry for him. I wondered if he was worried about his loan or about losing Joe and poor Carrie being in jail.

I hugged the children to me all the way home in the back of the pickup. They thought it was the best fun in the world to go riding in the winter air, and even Frank seemed happy now that he knew his mama was all right.

CHAPTER TWENTY

he days dragged on. Sue would amble over around ten or eleven o'clock every morning, too late to be of much help. She was just one more mouth to feed, but at least she was someone to talk to, when she would talk. She acted more sullen and ornery all the time, and we still never mentioned her condition.

One day, about a week after our visit to the jail, she dropped a bombshell. Sue always knew everything. She was lying on the bed, her arms flung out like they were dead. I was complaining about how I had hardly glimpsed Leighton during his stay at home and about living like this without going to school when she said, "Janet's pregnant as hell." Then she laughed loudly.

I was so shocked that I flopped on the edge of the bed with my mouth wide open. What she said began to sink in. I never would have noticed such a thing, but Sue would. I guess it took one to know one.

But Janet! She was a white girl and Miss Lou's daughter. She couldn't be pregnant, she just couldn't. Leighton's beautiful sister and her from the finest, nicest folks. This would be the end of the world if it was true.

"Sue, you're lying; it ain't so!"

She lay there poking out a mile and laughing. "I ain't lyin'. She done swole up. Just like me." She laughed and laughed. Finally she had admitted it about herself.

"And you know who done it?" she asked, cutting her eyes at me slyly.

My brain hadn't gotten that far.

"Jed Deiter," she answered and hee-hawed. It was the first

time I had heard Sue laugh for weeks. It surely took something to amuse her.

"Jed Deiter!" I repeated. "How you know?"

"You're so dumb, Ophelia, you ought to be that way yourself. You seen them messin' every night last summer. It was Jed all right."

I remembered then Janet's sickness, her vomiting all day, and her asking David to marry her. It was true. She was purely caught.

"You reckon her ma know it yet?" I asked sadly.

"I told you once if Janet swole up, Miss Lou'd think it was the Holy Ghost done it. But she ain't goin' to wish this away." She laughed at the thought. Maybe she had tried it herself.

"Janet ain't married," I remarked foolishly.

"Naw, she sure ain't, Dummy, and she ain't marryin' Jed Deiter neither because he's gone to Norfolk and joined the navy." This made Sue giggle. Misery does love company.

I thought about Miss Lou and Mr. Lockwood. Even murder wouldn't be this bad to them. It didn't seem fair—him worried to death about losing his farm and now this. I wanted to take Janet and beat her and scratch her, and I wanted to beat Sue, too, just like it was all her fault.

At that moment Geraldine started chasing Flea with the poker and my thoughts were interrupted while I disarmed her. She was mad as fire.

"How come you do that?" I scolded her.

She scowled at me. "He peed on me," she cried. "Nobody ain't peein' on me." For once I didn't blame her, and I spanked Flea with all my pent-up feelings. I think if they had called him Franklin Delano, his real name, it would have encouraged him to act more dignified.

Sue kept snickering all day while I cooked the collards and

dumplings, but I noticed she was ready to eat when I served them up. She slurped up plenty of pot liquor, but I felt sick. I wanted to jump in the collard pot and drown myself, the world seemed so topsy-turvy. I didn't dare think what was going to happen. Lord Jesus, these two children coming into the world and Sue's the uncle or aunt of Janet's! Those Deiters were common, just plain common. But they weren't all to blame; I had enough sense to know that.

I clammed up, pouted, and sulked the rest of the day. I was glad to see Sue go home. I wanted Mama.

When she came, at first I couldn't get up the nerve to tell her. I finally asked about how things were at the Big House with Mr. Lockwood and everybody.

"Terrible," she grunted. "Leighton left for school today and Miss Lou took sick and gone to bed."

Leighton had gone and I hadn't even gotten to see him again.

"I tried to take her a little broth, but she just kept her arm over her forehead and sniffled," Mama went on. My heart jumped. Miss Lou knew! They all knew!

"I told her Leighton would be back before she knew it, but she just grieved. Tell the truth, I was scared Mr. Lockwood couldn't send him back. It would kill his pride not to, though."

"Mama," I said trembling, "Sue told me something terrible today about Janet."

Mama cut her eyes at me and frowned, then shook her head. "I been 'specting it for a good while," she admitted sadly. I threw myself in her arms and sobbed.

"How they going to stand it, Mama?" I cried. "Janet ain't no better than a nigger."

"You hush up now," Mama scolded. "I don't want to hear you talking that way."

The children gathered around looking at me crying.

"What's the matter?" Frank asked, scared. "Have they hung my ma?"

"No, no, honey! Don't you worry about nothing," Mama told him, hugging him up to her. "Come on now, Ophelia, let's get these chillen to bed."

When Mama returned the next night, I dreaded to hear what had happened. She said Miss Lou just lay in her bed and stared at the ceiling all day, not eating a bite. Mr. Lockwood had driven off to Attamac carrying Janet with him. She was pale and quiet, Mama said. They had come home just before suppertime, and Janet had gone to her room and not come to the table for supper. Mr. Lockwood had sat there alone picking at his salt herring and batter bread. Then he had gone up to Miss Lou's room, taking her plate of supper with him, and closed the door. I could imagine him lighting the lamp in their bedroom and trying to get Miss Lou to eat and her not eating. Miss Lou was going through hell. This was worse than having Ginger Hill burn to the ground.

There was nothing we could do, nothing at all, except watch and wait and feel for them. I wondered if the news was out in Attamac yet. It would be a blow that the town would never recover from, I decided.

But life didn't stop, as it never does. School reopened, and though I hated not to be going, I made Frank go, and Sammy and Scooter along with him, to get them out from under foot. They needed some new overalls terribly, but they had to go in what they had. Mr. Lockwood had bought every one of them a new pair of shoes for Christmas, and that was a big help. It was sort of hard to tell whose shoes were whose with their feet so near the same size, for although Scooter was younger than Sammy, his feet were bigger. I tried marking them with a crayon I found, but the marks soon wore off, and one day, after the bigger boys left for school, I noticed Bobcat was wearing two right shoes, one bigger than the other. Poor Sammy had gone off with two left ones. Things like that are bound to happen sometimes in a family of that size, but the surprising thing is that we got on as well as we did.

Geraldine turned four. Carrie was right smart about the children's birthdays, keeping a list of them in her dresser drawer. We celebrated by making a batch of hot cakes, and I went over home and found one of my old dolls for her present. She liked it better than her Christmas celluloid doll, which she had pulled the arms off of. Bobcat gave her the rabbit's foot he always kept in his pocket, a real sacrifice. She had a good time getting Flea down on the floor and tickling his nose with it. He screamed and complained. Finally he blew out his nose on it and she cried, "Snot! You snotted my rabbit!" and bit him. We had to wash off the rabbit's foot under the pump and hang it up to dry.

I began to get tired out and fall behind with the washing, especially when it rained. Sue quit coming over altogether. The baby had to wear the damp diapers over and over, and the smell was terrible. Mama said I needed to go back to school, and I longed to, but first somebody had to be found to look after the children. Mr. Lockwood said he had been trying, he had talked to the Law about it. Carrie's mother was dead and none of Joe's folks had come to his funeral. I guess they didn't even know he was dead, wherever they were.

About three days later, a cold, icy, January day, when the whole world seemed lonesome and shriveled and the old cornstalks in the field reminded me of skeletons, I saw a black car making its way down the lane to the house. I was out at the clothesline hanging out wash that was freezing hard as soon as the wind hit it. The car chugged up to the house and stopped with a hiss. I didn't know who was in it, but I was glad to see them, whoever they were. Who should get out but Mama and then a big man and a big woman and four children.

"Ophelia, this here is Joe's sister, Mrs. Parue, and Mr. Parue. They've come for some of the chillen."

Mrs. Parue was stout and pleasant and smiled broadly, showing four gold teeth. She must have been rich as everything. We went in the house, and she began to look over the children. They took to her at once because she had brought them a bag of candy.

"Where you all live?" I asked timidly.

"In Conner Square," Mrs. Parue answered, shaking out her fur collar. "My husband is in the undertaking business there."

My mouth formed a big O. They were good and rich for sure. I never would have guessed Joe had such a wealthy sister. The four Parue children stood around looking like they hated to touch anything. The two girls had on bright red coats, white stockings, and shiny black shoes. Their hair was plaited in long pigtails and tied with red ribbons. They looked like pictures. The two boys, who were younger, wore blue serge knickers, white shirts, and overcoats. They had a nice scrubbed look. I thought, this is the way my children are going to look.

Mrs. Parue got right down to the children, looking them over, and they all looked up at her like she was a fairy godmother. They had never seen anyone so grand.

"What's your name?" she asked Bobcat.

"Bobcat," he replied, sucking up his runny nose.

She smiled. "Are you a good boy?"

He nodded his head so hard he shook out what he had sucked up.

Mr. Parue reached down and picked up Ethelene, lifting her

high above his head. "Look at this one, Decie! She's a cute little thing." Ethelene smiled gleefully.

When Ethelene was lifted up, I could see she hadn't put her pants on. If I had known the Parues were coming, I would have tried to clean the children up a little, but maybe it was just as well.

Geraldine was jealous. She ran at the smaller Parue boy, knocked him down, sat on his stomach, and stuck her fingers in his eyes. He screamed, "Mama! Mama!"

Mrs. Parue snatched Geraldine away and comforted the boy, whose eyes were red and bleary. Mama sent Geraldine upstairs, and she was eliminated as a prospective choice. During the rest of their stay she stood pouting at the head of the stairs and from time to time threw a stick of stovewood down. One piece hit Flea on the leg, and he screamed at the top of his lungs. Then we noticed a puddle of water forming at his feet as a result of his exertions. The two Parue girls withdrew from him as though he had the plague. I finally had to take him in the bedroom for dry clothes, and he was out of the competition. In the meantime Mama had dressed the baby in clean clothes and wrapped him in a blue blanket to show him off. Mrs. Parue took him and talked baby talk to him. He cooed and laughed out loud. She kissed him eagerly.

"Oscar, look! Isn't he cute?"

Mr. Parue tickled his stomach and little Herry-Kane laughed again.

"He looks just like Clarence used to," Mrs. Parue purred, kissing him again. You could tell she really loved babies. Clarence, the older Parue boy, moved over to see his likeness.

"Sure do favor him." Mr. Parue giggled. "He's your cousin, Clarence. What's his name, Cassie?"

"Herry-Kane. He came in the world on the big storm. He got to be something special. Lordy, what a night! And feet first!" Mama chuckled.

I shuddered at the memory.

"Let's take him, Oscar. He's so little he won't ever know we aren't his own parents."

I guess she thought Carrie would never want him back.

They whispered together, looking at the other children.

"We'll take her too," Mr. Parue said, pointing to Ethelene, who suddenly drew back, hid in Mama's skirt, and poked out her lip. "What's her name?"

"Ethelene. She's two. She's a good little girl," Mama assured them. "Ethelene, you're going to ride in the car, honey!" This cheered Ethelene up, and Mrs. Parue gave the baby to her husband and picked her up, giving her a big smile and hug. "You're going to be our little girl, Ethelene. These big girls'll be your sisters." The two girls drew near eagerly, cuddled her, and touched her cheek. Ethelene began to enjoy the attention. "Ride in car," she reminded them.

"Is she trained?" Mrs. Parue asked me.

"Mostly," I answered, embarrassed.

We packed up what clothes they had in a paper sack. I put all the soiled, smelly diapers in an old newspaper while Bobcat looked on forlorn. He was only five, but he knew he had been rejected and wasn't going to ride in the car.

Geraldine also knew she wasn't going. "Bitch! Grunt!" she yelled downstairs, throwing more stovewood, then an old poker, which came near hitting Mr. Parue on the head. Mama flew up the steps, grabbed her, and gave her a whaling then and there. Then she put her in the bedroom, bawling, and closed the door.

The Parue children looked frightened and went quickly outside when their mother told them to get in the car. The parents followed, each carrying a new member of the family. We went over to see them off. I kissed little Herry-Kane and Ethelene over and over.

"Tell Carrie we'll take good care of them, just like they were our own," Mrs. Parue said. "I wish we could take them all, but we don't have the room. And tell Carrie we sure hope they don't 'lectracute her." Mrs. Parue was a fine woman, I could tell.

They cranked up and rode off, everybody waving until they were out of sight. Then I let out the big sob that had been in my throat and ran inside to cry. I already missed the baby and Ethelene so much. It wouldn't seem the same without them, and I had a feeling I'd never see them again.

Mama comforted me with the fact that they would have a good home and all the nice things money could buy. Finally I dried my tears and played hide-and-seek with Geraldine, Flea, and Bobcat. Flea disappeared and we couldn't find him. We searched frantically until suppertime, even in the barn and outhouse. When Mama went to cook supper, she found him curled up asleep in the oven.

It set Geraldine wild because she hadn't thought of hiding there first. "We goin' to cook you!" she screamed at him. He crawled out, rubbing his eyes, and calmly made a big puddle on the floor. Mama shook him good and hard. "You're a big boy now, Flea. You got to stop that, you hear me?" she told him. There were no more dry pants, so he just went wet until bedtime, but it didn't seem to bother him at all.

When Frank, Sammy, and Scooter came home from school, they were surprised to find their brother and sister gone. We didn't tell them that Mr. and Mrs. Parue had come to choose among the children. It didn't seem right that they never even had a chance because they were at school.

That night I read my geography book until late, longing to get back to school and start learning again.

CHAPTER TWENTY-ONE

*T*hings *at the Big House were worse than ever, Mama* told me. Miss Lou lay in bed all day, never coming downstairs at all, and Janet kept to her room. Mama said she had heard her vomiting in the bathroom from time to time and that Miss Lou was bound to have heard the retching in that quiet house. Mr. Lockwood stayed gone most all the time. Mama said she didn't see any sense in cooking since no one was eating anything. She had given the scrambled eggs and bacon she fixed that morning for breakfast to the dogs, and Miss Lou had hardly touched the chicken broth she had carried up to her for lunch. Janet had drunk a Coca-Cola and tried to smoke a cigarette, but it had made her sick and she had run past Mama holding her mouth and rasping, "Get out of my way, Cassie!" between her teeth. I was glad I didn't have to go to the house these days.

"What's going to happen, Mama?" I asked sadly.

"I don't know to the Lord. But it can't go on. Miss Lou got to get up and eat or die. And not a friend been to see her. That means they know about everything."

That was worse than death, I thought. All the whispering that must be going on. It made me embarrassed that I lived at Ginger Hill. Janet had put a blight on the whole place and everybody in it, like some dreadful catching affliction. I was glad Leighton was off at school, and I wondered if he knew, hoping he didn't. In my imagination I could see him marching up and down with his head held stiffly like a tin soldier.

From Leighton my thoughts trailed over to James Odell, and my bones got a spongy feeling. Thinking of James Odell was the only pleasure I had those days. When would I ever see him again?

Friday night Mama came in huffing and puffing, very excited. While we were frying some perch that Reverend Halleck brought her, she told me the news. Mr. Lockwood and Janet had left early in the morning and been gone all day. Janet had brought home a pile of expensive-looking packages from Frederic, the next town west of Attamac. Miss Lou had come down to breakfast after they left and tried to eat a fried egg. In the midst of her coffee, with Mama standing nearby for comfort, she had burst into tears.

"Cassie," she had said, "Janet and David are getting married tomorrow." Then she cried into her napkin and Mama removed her delicate rimless glasses, laid them on the table, and patted her on the shoulder.

"Miss Lou, ain't I always said Janet and David would get married one day? He's sure the right one for her and she's going on sixteen. You eat your breakfast and we'll get busy!"

Miss Lou finally dried her eyes, and they cleaned and polished up the house all day. Miss Lou brought out all the heirloom silver, more than they could ever use, and they made chicken salad, cheese straws, and a huge white cake. Mama cooked the biggest ham from the smokehouse. "There wasn't time for soaking it," she chuckled, "but it'll have to do."

My eyes were fairly bulging out of my head with excitement. "What time is the wedding?" I wanted to know.

"Sometime in the morning," Mama said.

"I'm going to take the chillen over and stand in the yard and watch," I declared. She didn't tell me not to.

"And that ain't all," Mama continued. "In the afternoon,

here came Mrs. Farthingale to see Miss Lou. She came by herself and found Miss Lou dusting and cleaning, with a white towel 'round her head, and putting ivy and magnolia leaves in the parlor. I saw them hugging each other and Miss Lou crying all over her shoulder. They sat down to talk. I don't know what they said, but Miss Lou asked me to bring some hot tea. I was glad Mrs. Farthingale came. It don't seem so much like a shotgun wedding when people come."

"Mama, do they know . . . you reckon?"

"I guess they do, Ophelia, but you know they got to stand together and protect each other. And this means David's chillen going to come into Ginger Hill someday."

"But, Mama, this one ain't his," I blurted out before I thought.

"Well, nobody's s'posed to know that," she grunted. "Folks'll think it's his."

No, they won't, I thought, but they'll pretend to. In the white folks' world, like Mama said, they'll protect each other, cover up each other's sins. But the whispering will go on for generations.

The next morning was cold and frosty, but a pale sun was out. Maybe that was a good sign. I dressed the six children in the best they had and went to the Big House at nine o'clock. Mama told them they better behave and gave them some brown sugar to eat if they'd stay quietly on the back stoop behind the kitchen.

Miss Lou came to the kitchen in a flurry, her hair tied up in toilet paper and her hands fluttery. She looked dreadfully peaked.

"Ophelia, I'm glad you're here," she said. "We'll need you. Go up and help Janet with her packing."

"Yessum."

I went as she prepared to slice the ham. Miss Lou could slice a ham in beautiful, paper-thin slices. She was an expert in certain things like that and crocheting lacy bedspreads and making the best black fruitcakes in the world.

My heart was thumping as I left the kitchen. I saw that the dining room was decorated with all the gorgeous silver, flowers from the florist, and long white candles. It gave me a spooky feeling. I wanted to peep in the parlor, but didn't dare.

I went up the steps quietly and into Janet's room. With her hair rolled up and wearing her old bathrobe, she was sorting clothes out of her bureau drawers aimlessly, throwing underwear on the bed and some in an open suitcase. The bed was unmade, and the room was littered with boxes and dresses.

"Ophelia, these things have to be pressed," she greeted me.

I took all her underwear and new dresses to the kitchen and poked some coal in the stove to heat it up for the iron. Geraldine stood by with her sticky hands and wanted to touch everything I was ironing. "Get back over there or I'll slap you," I finally told her, after I nearly scorched one of the lacy slips. When I finished, I took the things back to Janet's room and she stuck them in her suitcase without question, smushed them down, and tried to close it.

"Help me get it closed, Ophelia," she demanded. "Sit on it."

I sat on the suitcase, and she finally got the snaps closed. Then she found she had left out her bath powder and we had to open it up again.

"Where you going?" I asked her.

"North," she replied, combing out her hair. "What do you think of me getting married?"

I laughed. "You're lucky," I told her, and I really meant it. "Ain't Leighton going to be surprised?"

"He sure is."

"Where you going to live?"

"In Attamac till school's out, then here," she said, tossing her long yellow hair around. I guess she felt she was really something, getting a husband at fifteen. She seemed to be forgetting she had a baby half made inside her and it not even David's. I kept looking at her to see it, and when she put on her wedding dress, I could. She was showing all right. The dress was a plain powder blue one, two sizes bigger than she ordinarily wore, which made her look thick around the middle. When her mama came up to look at her, she brought Janet a lace collar, probably one made by some old aunt in the family years before. The collar drew some attention up to her graceful neck. Miss Lou was doing the best she could.

Mr. and Mrs. Hollings arrived, and she came in the kitchen to see if she could do anything there and he went on in the house to speak to Miss Lou, his sister. I could imagine her crying on his shoulder just like at a funeral.

I helped Mama put ham in the biscuits. Every now and then I'd stick one in the mouth of one of the children, who had slipped in to watch. I saw Flea ease up to a platter of deviled eggs and lick one. "Flea!" I cried. "Now you got to eat it!" It didn't seem much of a punishment, so I set him on a high stool and told him to stay there. "And don't wet your pants," I warned him. He entertained himself by picking his nose while I carried the food into the dining room.

When I saw the Farthingales' old green car coming, I had a chill; I felt so strange—embarrassed and scared like some of this was my own fault, like knowing about everything made me guilty too. I ran back to the kitchen and stood close to Mama, who was busy making cream sauce for the chicken à la king.

168

"They're here," I whispered.

We sidled over to the window and peeked out. Mr. and Mrs. Farthingale in their Sunday clothes were slowly getting out of the front seat while David and Katie stepped solemnly out of the back. The expression on their faces was funeral, not wedding. David, the bridegroom, had the look of a poor, stringy chicken on a January morning when the corn has given out. He walked behind Katie with his shoulders hunched over and his face red with pimples. He looked plain caught. He had outgrown his Sunday suit, his pants and sleeves were a little short, but he did have a fresh haircut.

They walked quietly to the house without saying anything, and I saw Miss Lou open the door and plaster a smile on her powdered face. This was some sort of wedding day.

"Here come the bride," sang Frank in a loud voice.

"All dressed in white," Sammy added.

"Here come the groom with his britches too tight," Frank continued. They all giggled.

Soon another car came with Mr. and Mrs. Harper. Mrs. Harper was Mrs. Farthingale's sister and had that same look like things smelled bad. We wondered what they were saying to each other in the house and if anyone else was invited. We finally decided no one was. I guess with so many kinfolks and cousins in each family, Miss Lou just couldn't face them all.

In a while an old black Ford coupe drove up. It was Mr. Tillary, the Episcopal preacher. He looked solemn enough with his black suit and backward collar on. He went straight up the walk with his book in his hand. Mr. Lockwood greeted him at the door.

We hardly knew what to do except wait, but finally Mama told the children to stay inside the kitchen, and we went tipping and creeping into the dining room. We could hear them in the parlor. I guess the marriage was taking place because Mr. Tillary was asking things quietly and we heard Janet's voice repeating after him. Jesus, suppose she had a spell of vomiting now, I thought with horror. Then they were praying and I could imagine how Miss Lou felt with her only daughter having a shotgun wedding like this and breaking their hearts. Nothing would ever be the same with Miss Lou again; I knew that.

The next moment we heard the preacher pronouncing them man and wife. I kept wondering if David knew that the baby was Jed Deiter's and if he loved Janet enough for what he was doing for her. He was only seventeen, and nice white folks didn't get married at seventeen, especially boys. A nasty little poem jumped into my mind:

> Jed Deiter must feel very cute
> Far away in his sailor suit.

In a minute we heard a little burst of talk as everyone congratulated the newlyweds, and I could hear Miss Lou gasping out something and crying. She wouldn't have felt worse if Janet had been in her coffin.

Mr. Lockwood came out past us to the back porch and walked straight to the old woodhouse without even nodding. He was crying like I'd never seen a man cry, his shoulders throbbing and his eyes closed with tears. He stayed out there by himself until they got through eating. I knew he wanted to go drown himself in the river.

Mama had all the good food on the table, the ham biscuits, cheese straws, chicken à la king in patty shells, pickles, eggs, and wedding cake. The tea and coffee were ready for pouring into the eggshell-thin antique cups. Miss Lou was saying for everyone to come into the dining room and trying to act perky

170

and gay. But it seemed more like a funeral with the guests holding their plates and lining up quietly, trying to make polite conversation.

"Well, Janet, you'll soon be learning how to cook and sew," her uncle, Mr. Hollings, told her.

She and David were gazing at each other in awe. Here they were—married! They had taken that big amazing step reserved for grownups. She tried to smile at her uncle. "Guess I will one of these days," she replied dreamily. Everyone tried not to notice her dress poking out, but told her she looked pretty.

I ran back to the kitchen to get a fresh batch of coffee. They drank more coffee than anything else; I guess nobody was very hungry.

Presently I saw Miss Lou slip out to look for Mr. Lockwood. She stayed gone a long time, and then they came back together. I saw David and Janet cutting the cake with a knife together, like they had seen in a picture show, I bet.

Then it was time for the couple to leave. I was back in the kitchen stopping a fight between Sammy and Scooter when I saw David come down the steps with Janet's suitcase and put it in his father's car. Mr. Farthingale was letting them take his car. Everyone came out trying to smile. Janet had on a new blue coat and a hat that looked like a sailor cap, which brought Jed Deiter back to my mind.

"Ain't they going to throw rice?" I asked Mama.

She snorted. "That's a wish for having chillen," she answered. "Guess it ain't necessary this time."

Miss Lou and Mrs. Farthingale cried buckets of tears into their handkerchiefs as the couple prepared to depart. I guess Janet and David were glad to get away. David turned the old green car around under the pecan trees and away they drove with Janet waving gaily out the window just like they were going to get a bottle of pop at Macy's Cross.

The forlorn little band of the families stood out in the cold for a while and then went back in the house. Their duty was done; they had covered Janet's tracks the best they could. Soon the visitors came out again, leaving. Miss Lou was still red-eyed when she told them good-by.

We found out later that David and Janet went to Pineville, fifty miles away, to spend two nights at an old wooden hotel. Mr. Farthingale wouldn't let them drive any farther because David had never been away in the car before. I wondered what in the world they would do in Pineville for two days—go to the picture show, I guessed.

CHAPTER TWENTY-TWO

I *never felt as close to the river in winter, though it went* straight on feeling its way to the sea. It sparkled the very same way in the sunshine, but the flashes seemed cold and frozen like cracked rocks. And it was quieter; the gentle slush of the waves on the shore was muffled. Its life was withdrawn, like trees with their sap gone deep into secret hiding places.

> River in the wintertime,
> With your green and oily slime,
> I hear you cry but never sing;
> Are you grieving until spring?

I made up this poem walking over to our house, being free of the children for an hour or two. Mama said she'd keep them while I went over to see Sue. I went home first to check on everything and see if I could find an old sweater I had out-grown for Geraldine to wear because she had torn her coat on a barbed wire fence. It made me sad to go in the house, which looked lonesome as though it missed us. I found that ice had cracked Mama's big pitcher that we used for bathing water. It had come down from Mammy Bunny.

I felt gloomy as I walked over to Sue's. I almost hated to see her she was so hateful these days, but I'd promised to tell her about the wedding. And I hadn't seen Bucky for a long spell.

When I got there I found them in the back yard having hog killing. The huge iron pot was boiling out lard over a spitting fire, and the whole place stunk with the odor. Bloody red carcasses were laid out on some big slabs of wood, and Willie and Bucky were cutting into them with long knives. I was glad they had finished with the killing. It always made me sick to see a hog, squealing with fright, stuck in the throat, then the blood gushing. I saw the bloody mess on the ground near the barn where the slaughtering had been done.

It was up to the women to clean the guts for chitterlings and sausage. Bea and Sue were working over a small pot, cleaning the slimy, gray intestines. The smell was awful, but since I was company I thought it only polite to offer to help, which I did.

"How the chillen?" Bea asked.

"Fine. Herry-Kane and Ethelene have gone to live in Conner Square with their aunt."

"Hush your mouth!"

"Yeah. That's right. Joe's sister and her husband came to get them. He's a rich undertaker."

"Hush your mouth!" Bea couldn't believe it. She rubbed her nose, almost sticking herself in the eye with the knife she was using.

"Had a wedding at the Big House today," I went on, trying to work with the slippery guts, my nose turned up to heaven.

"We heard tell. So they married Janet off to the Farthingale boy. Sure some things happenin'."

"I saw it all," I added with importance.

"What'd she wear?" Sue asked with a scowl. "A smock?"

"A blue Sunday dress with a fine lace collar," I answered loyally.

"Bet the bride looked real pretty," Sue said sarcastically, slitting open a large intestine and squeezing out the slimy mess.

"Sure a lot of doin's on a farm nearabout fallin' to pieces; not but one tenant left and he got so much to tend to he got to kill hogs on a Sadday." Bea sounded bitter.

"What you mean, one tenant? Where's Mr. Deiter?" I asked.

"Fired. Mr. Lockwood done fired the fool out'n him. Give

him one day to pack and git. That's two weeks ago. Ain't you heard?"

"No, I ain't heard nothing but chillen crying." Here we were within a mile of each other and nobody knew what had gone on. I hated to think what Mr. Lockwood must have said to Mr. Deiter. It's a wonder he hadn't killed him in place of Jed.

"Yessir. Joe's gone and Mr. Deiter's gone and we're the only ones left. Bucky wants Joe's place," Bea went on.

This surprised me—Bucky a grown-up man and a tenant, with a house of his own. I looked over at him, cutting into the bloody hog carcass and emptying a bag of salt on some of the pieces.

"Well, I hope he gets it," I said. I didn't know whether Bucky could do a man's work yet, but it was the only thing I could say.

"He'll be needin' a wife soon," Sue remarked, flashing her dark eyes at me and laughing loudly when I got embarrassed.

"He ain't needin' no wife yet," Bea snapped, and spit a burst of snuff juice over her shoulder. I guess Bea thought they'd get part of his share if he didn't have a wife. I couldn't tell them about our engagement and that it had never been officially broken, but just neglected when I lost the stone out of my ring. I saw Bucky turn around and look at me and felt hot and queasy from the smell and the feeling that something big and frightening was going to happen.

"I got to get home," I told them suddenly. "Mama needs me to help with supper." I put the knife I was using down, rinsed off my hands in the bloody water in the pan, and wiped them on my coat. They went on working, not saying good-by or thanks for my help or offering us any fresh meat. I was angry that they could act so indifferent and common.

On the way home I saw a pale, ghost moon already high

175

in the sky above the thorny, black tree trunks. The fields looked bleak and deserted, like nothing would ever dare grow there again. I shivered. I thought of Mr. Lockwood and Miss Lou sitting in the evening stillness and wondered if they had lighted a lamp or were just enduring the coming darkness with hushed sadness. Poor souls, with their heavy burden. Oh, Jesus, can't anybody escape misery?

I hurried and soon could see a little glow from the lamp in the house. How good to get home to Mama and the children. I smelled pork chops frying the second I opened the door. Then we were sitting down to the table to eat, and my bad feelings melted. Mama made the children learn a blessing because Carrie in her busy days had failed to do that. It was Geraldine's turn.

"Bless the food we eats, Jesus," she began, and took a big mouthful of sweet potato. "Bless Mama in the jailhouse, bless her food. Bless Papa in heaven, bless his food." She took another bite. "Bless Ethelene and Herry-Kane, bless they food. Bless the hogs' food, bless the chickens' food, bless Jenny's food, bless all the food everywhere."

Geraldine had caught on to blessings all right. We finally started eating, letting her bless to her heart's content. At least it kept her from picking on Flea.

Mama cleaned up the dishes while I helped Frank with his school work. He was a smart boy. He did his arithmetic on his bright yellow tablet and read his story over and over out loud, using exaggerated expression. Sammy and Scooter hadn't learned much so far, but Sammy could print his name, making the "S" backwards, and Scooter liked to draw pussycats. Mostly they got in fights and played until Mama sent them to bed. I tucked them in under the crazy quilt and blew out the lamp.

176

They had plenty of fresh air with two window panes broken out in their room, but they didn't seem to know the difference. Life was fun to them every day. Still, they would have to get out of this house when a new tenant came. Where would they go? Later, I asked Mama and told her about Bucky wanting Joe's share.

"The Lord'll provide," she answered. "Mr. Lockwood'll find them a home. They ain't going begging."

I told Mama about Mr. Deiter getting fired.

"Humph!" she snorted. "I been 'specting that. Them Deiters sure were bad medicine. If that Jed show his face 'round here, he liable to get killed."

"What about Sue?" What a difference there was in Sue's fix and Janet's.

"Sue maybe done it for money and look what it's costing her."

"Who's going to pay for it, Mama?"

"Her papa and mama. Mark my word, Ophelia, it's the papas and mamas who pays." She sighed.

Sue later bragged that Mr. Deiter had given her twenty-five dollars before he left, like it was from love. Twenty-five dollars was a lot of money. I doubted if he had that much. Five was more like it, if any at all.

Toward the end of January we had another snowstorm, which really snowed us in. We made out with what food we had and with the stovewood that was banked on the back porch. Mama didn't try to go to the Big House since she didn't have any rubbers. The pump froze up and we had to melt snow for cooking and drinking. The children thought it was the greatest fun in the world and went out to play in it, like children will. Soon they were soaked to the skin and crying with icy hands and stiff, half-frozen feet. I thought their coats and shoes would never dry out.

On the second day, here came Mr. Lockwood down the lane in the pickup, slipping and slushing along and bringing us some collards and a hog jowl. He came in the house and joked with the children and told them he was going to take them to see their ma again soon. He said the pipes in the Big House were all frozen up, too, but hadn't cracked open. They had their own water tank up there, which was the pride of Ginger Hill. After a private talk with Mama in the kitchen, Mr. Lockwood left.

The sun came out and the fields got watery the next day. The chickens were soon pecking around in the melting snow and clucking nervously. When Frank and Sammy went out to feed Jenny, she neighed happily. Before long it got warm enough outside to wear just a sweater. Bobcat made a slushy snowball and threw it at Geraldine, who called him "Grunt Hog Pee Can," and tripped him. They tussled in the snow and got soaking wet again. Things were getting back to normal.

Mama told me that Mrs. Frizelle had offered again to take one or two of the children and Mr. Lockwood said we must try to get Carrie to agree. So on Saturday we all went back to Attamac in the pickup. The children were excited and looking forward to using Carrie's water toilet and getting ice cream cones.

We found Carrie in the best of spirits, fat and rested. I had never seen her eyeballs so white. She received us with "You all come on in," just like she was inviting us to a party. The jailer clanked to the door, and the children ran to the toilet with a fuss over who was to be first.

Flea regarded his ma with a puzzled look. I think he had just about forgotten her, but she joggled him up and down in her lap, and soon he began to grin and poke her breast with happy remembrance. She seemed pleased that the two babies had gone home with Joe's sister. "I never seen her," she explained, "but I heard about her from Joe, how rich they is." She smiled proudly.

We told her all the news, about Mr. Deiter getting fired, Janet getting married, and Sue's condition. We didn't mention Janet being pregnant because it seemed too indelicate.

"Jesus, hush your mouth!" she exclaimed. "Things sure happen in a hurry when you're gone. Well, I never!"

When we told her about Bucky wanting her place, she frowned. I guess she hadn't thought about having to leave the farm, since Joe was gone.

"Carrie," Mama began, "we got to make some 'rangements about these chillen. Ophelia needs to get back in school. Now, Mrs. Frizelle, she got a house all to herself and a garden and a cow and she's willing to take one or two. I know you blame her for what happened, but you got to blame Joe some. Mrs. Frizelle, she's high class. She'll do right by them. You got to alter your feelings to suit needs."

Carrie listened with a faraway look, her bottom lip poked out. She didn't say anything.

Mama continued. "Carrie, you got to forgive. This be Mrs. Frizelle's way of saying she's sorry about what happened. Now we figure if she takes Geraldine and Flea, Bea can take two of the boys and we can take the other two over to our house."

Carrie looked like she was thinking all this over. She fortified herself with some Rose Dream snuff she kept under her mattress. I wondered if the jail furnished it. She scratched her stomach and watched the children messing around the toilet. Flea had taken his pants slam off in his eagerness to make full use of it, so I went to make him put them on again.

"Miss Cassie, I been lookin' through the Bible every night," Carrie said. " I ain't read much, but it's helped me. I remember the part where it say 'Suffer the little chillen.' Miss Cassie, I don't want the chillen to suffer none, 'specially on account of the generations. I done wrong, I know it now." She hung her head and tears came in her eyes. Mama put her arm around her.

"Carrie, when you confess your sins you shall be forgiven. The Book says so. Let your burden go and trust in the Lord."

I felt like crying. I knew I would never forget Carrie in that jail cell repenting and Mama bringing her back into the fold of righteousness. Everyone was quiet for a moment, and I had to take some deep breaths to keep from choking. Then Carrie got up to go spit and Mama began to chuckle.

"What's funny, Mama?" I asked, perplexed.

"Rev'rend Halleck told me this was going to be a good day, a real good day." She grinned.

Suddenly it occurred to me that Mama hadn't had a chance to go to church in a long time and that the Reverend hadn't been to see her since we'd been staying with the children. But he had come around early that morning to say something to her. I had heard him mention Mrs. Frizelle. With jealous horror I wondered if he had been spending his Saturday nights with her, singing hymns and sharing his fish. I knew we had to get back to our home so things could be normal again.

"Now, chillen, you mind whoever keeps you," Carrie was telling them, "and behave. I don't want to hear of no mean chillen."

"When you gettin' out of jail, Mama?" Frank asked quietly.

Carrie sighed. "I got to have a trial, Frank. I done wrong to kill your pa and I got to be tried. It'll be in the newspapers," she told him comfortingly.

"Can we come, Mama?" he asked.

"I don't know, but I hope Mr. Lockwood'll bring you. I want all my family there to bear up my spirit."

"We'll come, the Lord willing," Mama assured her. "Have you heard when it is?"

"Naw. Somebody said they were waitin' for the judge." Carrie went to spit snuff juice again.

It was only eleven o'clock, but here came Carrie's lunch on a tray, and the jailer said it was time for us to leave. We looked at the food. There was steaming roast beef, mashed potatoes floating in gravy, snap beans cooked brown, and some kind of pudding. The children stared in awe. Then Geraldine stuck her finger in the mashed potatoes and Carrie slapped her hand.

"You do that with Mrs. Frizelle, she'll send you to the offnage," Carrie warned her.

"What you mean, Mama?" Geraldine asked.

"You and Flea goin' to live with Mrs. Frizelle."

Geraldine's eyes filled with tears; her mouth turned down. She faced the unknown for the first time in her life, and at that moment she changed into a feeling little girl.

"You wanted to go home with Mr. and Mrs. Parue," I reminded her.

She sobbed and rubbed her eyes. "I wanted to ride in the car," she explained.

Carrie took her in her arms and hugged her. "Mrs. Frizelle got a nice house with potted flowers," she told her. "She got a cow and lots of chickens, even a garden. She'll dress you up in a new dress and take you to church, you and Flea. She'll give you a new doll and put perfume on you."

Geraldine's eyes got round as big black grapes. She was so intrigued even the toilet lost its fascination. She stuck her finger in the mashed potatoes again, and this time Carrie let her.

"Time for ice cream cones," Mama announced, and we all kissed Carrie and filed out of the cell.

On our way out of town Mr. Lockwood stopped the pickup by a white frame house with a sagging picket fence and went to the door. It was the Farthingales', and in a minute I saw Janet hugging her father. She had on an old sweater and skirt that fitted too tight. I could see her stomach bulging out in a round ball. Her hair was rolled up and her face looked pinched, not like Janet at all. I saw Mr. Lockwood dig in his pocket and give her some money. She kissed him again. Then he was tipping his hat and bowing to Mrs. Farthingale, who appeared behind Janet. He got back in the pickup looking sad, his hat pulled way down, his neck red as a turkey's wattle.

Soon the cold air was biting us as we rode home through the winter countryside.

CHAPTER TWENTY-THREE

*W*e *were finally moving out. We packed up Geraldine's* and Flea's few clothes and possessions, the two dolls including the arms and legs that had come off, the rabbit's foot, and a certain stick Flea loved. Mr. Lockwood came in the pickup to take them to Mrs. Frizelle's. He let me ride with them and we all squeezed into the cab.

Mrs. Frizelle lived on the Poke Road a little way behind Zion Bethlehem. Her house sat in a clearing with a few tree stumps and she made a garden around them. I had heard that she owned her home, but this seemed a little farfetched to me. She had a chain swing on her front porch, and the house was painted a pretty green with very little of it peeled off. When we stopped at her door, we looked real hard to see if she was home. In a minute she came out all smiles and laughs, wearing rouge on her light cheeks. She had on a pink cotton dress, had her hair straightened and shiny as always, and smelled like perfume even in the morning. You couldn't blame the men for chasing after her, she was so friendly and inviting.

"Well, here're my children!" she greeted them, and held out her arms. "How're you, Mr. Lockwood? Howdy, Ophelia, how's your mother?"

Geraldine and Flea sat quietly in my lap looking at her, trying to take her in.

"Come on in, I just baked some cakes," she told them happily, and lifted Flea out of my arms. I took Geraldine and the paper bag of their things, and we all went in the house.

Inside, everything was spick-and-span, and the furniture hardly had a rip in it. There was a yellow, velvet-like sofa, not too faded, and on a fancy round table stood a big white kerosene lamp with pictures of swans on it, one of the prettiest things I had ever seen. The walls were painted green like the house, and the wood heater, which roared cheerfully, was bright silver. There were also two flowered parlor chairs in the room, a rug on the floor, and pictures on the wall. One of these was of an Indian man and girl riding in a canoe, looking like they were falling in love and trying to find a place to stop. Another one showed an old-fashioned girl with long, curly, yellow hair sitting in a tree swing with a prissy little boy pulling a rope to make it go. A picture of Jesus sat on one end of the mantelpiece and a photograph of a heavy-jowled, dark-complexioned man on the other, Mr. Frizelle, I imagined.

On top of all this beauty the house smelled of freshly baked cake. The children were awed beyond words. They had never seen anything like it.

Mrs. Frizelle came bustling in from the kitchen with a plate full of yellow cupcakes. She let the children take two each and didn't say a word about dropping crumbs. I took one and Mr. Lockwood ate two while saying what a good cook Mrs. Frizelle was. She smiled and preened her mouth. Any admiration I had had for her vanished, and I hated her. My mama was the best cook in the world!

"You children are really going to be happy here," Mr. Lockwood said. I took their things into the bedroom Mrs. Frizelle pointed to, a pretty room with a big feather mattress bed and an embroidered sampler on the wall behind it that said *Home, Sweet Home* in red, blue, and yellow.

"Look, you're going to have a big bed with just two in it," I told them, feeling very sad because I knew it was time to leave. "Here're your dolls, Geraldine." I placed them on the bolster. "Here's your stick, Flea. And don't you wet this nice bed," I added in a whisper. He started beating on the squashy bed with his stick and didn't look at me.

"We're going to get on fine," Mrs. Frizelle was saying, passing out the cakes again. We all took another one. Then Mr. Lockwood told her something about court and the trial and she nodded, saying she surely would do everything she could. I kissed the children and promised to come to see them real often. I felt like crying and hurried on out to the pickup so I wouldn't show how I felt.

When we drove off, I saw Mrs. Frizelle with an arm around each child. She was happy because at last she had a little boy and a little girl. But we didn't have them any more, and at that moment I was thinking more about missing them than of all the trouble they had been.

The next thing that happened, Mr. Lockwood told us he was going to give Bucky a chance at Joe's share. Bucky would get Carrie's house, and Sue would move over there with him to do his housework. I pitied Bucky. Frank and Bobcat would live with Bea and Willie, and Sammy and Scooter with us. I wondered where we'd all sleep, but I knew we'd manage someway, as we always had, hard times or not.

We were mighty glad to get back home, both Mama and me. The house had a cold, forlorn air when we first came back but soon perked up when we got the fires going and the bacon frying in the little kitchen. Mama threw out the broken pitcher with a grim face. "Ain't no more good," she muttered. "No use saving broken pieces of things."

We made the boys a bed of an old mattress we had brought from their house. They helped out by bringing in stovewood

185

and searching for eggs. Mama made them wash all over, regularly, every Saturday morning instead of night so we wouldn't be so long over the baths.

Finally we started to school again, and I was overjoyed to be going. Frank, Sonny, Monk, and Almalee joined us every morning for the chilly walk to meet the bus. We were glad to see Perry and all the children on the bus again. The smoking flue at the school had been fixed, and Miss Lovey gave us a big smile. She asked me to help with the small children's reading lessons. I took two children at a time and read about Baby Ray and the dog and cat and yellow chicks. I suddenly felt grown and wanted to be a teacher more than anything in the world.

"I don't want to do farm and house work all my life," I told Mama, thinking of Sue and what her life held for her.

"You got to have education, Ophelia. You're going places, you're going to amount to something. The Lord willing, you're going to college!"

I lay in bed that night dreaming of going away to college, of marching down a paved walk in a graduating robe and hat. Then I was standing in front of a big class of students, all looking at me eagerly while I wrote important words on the blackboard with a long piece of white chalk. I listened to the whine of the wind in the flue and the lapping of the river, urging me in some secret way to do daring, exciting things. My heart beat fast and I put my hand to my breast. Suddenly a sensation ran like lightning through my body. Through the flannel nightgown I felt not the beat of my heart but the size of my breasts. They had grown! They were big and round and full, strangers, come to worry me with something unknown. I touched them again. It felt good. I took deep breaths. I thought of Bucky, how he wanted to touch them . . . of James Odell, how it felt when . . . . I lay there hot, worried, frightened. Mama began to snore, and I smothered the shame of myself in the old, ragged comforter.

Mama now went back to the Big House regularly to do the cooking. She would mutter when she came home nights that it wasn't much use cooking since they ate so little these days. We all knew that Janet had cast a blight on Ginger Hill, the stain of which would never be removed and which Miss Lou would bear like the unclean beggar in the Bible. What had been such a gay, happy home the summer before had now become the saddest one in all the world. Miss Lou sniveled down in the morning in her old blue wrapper, her hair pulled straight back in a sloppy bun, to pick at her fried egg and stick little bits of toast in her mouth nervously, like she didn't want anybody to see her. Mr. Lockwood at least had those man-worries of the farm to dilute his misery and disappointment over Janet. Now Miss Lou, instead of waiting for Mr. Lock-wood to go to Macy's Cross for the morning paper so she could do the crossword puzzle as she used to, would tiptoe back upstairs and sit in a chair gazing out the window. Not looking at the river, but out toward the barren field, just staring with a sad and empty face, seeing nothing at all.

Mama kept an eye on her and tried to jolly her up. Suffering was necessary, it was the price we paid, Mama told me, but a good thing could be carried too far.

"Miss Lou's suffering without the fruits of the Spirit," she said. "Wasting away without any benefits. Be better to crochet while she suffers."

The worst thing of all was they hadn't been to church a single Sunday since Janet got married. Mama said it was bad enough not to face people, but worse not to face God with your sins. The trouble was, in Attamac, when you went to church, you had to face both at the same time. We grieved for them.

The first Saturday night after we moved back home, Reverend Halleck came the same as he used to, with his umbrella and a huge helping of fresh sausage. He was hobbling a little and said he'd had an attack of the rheumatism and the flues. We were mighty glad to see him, and Sammy and Scooter were as excited as Christmas when, after supper, Mama dusted off the old organ keyboard and tuned up with "All God's Chillen Got Shoes." Several notes were stuck from the long, cold winter and lack of use, but we all sang, even Reverend Halleck in a croaking, hoarse voice.

It was arranged that the boys and I would spend the night with Sue and Bucky so as to give Mama and the Reverend a chance to sing and socialize all they wanted to. So we gathered up some quilts and made our way through the cold, black night. When we got there, we saw that they were using all of Carrie's things, but Bucky had put in new window panes to replace the broken ones. When I admired them and told him he was smart, he grinned and lighted up a cigarette. The boys ran all over the house getting acquainted with it again and were tickled to find the old yellow dog in his same corner.

Sue, bigger than ever and glum as a wet cat, slouched on the sofa, picking little pieces of cotton stuffing out of one of the holes in it. She would hiccup from time to time.

"How you like your new house?" I asked Bucky.

"Fine. Sure like it fine."

"You're right smart, Bucky, to have a whole share."

"Yeah. Got to start plowin' Monday." He blew out some smoke.

Sue hiccupped.

"You got old Jenny?"

"Yeah. She was Joe's. I got to buy her from Carrie."

"Carrie sure ain't got any use for her where she's at," I said, then wished I hadn't.

Bucky laughed. "Sure ain't. How's Carrie doin', Ophelia?"

"Fine. She might be 'lectracuted."

"Yeah. Guess she's plum worried over it."

"But she's doing okay," I added cheerfully.

Bucky beat a tattoo with his fingernails on the table while we thought of what to say next.

"Sure been cold," he finally remarked.

"Yeah. I'll be glad when spring comes."

"Me too. Sure will."

Sue hiccupped. I wondered if she would be glad when spring came with what she had to face. Then I thought of the terrible night when Herry-Kane had been born right in this house and shivered.

"You cold, Ophelia?" Bucky politely asked. He got up and put a stick of wood in the stove.

"No, I ain't cold," I said.

"Let me show you the new pump," he said proudly. I followed him through the kitchen and out on the back porch. In the dim light, I saw a shiny, new pump handle.

"It's pretty, Bucky. That's real nice."

He came over near me. "Don't even have to prime it," he said in a low voice and put his arms around me awkwardly, drawing me up to his mouth for a sudden kiss. It took me so by surprise I didn't have time to shut my mouth, and his tongue came in and slithered around on mine. His spit tasted funny and I wanted to gag, but he held me closer, his hands on my breasts pressing hard. I threw him back against the pump.

"Look here, Ophelia," he hissed, "you done told me you

189

would marry me once. We been engaged. Now I got some rights."

"You, you ain't," I stammered. "I lost the stone out of the ring. It fell out by itself. You didn't come around all winter," I added with indignation.

"I ain't had a chance. Now we got a chance. After you and Sue go to bed, you creep on upstairs, you hear? She ain't goin' to hear you, she sleeps like the dead." He was rubbing my breasts again and I was trying to ease his big, cold hands off me.

"Look, Bucky. I want to be a schoolteacher. I want to go off to college. I don't want to be a farmer's wife with a dozen chillen to wash and iron for till I die. Now take your hands off me." Still, his hands were giving me chills, and I hated them for making me want to stay out there by the pump.

"You ain't goin' to no college," he said low and husky. "That's for white folks."

We stood there for a long minute, his hands searching my dress, hurting, while I made some weak efforts to make them stop. Finally I said, "Give me a drink of water please, Bucky."

In the dark he pumped and the water spouted. I took the dipper and held it until it overflowed, then took a deep gulp. "You've got a good pump, Bucky, not even to need priming," I said.

When I finished drinking, he took a drink and we went back inside. Sue was asleep on the sofa and the boys were playing with the dog. I took them in Carrie's old room and put them to bed, then crawled in with them. I felt flushed from Bucky's awkward caresses and disturbed with myself. "I'm getting common," I thought with terror and tried not to remember how his kiss felt.

CHAPTER TWENTY-FOUR

J *hated to face Bucky the next morning, so while he was*
out feeding the stock and Sue was still asleep on the sofa,
I bundled up the boys and we went home. It was a cold,
windy day, but the sun was shining brightly and flecks of white
clouds scudded across the sky. We ran down the road, happy
with the feeling of the noisy wind that jostled and rattled the
bare trees in a rough game, making jerky shadow pictures on
the ground. We had a race all the way home with the wind and
sunshine chasing after us. I forgot all about Bucky and his
fumbling hands and feeling common.

It was good to be going back to church that evening. Mrs.
Frizelle was there with Geraldine and Flea, both in nice new
clothes. Geraldine had on a red hat, the first one she had ever
owned in her life. She kept feeling it, making sure it was still
there. She had gotten stuck-up and acted as if she hardly remembered me. Mrs. Frizelle was all grins and oily pride showing off her children. She kept an arm around each one during
the preaching and let Flea play with her purse all he wanted to.
He took out her red powder sponge, her big black comb,
delicate pink handkerchief, and coin case. When he started
dropping the pennies out of it, she shook her head at him and
smiled sweetly. She had come out of the whole tragic mess
with her heart's desire—children. It made me mad; she looked
so happy, and poor Carrie was sitting in the jailhouse with
no children around her.

I craned my neck around until it hurt looking for James
Odell, but he wasn't there. I wondered if he had gone away
somewhere or had just quit coming to church. I hadn't seen

191

him since Christmas Eve. It had been a long two months, a long cold winter.

The winds of March came rising as always, cleaning up, carrying away dead leaves and branches, dust from the fields, and debris left by the hurricane. Miss Lovey at school taught us about Holland and windmills. She said March was the time to think about windmills. She showed us pictures of little yellow-headed girls and their mothers in neat, white caps sitting primly in chairs on checked floors paring vegetables with the big, flapping windmills in the background. They looked odd but pretty. I thought a lot about how big and strange the world was, and I wondered how people started doing such different ways. I asked Miss Lovey why we didn't have windmills since we had plenty of wind. She said they served as pumps and we had different pumps. Then I thought of Bucky's new pump and how funny it would be if he had to have a windmill on his house to get a drink of water.

On Saturday I went for a walk down by the river. I hadn't been near it all winter, only heard it gurgling and swishing in the night. Now it sparkled in the afternoon sun with millions of tiny flashes as though it was made of broken glass. It was running, running to the sea. It never gives out, I thought. It seemed to be saying, "Come on, come on, see how easy it is," and laughing over some secret. My heart beat fast, I didn't know why. The river knows something I don't know, I was thinking, and I want to know it. But how? Will I find out someday, maybe in college? Suddenly I felt sad. College, wherever it was, was far from the river. How would I find out so far away? And would I ever dare ask anybody? I felt confused. Still, it wasn't an unpleasant confusion.

I watched a gull hover over the twinkling water, suspended,

then glide up in a graceful spiral. Maybe he was looking for something secret, too. Or more likely a fish, I thought with disgust. I shook the sand out of my shoes and went on home to start supper for Sammy, Scooter, and Reverend Halleck, if he came. And he did, bringing a half of a fresh yellow pound cake that looked suspiciously like Mrs. Frizelle's.

Then Mama arrived in a lather of excitement. "They going to try Carrie next week!" she cried. "Mr. Lockwood come in to supper with the news. Court going to meet and she'll be tried!"

"Sure enough?" Reverend Halleck exclaimed. "Guess I'll have to attend and see Carrie. She'll need all the friends she's got, 'specially her preacher."

The boys were listening, their eyes wide. They knew something big and scary was going to happen to their ma, something to do with the Law.

I hugged them up. "This means your ma's going to get out of jail," I comforted them, and they believed me. Sammy gave a big, forced laugh.

"Mama, can I go? I want to go," I begged.

"Mr. Lockwood told me he would take some of us," she said happily. We wanted to talk over Carrie's chances, but didn't because of the boys.

That night Bucky came over. It was the first time he had ever come to see me deliberately. I was already excited about the trial, and when I saw him at the door in a clean shirt and ironed overalls and his old sheepskin coat, I thought my heart would jump off its hinges.

"Evenin', Miss Cassie. Evenin', Rev'rend," he said politely. "How you, Ophelia?" He hesitated, then got his courage up. "Want to go walkin'? One of my pigs got out and I got to find it. Want to help me?"

I never heard of such a poor excuse to come to see a girl. "I got to wash up the dishes," I told him indignantly.

"I'll wait for you," he said, took a seat, and accepted a piece of Reverend Halleck's pound cake.

"My mama goin' to be tried next week," Sammy told him importantly.

"You're lyin'!"

"Naw I ain't. Ask Miss Cassie."

"We're all going and bear Carrie up," Mama said.

I halfway washed the dishes and got my old brown coat on. "Be back soon, Mama," I told her. Bucky and I went out in the cold night, and the wind whipped across our faces as we walked down the lane, branches cracking under our feet. "Which way did your pig go?" I finally asked him.

"Think it's down near the river. I heard a squeal down that way comin' over here."

"Then how come you didn't go after it?"

"I set out to your house." He took my arm and gripped it, trying to stop me.

I pulled on. "Let's find the pig," I said.

He held me to a stop. "Ophelia, let's get married. I been thinkin' 'bout you all week. I love you." He grabbed me and his mouth came on mine, but I kept mine shut tight. I could feel the power and urge of him and it weakened me. He unbuttoned my coat and his hands went to my breasts, feeling and rolling them around in opposite directions. He jutted his loins into my stomach, holding my waist with his elbows. He was breathing hard and finding my mouth again. Suddenly I knew I'd be flat on my back in the next second if I didn't stop him. Panting, I jolted against him as hard as I could and he fell back.

"Bucky, I ain't getting in Sue's fix!" I gasped. "I ain't ruining myself. I'm going to college!" I cried.

"I'll marry you, Ophelia," he begged, reaching for me. "I'll marry you tomorrow. Tomorrow at church. I swear it. You ain't goin' to no college and you know it." He grabbed my arm.

"I ain't ready to get married, Bucky. I don't want any babies any time soon!"

"Maybe you won't have none," he moaned.

"And maybe I will!" I spat at him.

He stared at the sky in the darkness, his mouth drooped open. "Ain't no moon," he whispered. "It's real dark, Ophelia."

I studied on that remark while he kept trying to put his hands under my coat again. I buttoned it. "Your pig wasn't even out!" I reproached him, and started running home.

"It could of been," he shouted after me.

I was out of breath when I got home and found Mama and Reverend Halleck singing "It Ain't Gonna Rain No More, No More" to amuse the boys.

"Did you find the pig?" Scooter asked when they stopped singing.

"No," I replied angrily and went to the kitchen to try to get my mind calmed down by looking at an old *Saturday Evening Post* Miss Lou had given Mama. But I couldn't concentrate; my brain felt like a brier patch with porcupines running through it. I stopped up my ears with my fingers so I couldn't hear them singing "Gimme That Ole Time Religion."

How was I ever going to keep from getting married and having babies till time to go to college? I wasn't but fourteen years old and already it was a strain, waiting. Some terrible wildness was in me to let Bucky do those things that set me half crazy. I thought of the bootlegger who had tried to attack me that day at Carrie's, how horrified I had been, and how much I had changed since then. My own body is against me, I thought bitterly, putting my head on the kitchen table.

CHAPTER TWENTY-FIVE

*M*onday was the big day, the day of the trial. We got up at six o'clock and dressed in our best clothes. Frank came over to join Sammy, Scooter, Mama, and me. Mama had decided Bobcat was too young to go. After Mama cooked breakfast at the Big House, we met her and Mr. Lockwood and climbed in the back of the pickup, so excited we could hardly stand it. It was not only our duty but our pleasure to stand with Carrie on her day of trial. Miss Lovey would understand why we weren't at school. Sometimes there were things more important than school, Mama said.

Frank looked worried. "Your mama's not going to be 'lectracuted, Frank," I told him. "Leastways not today. She's going to be tried."

"What do they do?" he asked, frowning.

"Well, I'm not sure, but it's to do with the Law. They have a judge and it's serious. You'll see. Your mama'll be in the newspaper."

This cheered him a little, but not all the way up. He was old enough to know when he ought to worry.

We felt very important getting out of the pickup in front of the old brick courthouse in Attamac. There were lots of men, colored and white, standing around talking on the sidewalk. They had grim-looking faces and would spit every so often in a frightening manner. It reminded me of a funeral, especially when the bell began to toll for court to begin. Mama had planned on going to the jailhouse to speak to Carrie, but she didn't have time. We followed the crowd into the courthouse. The strong smell of musty offices, scary law odors, and winter-dressed bodies mingled on the stairway as we climbed to the courtroom on the second floor. Nervously I clutched Sammy and Scooter by the hand, and we found a seat halfway down on the colored side. Mama nodded for us to sit down. The court looked a lot like a church but unfriendlier and without any music. I saw a big desk up front like a pulpit and some side seats behind a rail to the right, as if for a choir. I hunched down on the bench, twisting my fingers.

Gradually I got up the courage to look around by cutting my eyes. The colored side was pretty well filled, and everybody was whispering with sharp hisses. Judgment Day, that's what it was. I couldn't have been more nervous if the Lord were descending from the firmament. I guess these court days were a trial run for the real thing. I felt I was on trial for all my sins; I thought of Bucky and James Odell, got hot flashes, and started sweating. I wanted to take off my coat, but didn't dare. Mama sat humped over in her coat, too. I wondered if she felt like I did. The children sat quietly craning their necks, their eyes big and their mouths open.

I looked over to the white folks' side. There were a few men over there, most not dressed up at all. One man was picking his nose behind his hand. Maybe he was nervous, too. It seemed as though we had all committed a crime. I saw Mr. Lockwood go down front and take a seat. This made me feel a little better, though he looked somber.

Glancing over my shoulder, whom should I see but Janet, sitting on the back pew, scrooched down in her old beige coat. I guess her curiosity was up over Carrie.

We had a long wait before anything happened, which gave me a chance to calm down, and I began to think that the Judge might not be coming after all. But just then a back door opened and in he swooped. I expected him to be a big man with a long beard, wearing a black robe, but he was small and thin, had a wrinkled, clean-shaven face, wore a plain gray suit, and reminded me of Mr. Lockwood.

Everybody stood up. A side door opened and in came the jailer and Carrie, followed by Mr. Bickford, the sheriff, and a police officer wearing a shiny silver star on his uniform. Mr. Bickford said something like "Oh, yes, oh, yes, oh, yes, Superior Court of Choanoke County is now in session," and we all sat down again. Then he motioned for Carrie to sit in a chair up front. The boys, seeing the important place she had, grinned and pointed, nudged each other and crinkled up their shoulders.

We noticed Carrie had on a new flowered dress, a sort of Mother Hubbard, and she looked scared to death. She didn't even look around for us. I guess her eyes were swimming and blurring. A young white man came over, sat down beside her, and whispered to her. She nodded her head weakly.

The Judge spoke to a mousy little woman with glasses on who was sitting up front at a desk. Then he turned to an old man with long, silver-white, flopping hair and said, "Mr. Solicitor, call your first case."

This old man rose up and faced the court. He wore an old-fashioned black suit that made him look like a spider, and he waved his arms around like he was spinning a web. His voice sounded oily and nasal, and he was the meanest-talking man I ever heard in my life. He began reading from a paper that said, "The State versus Carrie Batts," and then went on in a threatening tone of voice about how Carrie had viciously and with hate deliberately axed her husband, Joe Batts, striking him dead on Christmas morning, and the State would prove it and extract the extreme penalty from Carrie. It sounded dreadful with all those words he read. I could tell he was really against her and didn't have the least idea of forgiveness or

kindness in him. He said she had committed first-degree murder.
I shivered.

The Judge said to Carrie, "How do you plead?"

The young man sitting beside Carrie stood up and answered,
"The Defendant pleads *not guilty*, your honor."

Whew! I was glad of that.

Next, the Judge told the sheriff to gather a jury. A little white
boy started pulling names out of a box like at a raffle. The
sheriff would read out the name and that man would go down
front and sit in a square, box-like chair that faced us. The old
Spider would then ask the man questions, just as if the man
was on trial himself. He would ask if he believed in capital
punishment and if he had ever been in trouble with the law.
If he passed these questions, the young man beside Carrie
would ask the man some more questions. Finally they asked
Carrie if she liked the man. She looked at the young man by
her and if he said yes, she would nod. Twice he shook his head;
Carrie shook hers, and that man went back to his pew, looking
relieved. Those who were chosen sat in the choir stall up front
to the right. I couldn't tell why they liked some and not others,
but they had some way of telling, I guess. When they had
picked twelve men, all white, of different ages and clothes, to
sit in the choir, I whispered to ask Mama who they were.

"The jury," she whispered back.

I still didn't know what they were for. If they had started
to sing I wouldn't have been surprised.

It took nearly all morning to gather the jury. Then the Judge
said court was over until two o'clock. He rapped on his desk
with a hammer and everyone stood up. He left first, followed
by the sheriff and all the others including Carrie and the pot-
bellied jailer, who had left and come back in to take her in tow.

We went out with the crowd. Standing on the sidewalk in

199

front of the courthouse, we tried to think what to do till two o'clock. "First we'll go to the jailhouse to see Carrie," Mama announced. We walked there, but the jailer wouldn't let us in. I suppose it wasn't visiting hours. Then Mama said we would go to Miss Em's house.

It was a long walk, but we got there about dinnertime. Miss Em was surprised to see five head of us at her door, but she welcomed us into her clean house and sat us down to her dinner table in the kindest way. Her collards and side meat tasted better than anything after such a trying morning and long walk down the muddy road to her house. After dinner the boys went out to play, with a warning from Miss Em not to chase the chickens, and then she and Mama and I sat a spell in her sitting room.

"Thought I'd attend court," Miss Em remarked, "but I got behind with my wash on account of the rain."

" 'Fraid they want to 'lectracute Carrie," Mama said sadly.

"How you know?" Miss Em asked eagerly, paring an apple and munching little pieces of it.

"They're against her. They said so. 'Course she brained Joe, but he brung it on himself. They got a jury and Carrie got a lawyer."

"Sure enough?"

"They give you one if you ain't got the money. He's a right young fellow. Hope he knows the law."

"It'll all be up to the jury," Miss Em said, blowing an apple seed into the cuspidor.

I was listening with interest. "I thought it was up to the Judge, Mama."

"The jury says if Carrie be guilty or innocent," Mama pronounced with authority.

"Looks like they'd know that to start with from the newspaper," I remarked, wiser than I knew.

I asked Miss Em about Crystal, the northern girl I had met last summer. Miss Em told me she had never come back, but her grandmother said Crystal's baby had died of the measles. I felt sad and wished I hadn't asked.

There was a big commotion in the yard. We rushed out to find that the boys had chased off a big red setting hen. Miss Em picked a switch and it was time to go. The boys had already run up the road a way, laughing.

"That ain't funny," Mama scolded them. "You're not coming back tomorrow. You're going to school."

My heart sank. I knew I'd have to stay home with them.

We went back to court. The folks piled in fresh from their dinner, still using toothpicks and looking sleepy. Carrie and the young lawyer were already in their places when the Judge came in and rapped on his desk, signaling for everyone to be quiet. The jury sat down and looked curious.

"Mr. Solicitor, you may begin the case for the State," the Judge told the old Spider.

"I call Mr. James Lockwood to the stand," the Spider said.

I watched closely as Mr. Lockwood walked down front, swore on the Bible to tell the truth, and sat in the chair facing the people. It pained me to think anybody would believe Mr. Lockwood would tell anything but the truth.

"Tell us what happened on your farm on Christmas morning," the Spider said in his nasal voice.

Mr. Lockwood told how during breakfast Frank, Sammy, and Scooter had come running to tell us about what their mama had done to their papa. The boys held their breaths and looked around to see if everybody knew they were the ones. Then

Mr. Lockwood went on to tell how we had gone over to their house and found Joe dead by the barn, his brains knocked out.

Poor little Frank exploded with a sob, and putting his head on his arm, shook with the remembrance. Mama patted him comfortingly. Mr. Lockwood continued, saying how we had gone in the house and found Carrie sitting in a dazed condition and had taken her back to the Big House until the sheriff could come.

The Spider asked him how long Joe had been his tenant, what kind of man he was, and if he had ever been in trouble. Mr. Lockwood said he had worked at Ginger Hill four years, was a good worker, and had been in no trouble.

The next questions were if Joe was a good family man and how many children he had with Carrie. Mr. Lockwood said they had eight and that Joe was a good father so far as he knew. He added that Carrie was also a good worker and mother.

The Spider told him to answer only the question asked, then went on with, "Mr. Lockwood, what did you hear Carrie say was the reason for her crime?"

"She said her husband had spent Christmas Eve night with another woman."

Next, the young lawyer had a turn at questioning Mr. Lockwood, thank goodness. He asked about Carrie's character.

"I have never known a more devoted mother," Mr. Lockwood answered kindly, "and faithful wife."

This impressed me. I had never thought of Carrie as devoted and faithful, only worn-out and pregnant.

"Has the Defendant ever been known to do anything violent?"

"Not to my knowledge."

I thought of the time Frank told me she had bashed Joe with

a tobacco stick during a fight and how she slapped Flea when she got aggravated with him for wetting the floor.

"What sort of reputation does she have?" the young lawyer asked.

"A very good one."

I was amazed to think Carrie had a reputation. I would never have thought it of her.

Mr. Lockwood was excused, and he stepped down and took his pew. Then the Spider called Mr. Bickford to the stand. He told in detail how he had been called at his home on Christmas morning by Mr. Lockwood and had gone out to Ginger Hill to find Joe brained. He said in his opinion it had taken a mighty big blow from a very angry person to split Joe's skull like that, and, in fact, he had never seen anything so awful in his life.

Well, I agreed with that.

Then the Spider asked if Mr. Bickford thought Joe was hit without him knowing it was coming. He answered yes, because Joe didn't have his hands up or they would have been cut. The truth was, Mr. Bickford said, Joe had been in the act of relieving himself by the barn when he was struck.

This was news to us and made everything seem worse than ever.

The Spider asked what Carrie had said when they arrested her, and Mr. Bickford answered, "All she said was that she had done it and she was glad she had."

The Spider flashed a gloating smile at the jury and said, "No more questions."

Carrie's lawyer then had a chance at Mr. Bickford. He asked what state she was in at the time of her arrest. Mr. Bickford said she seemed in a kind of daze.

"You mean in a state of shock?" the lawyer asked.

"Yes," the sheriff answered.

There were no more questions, and Mr. Bickford was excused.

"That's the case for the State, your honor," the Spider said.

The young lawyer gave a little signal with his hand toward the back of the courtroom, and here came Reverend Halleck walking down the aisle to the front with Mrs. Frizelle following behind him. She had on her Sunday best, her feathered hat and her coat with the big fur collar. They sat down. I hoped Carrie couldn't see her. The Reverend looked around to find Mama and nodded to her with a reassuring smile.

Mama and I started to get more interested, but the boys were tired out. Scooter fell asleep against me. Mama drew some cough drops out of her purse and gave Sammy and Frank each one to suck on for comfort.

After studying over a paper for a few minutes, the Judge then asked Carrie's lawyer if he had any witnesses or evidence for the defense.

"Yes, your honor, I call Lida Frizelle to the stand."

She sashayed up to the chair, swore on the Bible, and sat down, crossing her legs and throwing her fur collar back some.

"Are you Lida Frizelle?" the lawyer asked.

"I am," she answered, smiling sweetly.

"And did the deceased, Joe Batts, spend Christmas Eve night with you at your house?"

She cast her eyes down. "Yessir, he did," she whispered, then added, "He came to help me set up my tree, and the time just went by. It was dawn when we finished. Decorating the tree, I mean. He didn't mean no harm."

There were snickers in the room, and the Judge rapped on his desk. Carrie hung her head.

"Now, Mrs. Frizelle, tell the court, had Joe spent the night with you before on occasion?"

"No sir, but he came over once in a while in the evenings just to pass the time or do a little fixing for me around the place, seeing as I don't have no menfolk to do those things."

There was a burst of laughter, and the Judge rapped harder and acted mad.

"Did you know that Carrie, his wife, was jealous?"

"No sir. Joe made out like she was glad to get shet of him for a spell."

There was more laughter, and the vexed Judge threatened to put everybody out.

Mrs. Frizelle went on. "If I'd a-known Carrie was jealous I would of chased him off," she said. "It's the Lord's truth, I would."

"No more questions," the lawyer said, and the Spider had none either.

Mrs. Frizelle stepped down daintily and stopped beside Carrie, who drew back as from a snake and glared at her. Mrs. Frizelle then patted her arm and went to her pew.

The young lawyer whispered to Carrie. Everybody strained their necks to see what he was going to do next.

CHAPTER TWENTY-SIX

"*J call the Defendant to the stand*," *the lawyer said, beckoning to Carrie.* She stumbled to her feet, her eyes blinking with fear. She swore on the Bible to tell the truth, and the lawyer motioned her to sit down.

"Carrie," he began, "tell us what happened on Christmas Eve."

Carrie's head lolled around like it ached, and her eyeballs popped as though a big light was flashing in them.

"We went to church," she said in a whisper.

"Louder," the Judge said. The room was quiet as a graveyard. Everybody could hardly wait to hear about her cracking Joe's skull.

"We went to church." She licked her mouth twice with a big, pink tongue. "Mrs. Frizelle ast Joe to go home with her and he went off." She licked her thick lips again and stared at the floor. "I took the chillen on home and waited for him." Her voice trailed off.

"Louder!" commanded the Judge.

"The chillen hung up their stockin's and I put them to bed. Joe didn't come and didn't come. I put candy in the stockin's and laid out the toys beside the wood stove. I drank some coffee. Then I laid on the bed, but I couldn't sleep none. Joe didn't come. I was layin' there wishin' we had a Christmas tree and wishin' Joe hadn't gone off with the Widow. I was mad. I didn't feel good. I got madder and madder. I cried, I was so mad. I must of slept some." She paused and panted a little. "It was light when I woke up and Joe wasn't there!" She rose partway out of the seat, her eyes were wild, and her face looked pained.

"Go on, Carrie," said the lawyer encouragingly.

"The chillen woke up and started hollerin' and playin'. 'Where Pa?' they ast me. 'Not here,' I told them. Joe left us on Christmas. I felt terrible low, Judge," she said directly to him, "and mad. Madder than I ever felt before. I look out the window. I see Joe goin' round the barn, sneakin'! 'Don't even have the guts to come in,' I say to myself. I run out of the house to the barn. 'Joe, you no-good dog!' I cry. 'You sneakin' lizard! You been after that woman once too often.' I run after him. He runs round the barn and hides somewheres." She stopped, panting like a dog. "I look for him and run round and round the barn. He runs from me. He won't let me catch him. I cry in a rage. Then I see him near the mule stall." She hesitated. "Doin' number one. His back be to me. I pick up the ax from the woodpile. I don't know what come over me. I hit him! I hit him!" Carrie began to sob, shaking all over. "Judge," she wailed, "I done wrong! Oh, lordy, I done wrong!" She covered her face with her hands and moaned.

We were overcome with Carrie's grief. Tears ran down Mama's face, and I thought my lungs would pop. The jailer had to take Carrie out. She kept shrieking how wrong she had done. Everybody shuffled their feet. The Judge whacked for order and declared a ten-minute recess. The whole courtroom burst into talk at once, and Frank asked in a scared voice, "What they done with Mama?"

"I don't know, Frank," I told him, "but the Judge knows she's sorry now; that'll help."

I needed to go to the toilet, but I didn't know where it was or if they let colored folks in. So I just sat there holding it. Some people went out, but we were too nervous to leave. We let the boys wiggle all they wanted to. They didn't know what to make of it all and I didn't either. But the worst was yet to come.

In a little while the jailer brought Carrie back in. They had given her a man's big handkerchief, and she was wiping her nose with it. Her sobs had quieted down. The Judge told her to take the stand and she sat down, hunched over and looking pitiful. Everybody waited eagerly. You know something terrible, they were enjoying Carrie's misery. I could feel it, white and colored both.

"Carrie," her lawyer said, "are you expecting a baby?"

"Yessir."

"When?"

"Sometime in the summer."

"You knew of your condition at Christmas?"

"Yessir."

"And did your husband know about it?"

"Yessir."

"What was his reaction to your pregnancy?"

"Sir?"

"What was his feeling about this?"

"I don't know, lawyer. He ain't said."

"Did he seem pleased?"

"He ain't said."

"Your witness," the lawyer said, and the Spider jumped up.

"Carrie," he began in his oily tone, "did you not lie awake all Christmas Eve night thinking of what you were going to do to your husband when he came home?"

"I laid awake a lot," she confessed.

"Planning to kill him?"

"Nawsir."

"What were your thoughts then?"

"I was thinkin' he was a no-good snake," she replied.

There were giggles. The Judge rapped with his hammer good and hard.

"Didn't it cross your mind that you would like to do something to him?"

She paused, studying. "I sure wanted to hit him," she admitted.

"And kill him?"

"Nawsir. Just hit him."

"Hard?"

"Hard enough he could tell it."

"Had you ever hit him before?"

"Yessir, and he hit me too."

There was more laughter. It didn't seem a time for laughing to me.

The Spider waved his right arm at Carrie. "Did you not lie awake so angry with Joe Batts for deserting you in your condition that you decided to put an end to him once and for all? Did you not brood over his going off with other women to the point that your hatred took hold of you and you deliberately and with malice aforethought planned to kill him when he returned?"

The young lawyer jumped to his feet and objected loudly.

"Sustained," said the Judge.

The Spider lowered his voice a little. "Wasn't your first remark after the crime that you did it and you were glad you did?"

Carrie drew back, her eyes wide.

"Weren't those your very words?" the Spider shouted, shaking his bony finger in her face and leaning toward her.

"I said it," she muttered hoarsely, "but I didn't hardly know what I was sayin'. I didn't hardly know what I was doin' either. It happened like a dream. Judge," she cried, "it's the worst thing I ever done!"

The courtroom buzzed, and Frank started to cry. Mama told me to take the boys out and I did, leading them down to the artesian well on the corner for a drink of water. I told Frank that the bad old man who was against his mama would be taken by the devil sure as the Bible told the truth. But inside I wondered. When you got in jail, the Law was more to be feared than the Bible. Repent and ye shall be saved, the Bible says. Carrie had repented, but it didn't seem to mean a thing to the Judge or the Spider.

We waited on the courthouse steps. Sammy found a wad of gum somebody had spit out and popped it in his mouth before I could stop him. Scooter lay down on the cement railing and made noises at the pigeons, while Frank sat quietly by me with a worried face.

"They're not going to 'lectracute your Mama, Frank. You wait and see," I said gloomily.

Finally all the people came out of court. I studied their faces to see if I could tell what had happened, but they were blank-looking, neither sad nor happy. I saw Janet slipping out, holding her coat close around her. "Hey, Janet," I said meekly. "Hey, Ophelia," she replied, walking off toward the Farthingale house. I thought of Carrie's crime and Janet's shame, wondering which was worse. I decided it was Janet's, because it was a secret shame while Carrie's was at least out in the open.

Going home in the pickup, Mama told me that Carrie's

lawyer had said a spiel to the jury that seemed to help some. He said that Carrie acted in anger and that she had enough to provoke her, being pregnant and it being Christmas, and then Joe running from her. He called it a crime of passion. This shocked me as it sounded like too common a thing to say out in public.

Mama said the Spider said terrible things about Carrie, how she plotted to kill Joe and how she deserved to die for it as the law demanded she should. Mama bit her lips and shook her head. "The jury'll decide tomorrow which one they believe," she added.

When we got home, Mama stayed on her knees a long time, praying for Carrie. She said we had to bear each other's sins. Reverend Halleck came, and he and Mama had a lot to talk over, so I went in the kitchen on the pallet with the boys. I snuggled up close to them because I knew they felt confused over their mama. It was a trying night for all of us, wondering what they would do to Carrie. I dreamed about a huge, screeching hog running from a big, black, spidery man with a long knife.

Mama made us go to school the next day. I hated to miss the climax of the trial, but she and Reverend Halleck planned to stay till the bitter end. Miss Lovey gave a spelling match, and I went down on the word *educate*, which mortified me.

That afternoon we ran the last half mile home. I knew by the curl of smoke out the chimney that Mama was back, and I wanted, but dreaded, to hear what had happened. We dashed in the house and saw her sitting at the kitchen table peeling white potatoes. She got up and came over to the boys with a smile. "Your mama going to be out of jail in four months," she said happily. "They ain't going to do a thing to her."

They jumped up and down with joy, giving out Indian war whoops and flying out in the yard to tear around in circles.

"Praise the Lord!" Mama said joyfully. "They changed Carrie's crime to manslaughter and gave her only four months."

Manslaughter. That sounded worse than murder, but I didn't care. Carrie was saved.

Mama said the young lawyer told Reverend Halleck they would probably let Carrie out of jail for good when she had her baby and would even take her to the hospital to have it and pay for it. He said Mr. Lockwood had told the Judge that after she got out, he would help her find a place to live, maybe in Attamac, where she could work in service. Then the boys, some of them anyway, might go and live with her.

It would be something new for Carrie to have a doctor to bring a baby. Being in jail had its advantages, I decided. Mama said Mrs. Frizelle's witnessing and Carrie's being pregnant helped a lot. It wouldn't be seemly to electrocute a pregnant woman. And of course Mrs. Frizelle wanted to stay on the good side of Carrie so she could keep Geraldine and Flea, whom she now called Franklin.

When Mama came home that night from cooking supper at the Big House, she said Mr. Lockwood looked as troubled as ever because of Mr. Hicks's embezzlement trial, which was coming up the next day. That poor, saintly man had more worries than a rabbit in a hound dog pen. And Miss Lou still hid in her room all day like she had the blight and the sunshine might snuff out her heart. "The misery they know!" Mama sighed.

Naturally Mr. Hicks's embezzlement trial was bigger and more important than Carrie's murder trial because he was a banker, not just an everyday person like most people. I finally got up the nerve to ask Mama what embezzlement meant, but she only grunted in reply as though it was too terrible to talk about. At the end of the week we heard Mr. Hicks was guilty of it anyway, but they gave him a suspended sentence. He never went back to the bank, however, just withdrew into retirement, and his wife went to teaching piano lessons.

CHAPTER TWENTY-SEVEN

*I*t was such a load off our minds with Carrie out of the shadow of death, we felt like singing and dancing. Then about the middle of March we woke up one day to feel that balmy air that creeps up to make you know the Good Lord hasn't forgotten to turn the world on around to something new. Spring! There were birds twittering in the apple trees and a promise of buds shining on the branches. Miss Lou's yellow bell was blooming its heart out and Mama's bridal wreath spirea looked like a water fountain of white foam. The river had a perky, fresh look with little whitecaps that reminded me of baby lambs jumping over each other, and the swish on the shore was an invitation to go wading. The boys and I went, down from the Big House so Miss Lou wouldn't see us, or Mama either, because she thought it was asking for the pneumonia to get your feet wet before June.

Mr. Lockwood must have gotten his loan straightened out someway, because the tobacco beds were all coming along just as usual. We took the white cloth off them in the daytime so the sun could nourish the plants. Then, on frosty nights, we'd cover them again to keep them from freezing.

A new white tenant moved into Mr. Deiter's house. His name was Mr. Bonnyham, and he had a wife who hadn't run off and left him high and dry. They were middle-aged and seemed to be hard workers. Their children were grown and gone. One son worked at a garage down in the Neck section and drove over on Sundays with his wife in an old, rattling Hudson, bringing three tow-headed children to visit. Mrs. Bonnyham was always at the clothesline or around the yard. She liked to dip snuff and was glad when someone would stop and pass the time of day with her for a few minutes. She had the rheumatism and high blood and liked to go over these ailments. Once she had had an operation in the hospital at Pineville, and she enjoyed telling about it. It seemed to be a landmark in her life, one of the real important things. She couldn't get over how nice the doctor had been to her, how mean a certain nurse acted, and how they kept giving her enemas every day. Once she pulled up her dress to show me the scar on her stomach. It was a long one, all right, and still pink and puffy after five years. Mrs. Bonnyham was very friendly and a little lonesome, I guess.

The Big House still looked bare and queer with so many trees gone. Mr. Lockwood planted some new ones, but they were just little switches at first. Mama worked on Miss Lou day after day, trying to get her to come downstairs and start crocheting again. She reminded her it was time to weed the iris bed and plant the zinnias. One warm day Miss Lou came out in the yard and walked around, and from that day she seemed to get a little better. It was a comforting sight to Mama and me too to see her acting peart again. Another day she came in the kitchen and said she was going to make a coconut-raisin cake. This made Mama deliriously happy. She said getting a taste for something was a good sign. Seemed like Miss Lou was finally recovering from her terrible illness.

Leighton was coming home for his spring holiday. I could hardly wait to see him. I made it my business to be at the Big House when Mr. Lockwood drove up with him one Friday night. He had on his uniform and looked more handsome than ever, his hair brushed and shiny in a big bulge on top where he had smoothed out the wave. It was his first visit since Christmas, since Janet's marriage and all the grief over it.

He dashed in the house to see his mama. From the kitchen

we could see him hugging her and she was crying. I felt like doing the same thing, and Mama had to dry her eyes on her apron. We went out in the yard when he came to get his suitcase. He hugged us both. I think it was a real comfort to him, we were so glad to see him.

"I want some fried chicken and hot biscuits, Cassie-style." He laughed. "And peach preserves. How you doing in school, Ophelia?"

"Fine. I'm aiming to be a teacher," I told him proudly.

"And you'll do it," he assured me and ran back in the house.

Janet and David came for supper. She was seven months pregnant. Leighton looked shy and embarrassed when he saw her, but tried to joke with them about being old married folks. David looked pained and didn't say much during the meal. Mr. Lockwood asked him how his school work was going. He said he was passing with Janet's help and that he was going out for baseball. Leighton had started to drink coffee for supper and was getting to be a real grown man. After supper they went in the sitting room to play the radio and talk and I cleaned off the table, happy they were together.

All the way home I thought of Leighton, how good and noble he was, and how lucky I was to live so near him, to see him and have him talk to me. I was singing I felt so good. When I got to the porch, a big shape startled me nearly out of my wits. It was Bucky.

"You scared me to death!" I cried.

"I been waitin' out here for you, Ophelia," he grumbled.

"Your pig out again?"

"Naw, but my temper is. You ain't never home. Where you go all the time?"

"On my business. I haven't seen you hanging around."

"Well, I been here."

"Yeah? What for?"

"You know I got you on my mind, Ophelia. It ain't right the way you do."

"Why ain't it? I do right, just right!" I felt sassy.

"You goin' to marry me or not? This's your last chance," he threatened. He tried to pull me over to him. I could feel his body all tensed up and his muscles like rocks. He wanted to get my coat unbuttoned, but he was too nervous. He squeezed my chest till I felt the breath go out of me.

"Quit it, you hear?" I yelled. "I can't breathe!"

He turned me loose long enough to draw a breath, then tried to hug me again a little more gently. "Ophelia, I love you, I got to have you. I think of you all day while I'm plowin' the field and feedin' the stock. Ain't you goin' to marry me? There ain't no reason why you cain't. I got a share of my own now."

"Bucky, I just ain't ready to get married. Can't you get it through your head?"

"That ain't no reason. This is your last chance. I mean it."

He forced me to kiss him. He was masterful, but I closed my eyes and tried to think of Sue and her condition and wouldn't let myself feel, even when he pressed my breasts through my coat and dress. "Stop it! Stop it!" I gasped. "I'm not going to let you!"

"You'll be sorry if you don't marry me, Ophelia."

"Stop it, you . . . you stinking billygoat!"

He threw me back against the porch and lumbered off the steps muttering, "You better not let me catch you out at night. You'll be sorry about this. I ain't comin' back."

I stood there breathing hard, trying to get calmed down. I didn't care whether he ever came back or not, I said to myself, trying to get my mind back on Leighton and pleasant things. Finally I went inside.

"Did you see Bucky?" Mama asked.

"Yessum, I saw him. Maybe for the last time."

"Have a fuss?"

"Kind of."

Suddenly I felt tired and sad. Bucky was my first boyfriend, and we had been engaged in a way. I knew instinctively he was gone for good and I would miss him. I couldn't do what Bucky wanted me to and go to college too. But college was nothing but a dream. Where would a poor colored girl get the money to go to college? Bucky was a reality, here and now. He had hard, comforting muscles and strong arms. Bucky wanted to do things to me, the same things I wanted somebody to do. I went in the kitchen, covered my eyes, and cried, trying not to let Mama see me.

One day before Leighton left, I saw him walking down by the river, his hands in his pockets and his head down. He threw some pine cones in the river as though he was trying to throw away his thoughts. I wanted to go down there, talk to him, and cheer him up. I knew he was in confusion over everything, his mama and Janet and Mr. Lockwood's money worries, trying to get used to it all. But I didn't dare go, just watched him and felt for him. He didn't go out at night a single time, not even to see Katie or that flirty Jo-Ann, he felt so shamed. In the daytime he rode with his daddy around the farm and sat in the pickup while Mr. Lockwood talked to the tenants.

When I went to make up his bed Saturday morning, his room seemed untouched, his suitcase still packed, his sheets hardly wrinkled at all. He must have lain still and tense all night in the cold sheets. Was he wishing to be back at school where things were ordered and dependable? For the first time in his life he didn't feel at home at Ginger Hill. Poor Leighton. Surely they had written him a letter about Janet's condition, or was it that Miss Lou couldn't bring her pen to write down those hateful words?

She tried to act natural, fretting over him, urging him to eat more fried chicken and hot rolls, and asking him about his studies. But when he answered, she sniveled, her rimless glasses slipped down on her nose, and she wiped the corners of her eyes. The strain never left them. They were like strangers trying to act polite.

After lunch Sunday Miss Lou rode with Mr. Lockwood to Pineville to put Leighton on the train to go back to school. We stood in the yard waving good-by. Leighton waved and gave us a smile. At least we were the same. I like to think that meant something to him.

Spring came on in spurts. There would be cold days when it teased us, windy nights when the pine trees moaned as though they were in pain and the smell of smoke blew down the flue into the house. We had nippy mornings all through March. Then, suddenly, there were the golden sun and warmth and blue skies again, with violets growing around the privy and red fliers on the maple trees.

And in spite of all the gloom, in spite of Carrie, Janet, Sue, Bucky, and Miss Lou's pride and suffering, I felt wonderful. I woke up in the bright warm mornings and my heart jumped. The air felt like silk caresses. My breasts felt alive like they wanted to do a dance right on my body. They actually tingled. My stomach was light and happy when I walked with Sammy and Scooter to get on the school bus. The pear trees and crab apples were blooming in white and pink ruffles along the lane. The daffodils and butter-and-eggs were almost gone, but

Miss Lou's hyacinths were patches of yellow, blue, and pink against the Big House. The air smelled like heaven, better than fruitcake at Christmas.

We met the children from Bea's house on the way to the bus stop. The boys were running ahead, tripping each other. Almalee, the only other girl, walked along with me. Her hair, as always, was in neat pigtails tied with red ribbons. "Bucky got a friend-girl," she announced, her tongue in the corner of her mouth.

"Who?" I asked, taken aback.

"Maggie Lamb. She near 'bout white." She was grinning and squinted her eye at me.

I felt jolted. Some of the spring went out of me. Bucky with the high-yellow gal from down the Neck—the one Sue said was old man Deiter's daughter? Godamighty! That Deiter family's never finished with us, I thought bitterly.

"He sure didn't waste much time," I said acidly. Just because I sent him off he didn't have to take up with some high-yellow trash! It seemed like an insult. That gal was scum; everybody knew it, white and colored. Where was Bucky's pride? I sadly reflected that his flesh had beaten him, corrupted him. It had beaten Janet, Sue, Carrie, Joe, and now Bucky, not to mention the Deiters. Would it beat me too? And Almalee and all these boys? The good feeling in my stomach turned sour, as though I had eaten too many green apples.

"Sue come home to have her baby," Almalee continued, wrinkling her nose and squinting again. My, she was full of news!

"She ain't had it yet?" I asked quickly.

"Naw, but it ain't long now. Mama said so. The baby done drapped."

220

"How you know that?" I asked, astonished. Almalee wasn't but nine.

"Sue let me feel where it drapped. It sure drapped all right," she said with authority. She paused. "She look like she got a watermelon in her stomach 'stead of a baby." She laughed. "S'pose she hatch a watermelon!"

"What does she want, a girl or a boy, Almalee?"

"She ain't said. But I wants a girl."

"Why?"

"I cain't stand the looks of that worm thing boys got."

"Hush your mouth, Almalee!" I giggled.

We rounded up the boys and got on the bus.

"I forgot my lunch," Sammy groaned.

"Come on, Sammy. I'll give you some of mine," I told him.

The bus ride was as noisy as ever.

CHAPTER TWENTY-EIGHT

The spring took hold of me and everybody else, putting us under its spell. It covered all the ugly broken things. The trees, battered by the hurricane, grew new limbs and were enfolded by silver-green leaves. The pine trees grew candles, having their own celebration. A glorious feeling covered our bodies, blotting out the dreary, bleak winter evils. The chickens started laying more eggs; the days got longer. Life was beginning again. The freshly plowed fields were black and beautiful with the first little corn shoots bright green against the raw earth. The men began to set out the tobacco plants, and the boys stayed home from school to help and laughed and shouted playfully. The girls all felt important for no reason at all.

> Redbird sitting on a sycamore tree,
> I talk to you and you to me.
> Don't know who is telling the truth,
> But it don't really matter
> 'Cause there ain't no proof.

I laughed to think that up. I saw redbirds, bluebirds, robins, thrushes, tomtits, mockingbirds, and jackdaws. And crows, flocks of them, sitting on the pine trees at the edge of the woods, watching the corn shoots, waiting their chance to gorge themselves. It gave me a strange feeling. Some thief is lurking around for every good thing, waiting its chance, I thought. Sometimes it's your own weakness, I realized with a start.

It was a balmy Sunday in April, and we could hardly wait to go to church. We were in the mood for dressing up, singing, praying, hearing preaching, and praising the Good Lord. I wore one of Janet's old dresses that Miss Lou had given me, a blue corduroy. It had a split under the sleeve, but I would remember not to raise my arm. Mama let me use some of her powder and cologne. Sammy and Scooter said they would stay home and play marbles, so Mama and I walked all the way to church, feeling like queens and nodding to people coming in mule carts and wagons.

The air was warm as summer, breathing love on everybody. I couldn't worry because I had lost Bucky to the high-yellow gal; I couldn't worry about anything.

When we got to the churchyard, the first person I saw was James Odell. He was standing in a crowd of boys under the umbrella tree in a slick blue suit and polka-dot necktie, grinning like everything. My heart bumped and jumped, and I felt weak. I hadn't seen him since Christmas. He left the others and came up to speak to me.

"Hiya, gal," he said. "What you know?" His light face was more handsome than ever and his brown eyes sparkled with excitement.

Mama went on in church to warm up the organ, and I stood there hardly able to think. "I don't know much."

"Who you been kissin'?"

"None of your business, James Odell." I felt myself perspiring under the arms.

"You're prettier than ever, I do say."

"Oh, you do?"

"I sure do, and I mean to do somethin' about it."

"And what you going to do?" I put my hands on my hips real pert, then remembered the tear under my arm and put them down again.

"Take you to ride in my car after church."

"Your car?" I was dumfounded. James Odell must have been older and smarter than I thought.

"Well, it's my car tonight." He pointed to an old Ford. It was a faded purple black and had a coon's tail tied to the radiator.

"Will it go?" I asked, delighted.

"Well, it come here," he grinned, "bringin' me and Willie Thomas. Hopin' to see *you*."

He had a fast line, and I grabbed onto it.

"It's not polite to go to church just to see a girl." I tossed my chin up.

"Well, it ain't impolite, now is it?"

"I'm not sure what it is. It might be a whopping tale."

"You ain't been here lately."

My mouth fell open. "You been coming to see if I was?"

"Gal, I been through the Battle of Jericho, I been through the waters of the Red Sea, I been to the gates of Zion, and on the banks of the river Jordan just to locate" (he made his mouth into a big O) "*you!*" He leaned forward and almost kissed me then and there.

Well, I never had a boy to get religion for me before. It was a lot more impressive than helping one look for his pig.

I noticed the people going in church and heard them start singing inside. "I got to go in now," I said, hardly caring whether I did or not.

"I'll go with you," he remarked, and gave a little signal to his friends under the umbrella tree. They all grinned.

I tell you I felt fine walking in church with James Odell, and him all dressed up and smelling like lilac hair pomade. My eyes blurred, the whole church ran together like waves on the river, the flowers on the women's hats became a floating garden. I never felt so good in my life. We held the songbook together and sang "Come to My Heart, Lord Jesus" like we meant it. Spring, love, religion, and bursting buds were mixing together. What could be a better combination on this earth?

Love. That's what I felt. I plain loved James Odell and I was sure of it. Without rhyme or reason, I loved him. Nobody knows why you love somebody. But loving him, I loved everybody else too. I loved Jesus better, I loved Mama more, Miss Lou, Bucky, Sue, and even Janet. I could forgive everybody for everything they had ever done wrong. God's whole world seemed perfect to me that day in church, maybe more so than ever again. I stood there in beautiful, perfect innocence, loving everything.

I confess I didn't even hear Reverend Halleck's sermon. It would have been better if I had. I remember his last words: *A place in His bosom for you. A place in His bosom for me.* Then he prayed. At least these final words sank into my brain and meant something later, and I said them over and over when there was nothing left to think.

When church let out, I went to tell Mama I was going riding with James Odell. Some of the loving spell was on her too, and she just nodded without giving me any warnings, which wasn't like her. But she was talking to Reverend Halleck, and they were closing up the organ and laughing about secret things. I went out to where James Odell was waiting, and he opened the car door, making me feel like a queen. Then he jumped over the door on his side, since it wouldn't open. Willie Thomas got in the back. I was a little disappointed when I saw he was going, but he explained that he was getting off for a hot date on the Neck road. I wasn't sure what he meant, but if my guess was right, I didn't think he should say it. I sat quietly and listened to the boys carry on and shout instructions to the balky Ford, which was rattling, backfiring, steaming, and shimmying in turn.

"*Be*-have, Ramona, you bitch!" Willie Thomas shouted.

"Damn you, you knock-kneed, bowlegged tin lizzie!" James Odell hollered as we bucked along.

There was a loud hissing when we stopped for Willie Thomas to get off for his date. His girl friend came around the house. She was light-skinned and skinny, with a wild look in her eyes, if I ever saw one, and sharp-pointed front teeth. I couldn't be sure if she was looking at me or James Odell or both at the same time. Her name was Brontella. She helped us get a bucket of water for the steaming radiator before we took off. I had a horrible feeling the Ford wasn't going any farther, but James Odell knocked on something in the fuming engine and off we went, leaving Willie Thomas and Brontella standing in the yard watching us.

We jerked along for half a mile with James Odell grinning at me and hardly looking at the road. We giggled. Finally we were off and alone.

He turned off the road into a little pine-straw lane through the woods, where car tracks were hardly showing. We went about fifty yards, and then the Ford gave a loud wheeze and died. The radiator steamed and hissed. It was about six o'clock in the evening and the woods were covered with quiet. It was still warm; the magic of the day lingered everywhere. Far off a rooster crowed, calling his hens to roost.

James Odell sat with his hands on the steering wheel, looking at me and grinning like "ain't we something?" I felt tingly, knowing he was going to kiss me and wanting him to. My stomach was watery and my heart was bubbling instead of beating.

He didn't say a word, just slipped over against me, put his

arms around me until I was up against his shoulder, turned up my face, and kissed me. I closed my eyes, feeling the kiss, then the next one and the next, each better than the last. They got deeper and deeper until they felt like they were inside me everywhere at once. He never stopped. Then he unbuttoned my dress, kissing me all the time, and his hands found my bare breasts and I couldn't stop them because they were making me tingle so happily. I was troubled in some far-off way because I couldn't stop him from carrying me on, on, to some rushing waterfall.

Then he was stopping, climbing over the door that wouldn't open, coming to my side, opening the door, and drawing me out of the car. He was leading me, still kissing hard while we walked, out under the trees, pushing me down on my back a little roughly, pulling up my dress, lying straight on me. I swear I knew what he was doing, but I didn't have the power to speak or think. The thing I had secretly imagined, dreamed of with embarrassment, dread, and longing, was going to happen. It wasn't like I imagined. He was so eager, so much sterner and more demanding. He never let my mouth go, so I couldn't even cry out with the hurt. Then waves of fire, pleasure, and joy! My whole body became vapor, went out and hung around the trees, up in the branches, everywhere and nowhere. I wasn't flesh and blood and brain, I wasn't a girl lying on the ground with a boy on top of me, but pure feeling mingled with the air, the world, the sky, and the stars. I was disembodied.

He groaned in his throat and was still, relaxing his whole weight on me, his mouth still tight with mine. I wanted more air but I couldn't get it. He hurt me, he disembodied me again, I floated up and then back to hear his moaning. Then stillness for several minutes. Then all of it again, but this time I didn't float. I was back in my body and it was hurting, the place inside was hurting, my chest and neck were aching. We had been locked together for a long time. I was glad when he pulled himself up.

I stood up shakily, pulled up my bloomers, buttoned my dress, and brushed off some pine straw. I felt dizzy; I was hurting and wanted to go home. I couldn't think; I was almost sick. Starting to get in the car, I saw I had only one shoe on. James Odell was trying to raise the hood.

"Find my shoe," I demanded. It was the first word either of us had spoken.

"I sure will, honey," he said. He hadn't even told me he loved me.

He lurched over to where we had been, found the shoe, and brought it to me, presenting it with an exaggerated bow. "You lost somethin' else too, ain't you, honey?" He giggled.

It made me cry, it was so mean. I covered my face with my hands and shook hysterically. He hopped in the car beside me, put his arm around me. "It won't that bad, was it? It felt fine to me."

"I loved you, James Odell!" I screamed. "I loved you and you hurt me! You did that to me. You took it from me. Don't you touch me! I hate you!"

He sat away from me. "It won't no good to you, now was it?" he asked quietly.

"I hate you!" I cried.

"I didn't take nothin' you didn't want to give. You gave me and I thank you for it. You ain't got to carry on." He patted my shoulder.

"Take me home! Take me home!"

He got out and fiddled with the engine again. The woods were almost completely dark now and scary, empty-quiet, except for my sobbing and a night bird warning us with a shrill cry. I was cold and began to shake. The wind stirred and the pine trees whimpered. He struck a match to see the engine. His face looked strange in the flicker of the little light. It took him a long time to crank up. I thought the old Ford had died for good and shivered in panic. Finally it coughed and sputtered and James Odell jumped in and backed it up to the road. I stopped crying and sat tense as he tried to find his way in the dark.

I had been so happy going out; I was so low coming back. I had gone in love and innocence, my whole self singing. I was coming back a different person, bruised, filled with pain and sinful knowledge. I had gone through a door, and I could never go back to the other side of it. I had merged with a boy and felt his nakedness. And what sickened me was that I went knowing what was going to happen and wanting it to happen. I hated myself. My body had betrayed me and I had betrayed my body. I didn't even want to think of Jesus or Mama.

The Ford stumbled along with one faint headlight showing the ruts in the road. Pretty soon James Odell started to recover from his exertions by whistling, singing, looking at me, and grinning like nothing at all had transpired.

> I got a gal, she's so smart,
> She shoo off the mule and pull the cart.
> Her feet's so big she wears canoes,
> But she sure is good at kickin' the blues.
> She loves me and I love her,
> And when we kiss she starts to purr.

He cut his eyes at me.

"You're making all that up," I muttered.

"Naw, it's true, gal. I love you. Come on over here near me."

I sat stony still.

"You ain't denyin' me a kiss now, are you? You kiss like you mean it. I like that in a gal."

"I ain't going to kiss you ever again."

"Ever be a long time. Come on. Might make you feel better." He scooped me up in one strong arm and dragged me over against him, shoving in the brakes and stopping the car long enough to kiss me again. I pushed hard against him, but he had my mouth; it was his and he knew it. He was caressing me again. My brain seemed to creak and I cried out, "No, let me go!"

He let go, and even as he did I felt that same weakness stealing through me and darts of light flashed behind my eyes. I was helpless. He stopped the car in the road and held me under him again on the front seat.

There was no use in crying any more. I knew and he did too that whenever he wanted to have me like this, he could. I was weak, I was common, I was enslaved. James Odell cranked up the engine and we drove on home, not saying anything, not even touching.

Love? I guess it was love, but it was more and it was a lot less. At the time I couldn't think what it was, I couldn't think at all.

I got out of the car up on the road above the Big House, jumping out quickly and running for home.

"See you next Sunday, honey," he called as I sped along the lane. The words sent chills down my spine. I stopped, covered my face, and whimpered in the dark spring night like a puppy that was hurt and didn't know where to find help. I could hear the Ford rattling off at a breakneck speed and James Odell yelling out wild wahoos in the night, shouts of triumph, echoing through space above the car noise until they died down in the distance.

I stumbled home wounded, wanting to die. I dreaded facing Mama. I stayed out in the lane a long time trying to get up the courage to go inside.

I heard the organ playing in the house and knew Reverend Halleck was there. I was glad—Mama might not look at me so straight, might not see the shame on my face. I walked in, hardly looking at her, and went hurriedly to the kitchen, took off my dirty clothes, hid them behind the stovewood, and crawled on the pallet with Sammy and Scooter, who were asleep. The music helped blot out the buzz of my brain and the hurting of my body. I didn't dare pray, but just lay there seeing James Odell's face in a blur, feeling his kisses and caresses, hearing his victory cry as he drove away. What had made me give in to him? I had stopped Bucky, and he wanted to marry me. I hadn't even asked James Odell where he lived or whether he worked or went to school. I hadn't asked him anything. Suppose he came back next Sunday. Suppose he didn't. Then for the first time the thought came: *Suppose I have a baby.*

I never thought of it out there under the trees. Dear God, I would swell, gradually, like Sue, my sin showing more and more every week for all the world to see. Maybe James Odell would marry me. Maybe he wouldn't. I'd never go back to school, never even get near a college. It wouldn't be as bad as Janet because I was colored, just a colored girl. But to me it would be as bad. I had to put my hand over my mouth to keep from crying out.

I could hear Mama and Reverend Halleck whispering now in the other room. Why didn't they play and sing some more?

231

In my sudden fear I went over the big storm and Carrie's anguish when Herry-Kane was born. I felt doomed and lay awake for hours, sweating.

When the first light of dawn appeared, I was still awake. The wind freshened, and I heard the waves on the river start to hit the shore in a lulling rhythm. Swish, swish, plosh, plosh.

"You don't know anything, River," I cried to myself. "You just go on beating and running; you don't know a thing. You don't have any brains or any feelings."

Swish, swish, plosh, plosh, over and over, insisting. Finally, I slept.

CHAPTER TWENTY-NINE

*W*hen *I woke up, bright sunshine was pouring in the* house. I squinted at Sammy and Scooter, who were sitting at the kitchen table eating a cold sweet potato. Remembrance of the night hit me with a pang, a stone of guilt weighted my chest down. My legs ached, my body was sore all over. Sammy pointed to me and Scooter threw a piece of potato at me. "We ain't goin' to school today," he told me happily.

I had forgotten about school completely. I pulled myself up, shaking my head. My hair tickled my neck.

"You're pretty, 'Phelia," Sammy commented.

That made me feel better. I went and got Mama's hand mirror and looked at myself. I didn't look any different, in the face anyway. I looked down at my body under my old nightgown. Nothing looked changed. Nobody could see the hurting and the difference.

"Miss Cassie gone to help Sue get her baby," Sammy said, his mouth crammed full.

"What!"

"Almalee come to get her early this mornin'."

"Miss Cassie say you go help at the Big House when you get up."

I didn't know what time it was, but it was late. I dressed distractedly and hurried over to Miss Lou's kitchen. I saw she had already cooked breakfast and piled the dishes in the sink. I glanced out the window and saw Janet in the yard in a long bathrobe, her stomach poking out, her blonde hair hanging down her shoulders. She was ambling along, looking at the hyacinths. Just waiting, I thought. She's home to have the baby, right along with Sue.

It made me so nervous to think about what was happening to Sue that I dropped the cup I was washing and broke it. I picked up the pieces, put them in a paper sack, and hid it. I'd throw it in the privy when I went home. I couldn't tell Miss Lou. It wasn't like lying; I just didn't want to see the pained look on her face if she knew. She had enough pain with a broken heart without a broken cup to fret her.

I helped Miss Lou with dinner. Janet grunted when I passed her the corn bread. Her face was swollen, her pretty features coarsened, and she was more ill-tempered than ever. They ate in silence, Miss Lou keeping her head down. The bright spring sunshine didn't cheer any of us up, but served as a big spotlight for our gloom. I made haste to clean up, banging pots and pans and nicking the dishes.

I ran home, told the boys to eat whatever they could find, threw the broken cup in the privy hole, and hurried to Sue's house. I became more nervous as I got near.

In the yard I saw Frank, Bobcat, Sonny, Monk, and Almalee in a group under the maple tree, chased out of the house, I knew, yet lingering as near the excitement as they could. Sonny was nonchalantly throwing a rusty pocketknife into the ground.

I went up to the porch, horrified but fascinated by the deep groans that floated out into the yard. Then Sue screamed and I could hear Mama telling her to bear down hard. I couldn't move; I felt face to face with my own fate.

Just then Willie came around the house with an ax in his hand and a big rope over his shoulder. I wondered if he was going to use them on Sue. "Hiya, Ophelia. You look scared half to death. Why don't you sit down?"

A moan came from the house. "How's Sue?" I whispered.

He scratched his head and contemplated. "She doin' okay. It ain't goin' to be much longer. The head already showin'," he said matter-of-factly.

Sue screamed full blast. I put my hands to my ears and closed my eyes. The children edged up close to the porch with eager, scared faces. "Go on, go on!" Willie hollered to them, shooing them away with the ax. They retreated to the tree, where Almalee burst into tears, laid her head on the trunk, and started picking at the bark.

Willie pushed the door open a crack and called inside, "It out yet?"

Some excited cries from within seemed to say no, it wasn't. Willie closed the door, sat down on the edge of the porch, rested the ax, and swung the rope back and forth around his foot. "Ain't goin' to be long," he said consolingly. "First one always sticks." He tickled his neck with the rope end. "You hear what happened last night?"

I sagged as Sue screamed again.

"A car run through the draw. Two head drownded. Ain't even found 'em."

It took a moment for what he said to sink into my brain. "Who was it?" I cried.

"Two boys been here to church. Had an old Ford. Goin' too fast and the brakes give way. Crashed right in the river, nearly hit a tugboat."

Now my insides stampeded. I didn't have to ask who it was; I knew. I heard the screams again. I gave a cry louder than Sue's and bolted down the path towards home, not even feeling my legs. I was inside falling on the bed, my head rolling from side to side, my eyeballs bulging with pain. I pulled my hair, groaned, and felt I was going crazy.

Finally I lay still and cried regular tears. It was the lowest point of my whole life to realize that James Odell was dead, drowned in the river, in the same river that had swished and ploshed me to sleep early that morning with such a soothing lullaby, and me telling it that it didn't know anything and had no feelings at all. It had swallowed James Odell and was gurgling contentment all the time. The river was mean and evil.

The wages of sin is death; it says so in the Bible. James Odell had died for our sin and I would die for it too. I would swell up and he couldn't marry me because he was dead, cold river-dead. A faint hope took hold of me in my desperation. Bucky might marry me like David had Janet. But even so I would die in agony, screaming like Sue. I resigned myself to it; it wasn't fair for James Odell to die and me not. I had to die too; I had done it as much as he had. He wouldn't be coming back on Sunday night or any other night. There would be no more kisses and loving under the trees. It was unbearable any way I thought of it.

I became aware of Sammy and Scooter standing beside me. "You sick, 'Phelia?" Scooter asked sadly. "I'll get you some water from the pump." He ran for the dipper.

"Is Sue dead?" asked Sammy, more practically.

"No, Sammy, she ain't dead."

I got up and drank the water and rinsed my hot face. My time hadn't come yet, and I had to live until it came. That's what Mama would say. I went in the kitchen and found I was starving. I hadn't eaten a thing all day. I scrambled some eggs and ate some stale crackers.

When Mama got home, I was hunched in the rocking chair thinking about James Odell floating about in the river with the fish, trying to realize I would never see him again. I felt more lonely than I ever had before. James Odell was the only boy I had ever loved that way and the Lord had taken him away. My heart was still beating, but it was a sickening funeral bump I felt. I wondered if Mama had felt this way when my daddy left her, or died, whichever he did. I didn't think about suffering for his sins, as Mama had told me I would. I only thought of my own misery.

Mama put her arms around me and said, "Don't you fret. Hush! Hush!" I buried my head in her shoulder with relief. My Mama knew how I felt. I didn't have to tell her what I had done; I could wait until it showed.

"Sue's got a girl," she told me with a grin. "Just as plump and white as white folks." Like Almalee, I was glad it was a girl.

"Go on over and see it," Mama urged me.

My curiosity got the best of me and I went. Bea was out in the yard boiling sheets in the big washtub. I ran in the house. Sue was lying in bed with glazed-looking eyes, but she smiled at me and said, "Hey, Ophelia." The baby was beside her fast asleep, a white-skinned, cuddly little thing. All the children were standing around looking at her with awe and taking her hand in turn, loving her already. Sue's baby might not have any daddy, but she would have plenty of love.

"Sue, she's pretty as a picture," I said. Sue smiled proudly, her maternal feelings already showing.

"I'm goin' to name her Alberta Yvonne," Sue said weakly.

"That's a pretty name!" I exclaimed. A fine-sounding name means a lot, and naming is free. I didn't blame Sue. If I had a girl, I would give her the grandest name I could think of. This thought cheered me up.

I found out from Willie the next day that they had fished out James Odell's and Willie Thomas's bodies. He said the

237

crabs had eaten out their eyes. I lay in bed seeing James Odell without any eyes, but with his big, enticing grin. My flesh crawled, and I tried to get used to what was coming to me. I dreaded more than Judgment Day the day when Mama would find out I was pregnant. I was sullen, quiet, moody, and mean to Sammy and Scooter, knocking them around when they did anything at all.

I thought of going to James Odell's funeral, but I didn't know his family or even where he lived. It was across the river somewhere. I asked Willie why those boys came to Zion Bethlehem to church if they weren't going to be buried there. Willie said they just came scouting around for fun. I felt terrible. James Odell had come just for a good time. Now he was gone, and I never even heard when his funeral was or where they buried him. I wondered if Willie Thomas's girl friend Brontella knew he was dead and if she went to his funeral. Reverend Halleck's words came back to me: *Room in His bosom for you. Room in His bosom for me.*

There was room in the river, too, for lots more.

CHAPTER THIRTY

*T*he very next week Janet had her baby. *I was at school* and not there to hear her holler, but Mama helped at the Big House all day. They sent for Dr. Perkins early in the morning, and the baby, a boy, was born in the afternoon about four o'clock. Mama said David had stayed on the front porch all day chewing on a splinter he had picked off the rail and looking scared and forlorn. They named the baby Robert Hollings for Miss Lou's daddy, who was long since gone and wouldn't know. Mama said he looked just like Jed Deiter, but nobody remarked on that, of course. She warned me never to mention it to a living soul.

Mama said Miss Lou was so nervous she had torn up three handkerchiefs. When it was over she cried and cried and kept saying how thankful she was the baby was normal.

Mr. and Mrs. Farthingale came to see the baby the next day. Mama told me they acted quiet and embarrassed and wouldn't stay to supper, although Miss Lou begged them to, urging them with "We've got batter bread; we've got plenty. Do stay." One look at the little dark-haired fellow was enough to confirm every suspicion they must have had.

Mama described the scene as we sat down in our little kitchen to the cold, left-over batter bread Miss Lou had given her. "Janet won't nurse the baby," she said. "Claims it'll ruin her figure. Miss Lou been boiling bottles all day and I been boiling diapers. Everything got to be boiled." She snorted. "And that poor boy. He ain't said two words."

"You mean David?"

She nodded sadly. "His mama and daddy took him home

239

and he sure seemed glad to go. They said he had better go on back to school, that he's the pitcher on the baseball team. Said they'd bring him back Sadday."

"You think he knows, Mama?"

"He can count, can't he? And he's got eyes."

"How in the world could they let him do it?" I asked, perplexed.

Mama stopped chewing and looked me in the face. "I might as well tell you. It's all leaked out anyway." She lowered her voice, and I felt a chill of shock start up my spine. "Willie found out something in town last week from his sister who cooks for the registry of deeds—he's the man who keeps all the legal books—and she heard him talking at supper one night about how Mr. Lockwood had give David half of Ginger Hill. *Half of the whole farm!* It's all in the law books right in the courthouse."

"Oh, Mama!" I gasped.

"Mr. Lockwood'd do anything to save his little girl's honor. She ain't hardly worth it, but that's the way it is."

"But what about Leighton?"

"He'll have a half, but he'll never get Janet out of the Big House. She'll live there forever, no matter what. She's the little princess and that's her castle. She's something as long as she's there, but if she left she'd be just a plain ordinary person."

I tried to take in all the sides of this new development.

"So David's got back the farm for the Farthingales," Mama went on, "and give the baby a name."

"But, Mama," I cried, "the baby ain't got his blood."

"A name's more than blood, don't ever forget it," she declared. "Maybe some people'll think it's his."

My thoughts raced. I could visualize Jed Deiter holding Janet down on the sand, his dark head bent over her. Then I saw him the day he got the persimmons for Sue, how he almost kissed her. The baby had his blood. I wondered if he would ever learn that Sue's little Alberta Yvonne was his aunt. That would be another unmentionable fact.

"Willie told me something else, too," Mama continued. "The way Mr. Lockwood got out of the hole was by Mr. Farthingale lending him the money. *After the embezzling*," she whispered.

I shuddered. Our life and home were threatened, our security swept away, all on account of Janet. She didn't like me much—would she tell David to get rid of us? My eyes filled with tears; I saw Mama through watery waves. Mama was getting old, and her high blood was a danger to her, the doctor said. She could die any minute. Oh, God, don't let Mama die and leave me, leave me pregnant. Miss Lou would cast me out like the leper in the Bible. "Oh, Mama," I wailed, throwing myself in her arms.

"Shh," she whispered, hugging me tight. "Nothing ain't that bad. Mr. Lockwood'll look out for us."

As the days passed, I sadly resigned myself to my condition and began to wonder if I went over to see Bucky whether he might ask me to marry him again. In my desperation I even decided I'd let him try me out if I had to, to urge him on. I would have done anything to keep my secret from Mama and Miss Lou.

Saturday afternoon I plucked up my courage, walked over to Bucky's house, and knocked on the door. Nobody answered. I pushed open the door and saw the house was neat and clean. A bright calendar with a big picture of a red tractor plowing a field hung on the wall. I thought of Bucky's fine new pump. He was a hard worker; he wouldn't be so bad to marry.

Maybe he had gone to visit his family. Encouraged by this thought, I headed for Willie and Bea's.

When I reached their house, I saw Bea hanging out diapers on the clothesline, her mouth filled with clothespins.

"Heyo, Miss Bea. Where'd Bucky get to?" I asked, smiling.

She removed the pins. "Gone to town to get married," she informed me, never stopping her work.

"Married!" I hollered.

"Him and Maggie Lamb," she said with a gloating smile.

I didn't even go in the house to see Sue's baby, but stumbled away, my last hope crushed.

I couldn't face Mama just then, so in my distraction I went to the shore and sat down on the sand, staring at the river, trying to think. The river was blue and silver the same as always, rippling in a thousand little designs, twinkling happily in the afternoon sunshine as though proud of itself. Proud to have swallowed up James Odell and Willie Thomas and how many others? "I hate you, River!" I shouted inside. "I hate you; I'll never touch you again." It would have been like touching the death of James Odell.

I began to weep tears of despair and frustration.

As the sunset faded and night came on, I prickled with the nearness of the water and its mysterious evil. It seemed to dare me to touch it, drawing me closer and closer. Its gurgling and swishing were an urgent whisper to come in, to surrender myself.

Suddenly, my heart leaping in fear, I took the dare. In the darkness I pulled off all my clothes and waded in, let the river have me right up to my nose. This was the same water that had baptized me, the same water that had held the body and soul of James Odell, life and death all at once.

The warm waves caressed and covered me. This very bit of water might be the same that touched James Odell when he died for our sin. I tried to believe it; I tried to touch and comfort him, to overcome my horror by feeling his death. I ducked my head under the black water, my lungs straining and nearly exploding. I came up in panic, gasping for air, and began to struggle through the murky water toward the shore. The water seemed thick and syrupy like glue, trying to hold me back and trap me. I thought I would never reach the bank and disentangle myself from its sticky grasp. Naked and shivering, I fumbled with my clothes, finally got them on and ran home to Mama, Sammy, and Scooter. I sat down, panting, in the cheerfully lighted room, thankful to be back in the world of people.

Repent and ye shall be forgiven, the Bible says. I don't know whether I repented or whether the river baptized me anew, but after that night I knew that, whatever happened, I belonged to the living. I would have to face Mama, Miss Lou, and the world and accept my punishment. I tried to strengthen myself for the day when Mama would learn the truth.

Then, maybe the Good Lord thought I had suffered enough, maybe I was simply lucky, but the next week I had the sign and knew I wasn't pregnant. The relief I felt was almost more unbearable than the agony of the past three weeks. It was a turning point in my life. I went out under the trees and said prayers of thanksgiving; I promised myself and Jesus I would never sin again. I swore I would be a teacher one day; I was going to be something to show the Lord my gratitude.

That night I made the boys a chicken pie and told them the story of the Battle of Jericho, how the trumpets and the shouting made the walls fall down.